FEAR

UNIVERSITY

Other Books By Meg Collett

END OF DAYS SERIES

The Hunted One
The Lost One
The Only One

DAYS OF NEW SERIES

Speaking of the Devil
Full of the Devil
Better the Devil You Know
Devil in the Details
Give the Devil His Due

STAND-ALONE NOVELS AND NOVELLAS

Fakers
Little Girls and Their Ponies

FEAR

UNIVERSITY

MEG COLLETT

ISBN-13: 978-1517002145
ISBN-10: 1517002141

There is something to be said for the night
The darkness holds a sense of promise, as if anything could happen
Maybe something good, like a handsome stranger
Or something with snarling teeth
That whispers pretty things as it eats you

Thus, the night is a test
A test of fear
And the sweet promise of pain

This is Fear University
Your enrollment begins now

ONE

"See ya tomorrow, Ollie!"

If I don't die first. The morbid thought sliced through my mind like a knife's cut, but I'd managed to be one step ahead of death for two years now. Tonight would be no different. Of course, I told myself that every night.

"Night, Cath," I called, waving at the pleasantly round woman who busily wiped down sticky, vinyl-covered tables across the empty diner. I slung my grungy backpack over my shoulder and shoved open the diner's door, the little bell above my head jingling. A blast of Kodiak's finest fall air swept through the little restaurant. The gust of wind chilled my legs, gooseflesh prickling, but I didn't shiver.

I was almost free of the grease-bathed restaurant when Cath hollered, "Are you sure you don't want these leftovers?"

She held up a to-go box full of fried goodness. Knowing Cath, she'd probably slipped in a piece of my favorite pie: lemon meringue. I gritted my teeth against my growling stomach and mentally told it to shut the hell up.

"I'm fine. Thanks though."

The door chimed closed behind me, and I took off across the dark parking lot, the diner's neon sign popping and flashing over my shoulder, sending shadows dancing around me. My backpack bumped against my spine, its straps growing wet in the drizzling rain. Kodiak was a quiet place this late at night, but I still slid my hand around the small gun I carried in my raincoat's pocket.

To some, it would be scary to walk six blocks home in the dark by themselves wearing a waitress uniform that barely came to mid-thigh. Not me. Only one thing truly scared me, and he was five thousand miles away. Everything else was a piece of lemon meringue pie. Had been that way since I was a little girl.

Guess that's what happens when you can't feel pain.

Child Services discovered I couldn't feel pain, a mutation of congenital analgesia, when my first foster daddy shoved me into a fireplace and broke my arm. He said I was being too loud. I took a fire-poker and dented his skull. Using my broken arm.

The incident had packed me on to foster family number two. Spoiler alert: that one didn't end well either.

Congenital analgesia meant processing pain stimuli was impossible for my brain, which wasn't as cool as it sounded. The doctors called my version of the disease a mutation, something messed up in my thalamus, because I cognitively recognized temperatures and touch. I'd been poked and prodded all my life, and I felt the poking and prodding—the pressure against my skin, the warmth of touch—just not the pain of it. No matter the reason for my freakishness, I'd made up my own rules: don't get too cold, wash my hands, never let anyone touch me, and shoot first and ask questions later.

I trucked along, the walk to my cash-only, pay-by-the-week apartment already feeling familiar enough that my teeth weren't on edge the entire walk, as if I expected cops might jump out from behind a car and finally arrest me.

We murderers were naturally a jumpy lot.

Glass storefronts lined the empty street around me, closed signs flashing. Streetlights buzzed above my head, and I slipped from patch of light to patch of light like a moth fluttering along.

As I walked, I listened to the thwack of my shoes against the sidewalk. I kept my eyes moving, looking down the narrow alleys, watching the empty cars lining the road. My thumb flicked the safety on and off. Between the weight of my gun and the natural ease I felt in Alaska, like it was a sacred haven for runaways like me, I almost hummed a song under my breath.

Almost.

I came to the unlit section of town, where the city hadn't bothered to replace the streetlights' blown bulbs. The darkness enveloped me so quickly that it was like stepping underwater. The only light came from the flashing red "closed" signs on the storefronts lining the left side of the street where I walked.

Normally, I walked right through, but tonight I paused and looked around. No one else passed me on the street, which wasn't unusual for this time of night, but my "shit's about to go down" radar sprang to life—a radar finely tuned from fourteen foster homes over the course of six years. Currents spread out along my skin, raising the hairs on my arms. My spine tingled. Slowly, I reached up and flipped back my hood, so it wouldn't hinder my peripheral vision.

Tick tock tick tock

The sound blasted in my ear, and I jumped in surprise. Reacting quickly, I pulled my gun and spun around, forefinger alongside the trigger. The ticking kept up, like a clock gonging right beside me.

I was the only one on the street.

Frowning, I dug my cheap pre-paid cell out of my pocket. One glance at the display told me the phone wasn't making the weird clock sound. The ticking trumpeted so loud, so close, it resembled a war drum in my ear.

Tick tock tick

I swiveled around, craning my neck to see deep into the shadows of the dark alleys between the small stores beside me. The shadows didn't move or tick, even though the ticking sounded like it literally came from two feet behind me. I spun in a circle again with my eyes roving the ground for something I might have stepped on. Faded concrete and old gum stared back at me from beneath the toes of my Converse. I stepped over to the closest store's window and pressed my face against the glass.

Tick tock

The clock sound faded slightly, and I glanced down the street, straining to keep up with the noise. It might have been a car, but none had passed by me. Lights blazed a few blocks down, but in front of me, darkness reigned, making the town's familiar streets suddenly feel like a foreign country with a population of one. And maybe an obnoxious cuckoo clock.

Or maybe just one cuckoo murderer: *me*.

The ticking continued to fade into a faint murmur. I flicked on the safety and put the gun back in my pocket.

Tick

I spun around, the sound a whisper against my ear, like someone had blown a kiss inches from my face.

Tock

The sound came from my head now, directing me toward the alley next to me. Slowly, I turned and looked.

A dog with dramatically pointed ears materialized from the shadows, its black fur rippling like silk in the silver moonlight. It drew to a stop a couple feet away, obsidian eyes sweeping up my body in a way that gave me the very distinct impression it was cataloging my most tender parts. Its nostrils flared, breath condensing in the still air between us.

I didn't move and neither did the dog, as if we were locked in a game of chicken to see who would turn away first. After a few blinks, the dog cocked its head and huffed a heavy breath, like I'd disappointed it by not playing the game right.

Over the past week, Kodiak had reported a series of animal attacks, but it felt like a mistake to consider this creature just a dog. At any moment, I expected it to throw back its animal pelt and reveal a man beneath, laughing at playing a joke on me.

Tick

I leaned closer, bending slightly at the waist. The creature stiffened, but I focused on the black inside its eyes. A store's sign flashed above me, giving me all the light I needed to see.

My reflection was upside down, which wasn't right at all.

Tock

"What the hell are you?"

The one to end you, brave girl. To lick the marrow from your bones and dine on your fear.

The shock at hearing the dog's voice *in my head* saved my life. With a gasp, I recoiled, stumbling backward right as the creature lunged, its snapping jaws sending a pungent breeze across my face. Its front paws, massive with curling yellow claws, hit the concrete right where I'd previously stood.

Not willing to turn my back on the dog and knowing better than to run, I backed into the street, hand reaching into my pocket for the gun. The dog followed, letting out a low rumble that shook my bones. As it stalked me across the street, keeping close enough to reach out and touch, I stared back at my upside-down face in its empty eyes.

Why aren't you afraid, brave girl? Why don't you feel my pain?

I drew my gun and aimed, refusing to believe a dog's voice was in my head.

Tick

My heel hit the street's curb and I stumbled. My arms pinwheeled for balance and the gun went flying. I fell backward as the dog leapt at me, jaw stretching open wider and wider, like it was going to consume me whole.

Together, we hit the ground, the air gushing out of me with a gasp. The dog's claws ripped my rain jacket, its weight bearing down on me with enough bruising force to bend and crunch my ribs.

The dog's lips pulled back in a snarl, teeth dripping with long ropes of saliva. On instinct, I braced my hand against its neck, locking out my elbow until the joint bent dangerously backward. The dog snapped repeatedly, its razor-sharp fangs coming within an inch of my cheek. Judging solely by the angle of my joint and the surge of heat straight to my fingers, my arm would break soon if I didn't do something.

I cursed, the words running through my head before they hissed out my mouth. The dog, I swore, laughed at me.

With my other hand, I grabbed the dog's ear and yanked, an unnerving warmth spreading through my damaged elbow from holding up the dog's weight. I'd nearly ripped the appendage off before I realized the dog didn't care about its ear. Deep in my elbow, something popped and snapped, but the pain accompanying a dislocated elbow was absent, and I managed to keep holding the dog off of me.

This dog had met its match.

At least I thought so until it feinted to the side, rolled off me, and charged again. I scrambled to my feet right as the dog hit me in the side and knocked me into the store's window front hard enough to send a spiderweb of cracks through the tempered glass.

I gritted my teeth. I would be damned if some freak-ass

dog was going to take me out.

I sprang forward, ready to try running away, but the dog latched on to the hood of my jacket and slung me backward with a vicious shake of its head. I hit the pavement again, the air in my lungs jarring up my throat. The dog sprang onto me before I rolled away, the heat from its thick fur stifling. It lunged for my throat, ready to rip it out, but I just managed to raise my hands in time. My fingers pried deep into the dog's mouth, the backs of my hands digging into my neck and choking me along with the dog's hot breath that stank of rotten meat.

The dog tried to sling off my grip as it shifted to try a new angle. I grunted and shifted with it, forcing my hands deeper into its mouth. I maneuvered my fingers and curled them around the dog's upper and lower jaw.

I pried.

A force, like twisting open a tightly sealed mason jar, worked up through my cramping fingers and hands. The flare of concentrated heat, normally my first warning sign of injury, spreading up my arms was unlike any I'd ever felt before. I didn't know the dog's teeth had cut my palms until blood gushed down my arms.

For a split second, I wished I felt the pain. To feel normal for a moment.

No such luck, so I ignored the warning waves of heat in my arms and pressed harder. The dog's jaw stretched farther open until the skin along its mouth tore. Its eyes blinked in pain, flickered bright white, before returning back to black. It scrabbled backward, feet scuttling against the pavement, a whining scream building deep in its throat, but I kept pushing my hands apart as it struggled against me.

No, the dog said, voice crystal clear in my head.

Maybe I was half-crazed from the warmth growing into a fire inside my hands, where the dog's teeth likely shredded my palms, but I answered back. *Screw you.*

The dog paused, as if he heard me plain as day. There was a sudden release, like the reluctant jar's lid finally springing loose, and a loud crack echoed against my hands. With its jaw dangling loose in my hands, I adjusted my grip and went in for the kill. Another snap punctuated the silent night and reverberated up my arms. The creature finally stilled, neck broken. With one last heave, I shoved its body off of me.

Slowly, I rose, checking out my hands. Along the palms, right below my fingers, deep punctures cut into the fleshy tender parts, glistening with blood and exposed muscles. The sight worried me plenty, but from deep within my hands, the fire spread farther, which concerned me even more. The sensation went beyond my normal warning signals and became something else entirely—something else being what I imagined pain felt like. But I knew better than that, which meant the dog probably had some disease.

Thinking how expensive a black market rabies shot would cost me, I crouched beside the dog and lifted its mangled head with my good arm. In its eyes, my reflection was right-side up. No more clock noises. It was just me, alone on the street, staring at myself in a dead dog's eyes. A dog that I would've bet my life on had spoken to me. And I had answered.

"Well," I said, cradling my hurt arm, "that's new."

"Believe me, hot legs. You have no idea."

I whirled around. Two guys stood behind me. The one who'd spoken busied himself with checking me out. He had electric-red hair and a series of jagged black scars spreading from the right side of his forehead and over his eye, making the damaged iris a shockingly bright gray color. The longest part of the scar stretched down his cheek and into the corner of his mouth.

My attention quickly flipped to the second guy, who studied me with a dark, shadowed expression that instantly raised my hackles. Every instinct I had screamed he was the dangerous one. And you always kill the dangerous ones first. Only then did I notice they were both dressed in thick black pants laden with all kinds of gleaming knives. They wore vests resembling Kevlar but with a thinner piece wrapped around their necks.

Obviously this was my night for running into freaks. I glanced around for my gun. "Who the hell are you?"

"I'm Hatter and this is Luke. We are very happy to have your acquaintance," the one with red hair—Hatter, apparently—said.

"Like the Mad Hatter?" I spotted my gun beneath a parked car ten feet away.

"Oh, you're good. She's good, Luke."

My eyes flicked toward the other one with dark hair and blazingly bright green eyes—Luke. He nodded toward the dead dog beside me. "You do that?"

His voice was deep and even, like he controlled every

syllable as it left his mouth. As I watched, he pulled out something from his pocket and began unwrapping it. A hard caramel candy fell into his palm. I blinked, suddenly remembering the dog beside me as Luke popped the candy into his mouth.

I sniffled, letting my eyes moisten. Slowly, so it didn't look overdone, I trembled and cradled my hurt arm. The victim act worked on some guys. While looking as helpless as possible, I tried to work out how to reach my gun. "It attacked m-me."

"How were you able kill it?" Luke asked, unimpressed with my act.

"And when do your legs open for service?" Hatter grinded his hips toward me.

A red haze rose up through my body, starting in my bones and leeching out into my blood. I'd felt this way before when I'd killed a man. This feeling, this heady rush of *rightness*, was like an old friend. It's how I knew I was the violent, killing type.

In a blink, my eyes cleared and I straightened, dropping my hurt arm down to my side in case I needed it. "You two better move on before I crack open your jaws too."

"Answer the question." A motion down by Luke's side caught my eye; the fingertips on his right hand danced against each other in an odd sort of tapping rhythm. He sucked hard on the candy in his mouth, almost like it was therapy to him.

"Which one? There were a few."

"What's your name?"

"Name's none of your business, asshole."

ll

"How did you kill the 'swang?"

"The *what*?"

Luke watched my face for a long moment, his eyes flicking between my nose and mouth and back up to my eyes. He even stared at the pulse in my neck for a moment. Finally, he crunched the caramel candy up and swallowed it before responding. "You really have no clue, do you?"

"Look," I said, wiping my bloody palms on my bare legs, "I don't have time for this shit."

I moved to walk past the guys, but Luke grabbed my arm, his entire hand wrapping around my forearm. I've had a very strict "no touch" rule since I was ten and put into foster care. I reacted on pure instinct. My hand shot up, the heel of my palm smashing into his eye socket. I could only imagine the pain he was in. Literally.

The punch did a little to alleviate the heady need for violence pulsing in my blood. If they didn't let me go soon, I would kill them.

Luke staggered back, bent over at the waist, and howling in pain while he clutched the side of his face. "Hatter," he managed to choke out.

I turned my attention to Hatter, who took his sweet time pulling out a little plastic gun from the back of his rugged black pants. I pointed my finger at him. "Don't do it," I warned and then paused, cocking my head to the side. "Is that a water gun?"

"Kentucky fried chicken!" He sing-songed the words as he pulled the trigger. Two wires shot out of the end and straight at my chest.

Prongs tore my uniform and blasted into the skin right beneath my collarbones. With a frown, I glanced back up at Luke and Hatter. Their mouths fell open in shock at my lack of response. But something spread through my body like a great humming or a bone-jarring vibration. My body flashed warm then cold, another warning sign. I crumpled to the ground, confused as to why my body twitched and flailed about. The back of my jaw locked tight, and my eyes fluttered into the back of my head. I could've been adrift on the sea of pain for hours or seconds while I peered down into the murky depths, wondering what was wrong with me.

Strong arms lifted me into the air, and Luke's caramel breath swirled across my face. The night's breeze tickled along my legs, fluttering the hem of my skirt. I groaned. Not because I hurt, but because my body refused to move. It betrayed me. The pain remained as foreign as it always was. Yet, I was too numb to move.

"Ugh," I moaned, my throat refusing to form actual words.

Luke carried me a ways down the street, my head jostling against his chest, and we turned a corner into a narrow alley, where a discreet black van was parked. I wanted to threaten them, to lash out and shred Luke's face with my nails, to fight back, but I only managed a sick little whimper that sent a surge of self-hatred through me. As Hatter went ahead of us to open the van's back door, Luke squeezed me tighter to his chest, murmuring something I couldn't make out through the fog that had descended around me.

When we were at the back, Luke carefully laid my body

out on a cold metal floor, like he didn't want to bang up my elbows, which was nice of him considering if I hadn't been paralyzed I would've ripped his nuts off. He turned away from me and disappeared. The breeze coming through the open door ruffled my hair. A long, silent moment later, he and Hatter came back into view with the dog's body lifted between them, arm muscles straining against their dark thermal shirts.

I wanted to tell them they better not dare to put that thing in here with me, but I'd lost my voice. They tossed the dog in next to me, and its broken neck flopped over in my direction. Open eyes, cloudy and vacant, stared right at me, but my head refused to turn away.

I was paralyzed on the floor of some van with a dead dog-thing beside me. This was bad. This was really, really, really bad.

The van's front doors opened with a squawk of worn metal and the guys climbed in, the engine rumbling to a start a moment later. They tossed their vests and throat guards into the back with me, and someone rummaged through the console by my feet. No one spared a glance back at me. They hadn't tied my wrists, so they must be fairly certain I'd still be out of it when we arrived at our destination. I shivered, feeling a lick of fear crawl up my spine. What would happen to me when I got there?

"We have a situation," Luke said from the direction of the driver's seat. By the lack of Hatter's response, I realized Luke must be on the phone with someone. "A civvie killed one."

Muffled, hurried words sounded from the other person on

the phone, but they were obviously talking about me. I strained my body until my neck finally moved, and the front of the van came into view.

Luke interrupted, his voice clipped, giving me the distinct impression he didn't care for the person on the other end of the line. "I don't know how she did it, but does it matter? We don't bring in civvies." The voice on the other end raised to a static-filled yell. "Well, I think we should let her go. There's no point—"

Luke paused for a long time, listening to the other person and occasionally answering with a clipped yes or no. He glanced back at me, his expression unreadable as his green eyes searched over me, as if my life's secrets were written across my exposed skin. If anyone else would have looked at me like that I would have gagged, but I stared back at him, unblinking and unyielding. He turned away first.

"Have the plane ready for us then," he growled before disconnecting the call. He shoved the van into drive and steered it back onto the street, the wheels bouncing over a curb.

"Wh—" My throat closed up. It took a couple tries before I spoke again. "Where are we going?"

Hatter looked over his shoulder, his wild eyes dancing with delight. He looked crazy. I shivered. "You killed a 'swang, hot legs! You get special attention, now."

"Wh-what?"

"It's not every day a civvie kills a 'swang. Especially at night. We gotta know who you are. We could use you on our side."

"Shut up, Hatter." Luke examined his slightly swollen eye in the rear-view mirror as he drove down the quiet street.

"Come on, Luke. You know we could use her too. She took it down with just her hands! Could you imagine what she could do with a sting whip?"

"What's a sting whip?" I asked, trying to keep up, but it was like they were talking in another language.

"No civvies." Luke's fingers tapped a mad jig against the steering wheel, tension simmering off of him like hot pavement in summer.

"Civvie or not," Hatter said, "Dean said to bring her in, right? So we bring her in."

"Please," I begged, my voice rasping. Both men up front stilled. Luke glanced into the rear-view mirror, eyes hard and unrelenting in the face of my fear. And I was definitely afraid. I had the sinking feeling that my greatest fear wasn't as far away as I'd thought he was. "Please, where are we going? Did Max send you?"

"Who's Max?" Luke asked.

But Hatter grinned, his smile slashing across his scarred face like an exclamation point. "You took down a 'swang, and you're worried about us?" He laughed, like belly laughed, for a long moment. "Nah. You don't have to worry about us. We're taking you to Fear University."

TWO

I'd never been tased before, and I never wanted to be again. The powerlessness was awful. I'd felt this way once before, and I killed a man because of it.

The van moved fast, likely far away from the street where the dog thing attacked me. There were no windows in the back to orient myself to what direction we were heading. But I knew the destination.

Fear University.

At the name, a chill crept down my spine. A shiver swept up my throat.

"If you don't know Max then who are you and why are you taking me to a university?" I asked to keep myself from panicking. I tried wiggling my fingers to work out the numbness.

"Stop with the questions," Luke snapped. "How many

volts did you hit her with? Why isn't she out cold?"

Hatter looked down at the device in his hand. "Uh, like all of them?" He twisted around in his seat and leveled his two-toned gaze at me. "Hey, why aren't you out cold?"

"I don't know," I lied.

"She doesn't know," Hatter told Luke.

"I can hear her fine. Check her hands."

"For what? A wedding ring? You're too old for her, bro. On the other hand, I'm just right." Hatter turned to look back at me. I cocked a brow and glared back. "Show me your ring finger, goodlookin'!"

"Screw you."

"I think she likes me."

"Hatter," Luke growled, the sound sending a hum through me completely unlike getting electrocuted by the stun gun, "check her palms. She's bleeding."

"Oh, right. Lemme looky look . . ." Hatter leaned back over the console, his torso stretching toward me. Grabbing my ankle, he hauled me closer to the front of the van and, with a grunt, pulled me upright to prop me against the console. Up this close and personal, I had an eyeful of dirty red hair, monstrous black scars, and dazzling white teeth grinning manically at me. Once I sat in position, letting him believe I was still completely numb, he examined my hand and probed the injuries, checking my face every now and then to see my reaction. Curiously enough, he leaned in close and took a sniff. Like he'd stuck his face in sweaty underwear, he reared back, eyes wide and flashing.

"Holy cock monkeys! She's been bitten!"

Instantly, the van jerked to the side of the road, banging me around in the back like a ragdoll. I gritted my teeth, not because it hurt, but because it was annoying. These assholes were crazy. But if the van stopped, I might be able to escape.

"Let me see," Luke said, replacing Hatter between the front seats. His wide, muscular chest didn't fit as well, and he had to shoulder himself through.

He grabbed my hands and jerked them closer, his big hands wrapping around my wrists. Heat from his touch flooded through me and made me slightly dizzy. My stomach fluttered like I was on a first date or some shit. He smelled like caramel and cottonwood trees, a scent I told myself I hated.

He stabbed his finger into one of the bite marks on my palm and brought the finger to his mouth, tasting my blood with his tongue.

"Ugh!" I shouted, beyond disgusted, and tried to jerk away from him. "You're insane!"

Luke released me and sat back in his seat. "You're right. She's been bit," he said to Hatter.

Hatter didn't act like Luke's little snack was suspicious, which worried me more. I studied the two of them, thinking how they kept going on about how I was bitten and what my blood tasted like. *Motherfucker*, I thought, *I'm in some* Twilight *shit.* "Are you two vampires or something? Am I turning into one since that dog thing bit me?"

Hatter snorted with laughter. "There's no such thing as vampires—"

"Werewolves?"

"Oh, girl," he said, rolling his eyes to the roof of the van, "I *wish* we were dealing with werewolves. Sadly, they don't exist either."

But apparently there were dogs that ticked like a clock and spoke inside your head. I decided to keep that last part to myself. "Then what was that thing?"

"Why aren't you unconscious?" Luke asked. Not bothering to hide his frustration with my questions, his voice contained a dangerous edge. I knew violence well enough to recognize it when I heard it. I screwed my mouth shut and waited.

When you tell people you can't feel pain, sometimes they like to test the theory. I've had a few foster parents and siblings try that one out. Obviously their tests never hurt, but some things cut more than the physical stuff.

I waited too long. Luke snapped. He surged through the gap between the front seats and grabbed my throat. "You've been bitten," he hissed into my ear. "Why aren't you writhing in pain? Hell, with those bites, you should be out cold."

The air coming up my windpipe wheezed and sputtered, my lungs instantly constricting from the lack of oxygen. I tried to escape his hold, but Luke held me tight. "I can't feel pain," I managed to choke out the words.

Luke's grip slackened. He released me but didn't get out of my face. I shifted away slightly, not wanting him to touch me again. Over his hulking shoulder, Hatter craned his head to see me, his scars flashing almost silver in the moonlight. "What did she just say?"

"Don't lie to me." There was that soft voice again,

practically a whisper but as threatening as if Luke pointed a gun at my head. Hatter eased back slightly. So did I. I'm not stupid.

"I'm serious. It's a medical condition that affects how parts of my brain process pain stimuli. I've had it since birth."

"So you can't feel anything?" Hatter's raised brows made his scars twist and contort.

I decided to tell the truth, at least for this. "I can feel temperature and normal sensations like everyone else. I just can't feel pain." I lifted my injured elbow. "When I get hurt I feel heat. That's it."

Luke's face drew together into a dark scowl, and I didn't know if he believed me or not. "How did you survive with that?"

"Not many people do survive with it, but I'm tougher than the normal person."

"Clearly," Luke muttered. I swelled with pride at the words, which was totally sick. I'd never needed anyone's approval before.

"Dude," Hatter said quietly. "If she's telling the truth—"

"I am."

"She's a civvie." Luke ground out the words between his teeth.

"What's the big deal?" I asked, looking between the two of them. The numbness from the taser was dissipating. Soon, I would be able to check the back door to see if it was locked. After I got a little more information, that is. Call me curious.

"At least tell me, what was that thing I killed?"

Luke glanced at Hatter. They must have spent a lot of time

together, I guessed, because they silently communicated with slight shrugs and tiny nods. Luke ended the conversation with raised brows and a relenting sigh. I'd won. I fought the urge to cheer.

Hatter was the one to explain, while Luke went back to the task of driving, easing the van back into drive and continuing down the road. "That monster was an aswang but—"

"A what?" My brain caught over the foreign sounding word. I'd never heard it before, but it felt familiar, like I knew its twists and angles would roll easily off my tongue, as if I'd spoken it a million times. The word was black smoke, lithe and twisty, dark but thrilling nevertheless. *Us-wung*. My heart contracted a little each time I said it in my head. *Us-wung*. I kept repeating it to myself just because I liked the way it made me feel. *Us-wung*.

"Aswang," Hatter repeated, "but we call them 'swangs."

"'Swangs," I whispered. *'Swungs*—the word tasted delicious, like crispy, warm crème brûlée.

Hatter continued, ignoring me. "They mess with your head and make you think you're feeling pain then they eat the fear out of your body. But you're a little . . . ." Hatter swirled his finger around his ear, like I was the crazy one in this situation. "So you didn't feel the pain, which probably confused the hell out of that 'swang. We," he motioned to him and Luke, who eased the van back out onto the road, "are 'swang hunters."

"Right." I drew the word out as I recalled the way my reflection had been inverted in the dog's eyes and how something so *human* had been staring through its eyes. Did I believe these guys? Probably not, even if they used beautifully terrifying words. Did I believe they could be crazy and that they had my figurative balls in their hands while they were taking me who-knows-where? Yes. Yes, I did.

"How do they make you think you're feeling pain?" When I got no answer, I tried again. "What is Fear University? Who were you talking to on the phone?"

"You'll have to get the rest of your answers from Dean," Luke said, turning down a bumpy road that made the van's suspension creak and groan.

"Who's Dean? That's who you were talking to? Why does he want you to bring me in?"

No one answered. Luke's conversation on the phone had ended with him telling the person to have the plane ready. Kodiak wasn't a big city, and we would be to the airport soon enough. From the front, Hatter bopped his head to nonexistent music, and Luke was doing a very good job of pretending I didn't exist.

Clearly, I wasn't getting any more information. Honestly, I didn't really want more anyway. I cut my eyes toward the dead aswang next to me and bit my lip. I needed to get out of this van. Hopefully we were going slow enough that I wouldn't break anything when I jumped out.

Taking a deep breath, I flung myself backward, sliding across the exposed metal of the van's floor. I banged into the back door with a loud metal clatter. Not looking to see what was happening up front, I grabbed the handle and gave a hard tug, prepared to fling myself out the door and roll to cover.

Nothing. The handle wouldn't budge.

"It's locked," Hatter said casually.

I glared at them. They hadn't even turned around. "We have to stop sometime. You know I'll get away then."

"We're here. Now's your chance," Luke said dryly. I hoped that wasn't his attempt at a joke. He put the van in park and turned off the engine.

Hatter shot Luke a wild grin and smacked him on the shoulder before opening his door. "Try not to scream like a little girl when we take off this time, okay? It's distracting."

They both got out and walked to my door. Outside, they took good-humored shots at each other. I heard a sound that might have been Luke's laugh. My stomach tightened as the door slid open.

Behind them was a small airplane hangar. A little bush plane sat idling on the runway.

With a quick jerk, the guys pulled the 'swang out and let it hit the ground beside the van before Hatter started packing their gear with quick efficiency, suggesting they'd done this a hundred times or more. Luke climbed into the van and crouched beside me, ducking his head against the roof because he was so tall, his hulking frame casting a large shadow over me. He rummaged around in a box behind the driver's seat and pulled out a large syringe. I watched closely as he removed the cap with his teeth and spit it on the ground beside my feet.

"What the hell is that?"

"A sedative. You can't know where we're going."

24

I scrambled as far away from him as possible, but Luke pressed in tighter next to me, cornering me. Carefully, I moved my knee so it wouldn't brush against him. I wondered if anyone would hear me if I screamed.

"I know it looks like we kidnapped you, but we really didn't."

I glared at him. A bit of liquid squirted out of the needle's tip. "Is that supposed to be comforting?"

I swear the corner of Luke's mouth twitched, like I might, just maybe, have made him almost smile. "You're a tough girl. You can handle it. We're staying on the island, though, if that helps."

"It doesn't."

Luke took my wrist, his grip tight but not tight enough to bruise, and exposed the crook of my uninjured elbow. The pads of his fingers were rough and calloused, making me wonder if his habit of tapping his fingertips caused their roughness. Too busy wondering about his twitch, he caught me off guard and injected the sedative in my arm. "You're lucky you'll be passed out during Hatter's flying."

I blinked up at him. I bet he scared a lot of people with his tightly leashed temper and dark look, but it didn't bother me so much. His face was chiseled and distinguished, and he could've been handsome if this was any other situation. I caught a hint of a black scar behind his ear. "I should be running," I managed to say. My words slurred together.

Luke watched me as I wavered back and forth on the edge of coherency, mumbling about my escape. "What's your name?"

"Ollie." My voice sounded foreign to my ears, and I bit my tongue a little as I spoke.

"Ollie with no last name?"

"Ollie . . ." I thought really hard, straining to come up with something. "Polly. Yeah. Ollie Polly. That's it."

Luke cocked a brow. "Who's Max? Why did you think he'd sent us?"

"Not a fun guy."

He steadied me when I slumped to the side. The edges of his face blurred as he watched me for another long moment before speaking again. "We're taking you someplace where you'll be safe while we figure out how you killed that 'swang. I promise, okay?"

"Trust you?"

"Yeah. You should."

I tried to snort, but the sound came out more like a snore. "Never trust."

Blackness edged in around his face, his bright eyes blurring as he said, "You should try it sometime."

I surfaced groggily once during the flight.

The sedative scrambled my body functions, and my eyesight blurred hazily as my head flopped over to the side. Right next to me, on the floor of the rumbling and shaking plane, laid a dead body. A young man with a closely shaved head and dark, unseeing eyes. His jaw and neck were broken.

From the front of the plane, someone crowed with delighted laughter. The bush plane dipped abruptly, bouncing me into the body, the skin waxy and cool against my own. On the other side of me, someone cursed viciously. "Calm the hell down, Hatter! This isn't funny!"

Hatter's only reply was to howl like a wild wolf as the plane shook and wavered in a gust of wind.

A hand reached down and gripped mine tight enough to suggest they weren't trying to comfort me. With every ounce of will I had, I turned my head the other way and looked up.

Luke sat strapped into a seat, his face pale and clammy, his other hand gripping the armrest. In the morning sunrise streaming through the window next to him, he looked like the most beautiful person I'd ever seen.

Clearly, I was delusional.

When I woke next, I was strapped down to a cot beneath a blindingly bright fluorescent light. People were talking near my bed.

"—found her right next to the 'swang with blood on her hands. Said she broke its—"

Don't do it, I told myself. *Don't do it*. I couldn't help myself. "I *did* break its neck. Now, untie me," I said, sitting up as much as possible on my cot.

Luke, Hatter, a young woman about my age with black hair and the smoothest golden skin I'd ever seen, and an older man with a large handlebar mustache all looked over at me like I'd grown two heads. Well, Luke's expression was more of a dark scowl, like someone had just pissed in his cereal. They didn't untie me before turning away and lowering their voices. I sighed and looked around.

More cots lined the wall next to me, one of which was

occupied. The patient's blond hair was lank and brushed back, and a thick bandage wrapped around his neck. The bandage dipped oddly in the middle, like a chunk of his neck was gone. He was hooked up to a ventilator puffing out his chest every couple of seconds with a mechanical wheeze.

I looked away, looked anywhere but the broken young man on the cot, and squinted up into the bright fluorescents. My nose itched with the burning, antiseptic hospital smell. White cabinets with glass doors full of bottles and packages of medical supplies lined the opposite wall with pristine counters beneath them. Seeing all those supplies made me heady with excitement. I could keep myself healthy for years with all that.

When I looked back to the people in the room, they'd all ignored me except for the girl. She peeked over Luke's shoulder, big doe-like brown eyes blinking at me behind prim glasses as if I were the Loch Ness monster or some shit. I narrowed my eyes at her.

"She shouldn't be here," Luke hissed to the guy with the mustache. "No civvies. It's too dangerous. They can't handle this lifestyle."

"You said she can't feel pain?" Mustache Guy asked.

"Not a bit. We checked." Hatter smiled as he spoke and shot a wink at the young girl, whose round cheeks turned a ferocious red beneath his gaze.

"That doesn't mean anything—"

"It means everything," the Mustache Guy snapped, interrupting Luke. They were squared off against each other, like two fighting dogs. I knew this was the guy Luke had spoken to on the phone from the hatred boiling between them. Luke opened his mouth to argue, but Mustache held up his hand. "Bring her to me in the morning. I want to talk to her."

Clearly biting back his argument, Luke dipped his chin in quick acknowledgment, though his jaw clenched tight, making me think he hated having to give in to this guy.

"What about her injuries, sir?" the young girl asked, her voice trembling slightly.

"Get her patched up, Sunny. And thanks for working tonight." Mustache Guy patted her on the shoulder before he left with Luke and Hatter. As the door swung closed, Luke glanced back at me, his eyes hidden beneath his dark brows. I took the liberty of flipping him off, even though I had to twist my hand around in the constraints. He still got the message though: sedate me again and die.

I turned my attention to the girl. "Your name's really Sunny? Did your parents hate you?"

Sunny's mouth flopped open and closed a couple of times before she managed to say, "Uh . . . it's more like a nickname, I guess."

"Right," I drew out the word and threw in as much sarcasm as humanly possible. "Well, *Sunny*, why the hell am I strapped to this bed? And where the double hell am I?"

Sunny pushed over a little rolling tray full of bandages, a stitching kit, and some pills. She took a deep breath, shoulders heaving, and met my eyes. "You're strapped down because Luke said you were a flight risk and would try to threaten me to let you go. He said you were a pain in the . . .

29

the *bottom*. And you're at Fear University. Also," she added with a sniff, "I would prefer it if you didn't curse in my ward."

"You're too young to have a ward."

"Well, technically, it's not mine, but I'm the nurse on duty tonight."

"You're too young to be a nurse."

"Nurse-in-training."

"What happened to that guy?" I jerked my chin toward the dead-looking patient a few cots over.

My question clearly threw her off guard; she stumbled for a moment, her eyes flickering over to the other occupied cot. "He's hurt."

"No shit, Sunny. How did he get hurt?"

"I'm not allowed to share that with you."

"Am I a prisoner?" I asked, scraping my leather restraints against the cot's metal frame.

"Not at all! I'm just not supposed to be talking to you."

"Why not? Because I was kidnapped and you're working with criminals?"

"No! We aren't criminals." She huffed out a breath, clearly flustered. "This is a good place. You're safe here."

"Oh! So *that's* why they tased me, tossed me in a van, drugged me, shoved me on a plane, and then tied me to a cot. Because I'm *safe*."

"They tased you?"

"Do you think I jump into strange vans for fun?"

"I mean, no. I guess not. That would be odd."

I sighed. Our little question roulette had worn me down.

Sunny positioned her tray beside my bed and then went back for a stool, her practical white shoes squeaking on the tile. After she was settled and had meticulously rearranged the supplies, she snapped on a pair of latex gloves. Up close, she was a pretty girl with her almost black hair and exotic eyes, chubby cheeks, and soft hands. But there was an obvious kindness in her naive questions and innocent, gentle approach, in her dull-gray scrubs and no-nonsense glasses.

"I'm sorry," Sunny said, taking my hand. I fought the urge to yank it away from her. "I don't have the keys to undo your restraints, but I'll be as careful as I can, okay?"

"Fine. Just make sure to clean them good. Don't use that cheap shit soap. I want the hospital-grade stuff. You'll have to start me on a round of antibiotics, preferably Augmentin. Two doses twice a day for a week at least. I need a tetanus and rabies shot." I took a breath. "Also, you'll have to reset my elbow. I can walk you through how to do it."

Sunny stared at me, stunned, for a moment. "That's what I plan on doing. Except for the rabies shot. 'Swangs don't carry it. And I know how to reset an elbow, but how do you?"

I couldn't exactly tell her that I was on the run for murder, which meant hospitals weren't an option. "I take care of myself."

"So you were bitten?" she asked, probing the wounds along my palm with swabs.

"Technically, no. I pried open the dog's—"

"Aswang," Sunny corrected.

"Whatever. I pried open its mouth to break its jaw, because it was about to munch on my throat. Then I broke its neck. Its teeth sort of *dug* into my hands."

"You just," she said quietly, swallowing loudly, "killed it? You weren't even scared?"

"Why would I be?"

Sunny stared at me a long moment before shaking her head. "What's your name?"

"It's Ollie. And don't change the subject."

"I'm not. It's just . . ." Sunny's eyes went to the door, like someone might sneak in, her voice lowering to a whisper, "Can you really not feel pain?"

"Why is that such a big deal? Because those things make their prey feel pain?"

Sunny bit her lip, eyes going to the door once again. "I can't talk about that stuff with you. Dean told me not to."

"Dean was the guy here earlier?" She nodded. "Do you always do what he says?"

My question clearly stunned her. "Yes. Of course."

I wasn't getting anything else out of her. I sighed in frustration and sat back on the cot. Metal tools scraped about on Sunny's tray. I sensed her pause, her bright eyes watching me, but I didn't look at her. Finally, she turned her attention back to my hand and began cleaning the wound. I scrutinized every move she made, ensuring she did as good a job as I would have. Later, as she made her clinical, precise stitches, my skin popped beneath her needle, like a finger poking through tissue paper. As she worked, she occasionally glanced up at me. I looked away, my eyes falling on the dead-looking guy.

Every now and then, his hand would jump, his legs

twitching, caught in a nightmare, like he was running from something. Or trying to.

Sunny bandaged my hand, packing and wrapping my wounds with a skill even I admitted was good.

"Are you doing okay?" She finished with my right hand and rolled around the end of the cot.

"I'm fine."

She settled her tray on the other side of the bed and turned over my left hand. "What's it like?" she asked so quietly I barely heard her.

"Not feeling pain?" When she nodded, I continued with a heavy sigh. "It's a pain in the ass. I never know when I've really hurt myself or if I'm sick unless the signs are obvious. I can tell if water is hot, but I don't feel if I've scalded myself. I have to spend a lot of money on medical supplies instead of normal things like rent and food or cool shoes."

"Why can't you go to a hospital?" Sunny kept working on my hand, digging into the bite marks and cleaning them with rolls of gauze.

"I just can't." My eyes trailed back to the wounded guy. I hoped Sunny would drop the hospital thing. I didn't want to explain I'd been on the run most my life, never used my real name, and was always too afraid that Max would find me if I checked into a hospital. I had to be a ghost.

"That sounds amazing. I wish I didn't feel pain."

I didn't respond. Even after all I'd been through, I would trade not feeling pain for a normal life any day. Sometimes I wondered if my mom would have never left me if I wasn't such a freak, wasn't so hard to care for. But those were bad thoughts, and I swerved around them now, closing my eyes to them like they were a part in a scary movie. *Don't look*, I told myself.

Sunny worked quietly after that, which I was thankful for. She stitched up my left hand and bandaged it. My elbow was another matter altogether. She had to reset the joint, telling me it was going to hurt before she remembered. With a cautious look, she set the joint, eyes wide while she took in my lack of response. She recorded my basic vitals and gave me a shot then helped me take the antibiotics due to my restraints.

Before the water was even to my mouth, I knew something was wrong with it. I jerked my head away from her. "What did you put in that?"

My harsh accusation rocked Sunny back on her heels. She looked between the water cup she held and me, finally realizing what I meant. "Oh! Nothing is wrong with it, I promise! I added some garlic and chile to it."

Not what I was expecting, but now that she said it, I recognized the tingly hint of garlic in the murky water. "Why?"

"I'm sorry. It's a habit. My mom's side of the family is Filipino, and she always said a person should drink water with garlic and chile in it after being bit to reduce the risk of infection."

My brows rose. "Wouldn't the antibiotics do that?"

"Not from that kind of infection." Sunny smiled. "It's to keep you from turning into a 'swang."

I lurched against my restraints, horror making my throat

thick. "What the fuck? I might turn into one of those things? Shouldn't you have mentioned that earlier?"

She shushed me. "Don't yell! And the chance is very low. Normally only children turn into aswangs when they're bitten."

"Not comforting! Is this just Filipino lore or is this based in actual medical research?"

Sunny shrugged. "No one was ever infected under my mother's watch, and she believed in all the superstitions."

I gritted my teeth. Never one to believe in hopes and chants, I put my faith in the antibiotics. "Fine. But I want two weeks of antibiotics."

"Sure thing." Smiling brightly, she helped me swallow the pills and drink the infused water, which I choked down as my eyes watered. When I finished, she murmured under her breath, "Perausog. Perausog."

"That was disgusting. And what did you just say?"

Sunny took the cup from me. "Warding off the *usog*. The evil eye. My grandmother says it all the time for protection from aswangs." She shrugged. "I thought it couldn't hurt. And it sounds cool, you know?"

"Sunny," I said, feeling suddenly exhausted, "I don't care what you have to say to keep me from turning into one of those things. Send your grandmother my thanks."

"Sure," she said, still smiling, and turned away to tidy up. I sensed the tools and this dark ward gave her comfort, even though I didn't know what a pretty, quiet girl like Sunny needed comfort from, but, then, I guess we all have those bad parts in our lives.

I was almost asleep when Sunny spoke again.

"Will you be okay alone?" In the long pause after her words, I realized she wanted to know if I was scared and didn't want to stay down here by myself. No one had ever asked me that before. I managed a tight nod. "Okay. Try and get in a quick nap. Luke will come for you soon."

"Great."

"I'm sorry I couldn't tell you more," she said, still looking down at her tray. "But maybe . . . maybe if you stay, we can hang out some." Her words were so carefully casual, so carefully full of hope, I knew she didn't have many friends, which surprised me. "And I can tell you everything then. If you stay."

"Do I really have a choice?"

Sunny frowned and finally met my eyes. "I hope so. Because we could really use a hunter like you to save us."

THREE

Weird dreams haunted me during those early morning hours when I napped. Dreams I'd never had before. I dreamed of a woman with blonde hair like mine and a kind smile that made her cheeks dimple prettily. My mother. But the dream didn't let me hate her. Instead, I walked beside her, hand in hand, like a normal mother and daughter. It was wrong. It was a lie.

Then I was a little girl again, squeezing myself into the back of the closet and looking up at my mother with love and trust.

"Olesya," she whispered, her voice quaking with fear, "Stay here. Stay hidden. I'll be back for you, sweet girl. I promise. I'll be back. I love you."

She never came back.

I woke with a start. Someone was shaking my shoulder.

Groaning, I tried to roll away from the jostling and go back to sleep but my wrists were still bound.

"It's time to go."

I cracked an eyelid at Luke's impatient morning voice. I smelled coffee on his breath, and it made my stomach rumble with hunger. "What?"

He dumped a pile of clothes and a small bag on the bed next to my hip before roughly unlocking my cuffs. "Get cleaned up and meet me outside in five minutes." He jerked his chin toward the door before leaving.

I stretched out my arms and opened the bag. He'd brought me a pair of linen pants and a white shirt along with a pair of flats that looked like slippers. Also inside the bag was an unopened toothbrush, a travel-sized tube of toothpaste, a hairbrush, and a pair of lacy panties. I hooked them on the end of my pinkie and brought them up to eye level. Not that I minded a new pair of undies, but this was interesting.

I made quick work of changing, glancing over my shoulder every couple of seconds to make sure the other patient was still asleep. He didn't move. I pulled off my tattered and bloodied waitressing uniform, keeping my bra on, and wiggled into the panties before slipping the pants on. The material was strong and snug over my hips and sat high on my waist, but I liked them even if they weren't exactly my style. Give me Converse and a leather jacket any day and I would be happy. I slid my feet into the slippers and carefully folded up my old clothes before using the sink to brush my teeth and wash the grime off my body. By the end, I looked halfway normal, and the guy on the cot still hadn't stirred.

Luke waited outside the door like he's said. He'd changed into dark jeans and a clean gray thermal that pulled across his chest, outlining an impressive display of muscles. He gave me a brisk once-over before saying, "Follow me."

"Do you give all the girls new panties?" I asked, smiling sweetly up at him.

"Who said they were new?"

His retort stunned me too much to come up with a snappy reply. Without waiting for me, Luke set off down the hall outside of Sunny's ward.

The passageway was windowless and too bright with humming lights. I trailed behind Luke, letting my eyes slip over the metal doors spaced along the hall. Wanting to know if the doors contained prisoners or patients, I glanced at Luke before veering closer to the nearest room and peering into the small window at the top of the door.

A withered old man laid on a starched white bed with wires and devices hooked up to him. It took me a moment to get past the equipment and actually see the man beneath it all, but when I did, I fought to hold down a gasp. The man's face was disfigured, heaped with scars upon scars, all inky black. His nose was off center with a deep twist in the bridge. Black chasms resembling claw marks hollowed out his sallow cheeks. His right eye blinked back at me with a milky white color, his left one gone.

"The nurses do what they can." I jumped at Luke's voice coming from right beside me. He gave the old man a nod and pulled me aside.

"What's wrong with him?" I shivered in the damp coolness of the hospital.

Luke shrugged. "He's a hunter. *Was* a hunter. Dying in a room like that, looking like that, driven half mad by 'swang saliva is a hunter's future. Could be you in twenty years or so if you stay."

"But he looks so old."

"He's thirty-nine, which is old for this lifestyle."

I kept seeing the hunter's black scars and thought of the ones on Hatter's face and those poking up from the hem of Luke's collar. "Why do the scars turn black?"

Luke lifted a shoulder in an uninterested shrug. "Doctors say it's a localized infection, but we really aren't that sure. Get too many, though, and you might turn into a 'swang."

My thoughts instantly returned to Sunny making me drink that water last night. I would have to thank her later. I still wanted extra antibiotics, though.

Luke turned and walked off. With one final glance at the door, I hurried after him, a shiver creeping down my spine at the thought of spending another moment in here. Hospitals, when I'd gotten to go to one, had always comforted me. They were safe. But not this one. There was no healing here. Just death.

"What is this place?" I asked.

"Fear University."

I rolled my eyes. "I know that, but why are there sick people here?"

Luke glanced at me as we walked, our steps echoing off the floors. I had the distinct impression we were underground, which made my skin itch. "This place trains hunters, but we also operate as a hospital for hunters who get injured in the nearby area."

"Must be a pretty big school."

"It's a prison."

I screeched to a stop. "Excuse me?"

Luke paused, cataloging my wild-eyed reaction. I knew I looked wild because I felt like one of those big animals locked in a small cage in some cheap zoo that smelled like shit and bleach. "The school operates under the cover of an old prison, but it's not an actual prison. We used the pre-existing estate for the security and space."

His casualness made me snort. I shoved my hands behind my back to hide their shaking. After all this effort, all this running, I'd ended up in a prison anyway. "Oh really? You're going to drop a bomb like that and act like it's no big deal? We're in a fucking prison!"

Luke blinked. "So?"

He waved me forward before continuing down the hall again. After a long reluctant moment, I followed. A large elevator took up the entire wall at the end of hall. It looked big enough to fit a gurney and a menagerie of doctors and nurses, possibly even the ambulance itself. But Luke avoided it and started up a twisting set of stairs made of crumbling concrete. This part of the prison showed its age in the slick tread worn down the middle stairs. Crude electrical wiring ran along the wall, connecting one light fixture to the next. That shit couldn't be up to code, and I made sure to keep plenty of room between me and the wall.

"What's wrong with 'swang saliva?" I asked, thinking how Luke had mentioned old hunters were driven mad by it and wanting to distract myself from the fact that I was *in a freaking prison.*

Luke grunted and picked up his speed. I caught glimpses of his back as he spiraled up the stairs faster and faster. I picked up my speed, my breath coming in shallow pants, my legs likely on fire from the exertion, but I didn't feel their complaint. At the top, Luke glanced back at me, noting my lack of breath. He cocked a brow. "You're out of shape."

"Bite me."

Luke's expression stayed neutral, impassive, but his green eyes contained a promise of violence. "Not a good thing to say around here."

"Might get what I wish for?" I finally got a reaction from him when his jaw clenched. He didn't like me talking back to him.

He left the dark stairwell and stepped out onto the third floor. Windows filled the walls, letting the morning light stream in and warm the stone at my feet. For this place to be a prison, I hadn't seen any barred doors or such yet. Actually, apart from the dark, confined ward, this floor was airy and bright though the stone floors and exposed bricked walls were a little dated. In contrast to the old architecture was a series of fluorescent lamps swaying slightly above our heads, their light reflecting off the windows.

The third floor stretched out like a long runway in front of me, the right side lined with empty classrooms containing desks and wooden chairs lined neatly over the stone floors.

One room was filled to the brim with so many weapons it looked like a torture room. The students' desks were crammed somewhere in between the weapons protruding from the walls and floor. Abruptly the classrooms stopped, and the wall turned to one of solid glass that stretched the entire length of the hall. It was a large gym, where a handful of students sparred with each other, practicing on the weekend. They wore loose pants and white shirts like mine. Their feet were bare.

As I passed, the students froze, fists still raised and mouths gaping open. Their eyes roved between me and Luke, their expression turning from one of disbelief when they looked at me to respectful intimidation when their attention went to Luke. Who was he that these students watched him like he was some kind of god?

"What are they staring at?" I asked, glaring back at the students, refusing to be the first to look away.

"Civilians aren't meant to be here."

"Yeah, yeah," I muttered. "You keep saying that. So this really is a school." I was kind of surprised. I guess I assumed everyone was lying to me when they called it Fear University.

"You're a sharp one."

"And you're a jackass."

Down the hallway, away from the gym and other classrooms, someone screamed. "What the hell?" I grabbed Luke's arm to slow his quick pace.

"Fear simulator. It's normal."

"It's normal for people to scream here? And what's a fear simulator?"

He started walking again, calling over his shoulder as he went, "What does it sound like?"

I rolled my eyes at his back but I had no choice but to follow him. I really wanted to meet this Dean and see what he had to say since he was apparently an important person here at Fear University. I kind of hated to admit it because I never liked getting my hopes up about anything—it left too much room for them to be crushed—but I was actually intrigued by this place.

These people had nothing to do with Max, or else I would already be dead. And the school didn't even look like a prison. Maybe it would have been more normal to be afraid, but I was just excited.

We turned a corner, and I finally caught my first view of the prison's estate. I screeched to a stop, shocked by the view. I ignored Luke's impatient sigh as he waited for me.

A bank of floor-to-ceiling windows lined the wall in the narrow alcove of offices. Outside revealed the familiar landscape of Kodiak Island, which meant Luke hadn't lied about us staying on the island. Thick cottonwood and birch trees rose up into the crisp fall air; the sky blazed a clear, crisp, bright blue. There were buildings and even a small grouping of wind turbines peeking above the treeline. And beyond that . . .

"Is that a fence?" I asked, shocked. It appeared gigantic, a massive wall of impenetrable stone, even from a distance. I made out the thick spirals of razor wire along the top and the watchtowers stationed at intervals along the fence.

"This is a prison."

"It used to be," I said, needing to clarify, but Luke walked farther into the alcove without a word. He stopped beside a thick cherry door. Before I knocked, he caught my wrist and pulled me to a stop. He loomed over me, a mere inch separating our bodies. I forced myself to meet his eyes even though he was doing a damn fine job at this intimidation game, but I wouldn't back down. Heat rolled off of him in suffocating waves until I had to bite my tongue to keep from panting. I tried to jerk away to catch my breath.

"This place *will* be a prison for an outsider like you. A death sentence. Whatever Dean asks you, you need to say no. Go home. Go home or you'll die here."

I finally wrenched my arm free. "God, you're so cheery, you know that?"

"I'm serious, Ollie. This isn't the place for you. If you have problems with that Max guy, I can take care of him for you. But you can't stay."

His words startled me, shoved me off kilter. My harsh reply died in my mouth and I blinked up at him, wondering if he really meant what he said. But as I thought it, I knew the answer. He did. His squarely set shoulders, determined eyes, and tip-tapping fingers told me that he would follow through on any violent promise. I loosed a breath, and his eyes swept down to my lips.

I froze. What was he thinking when he stared at me like that? Heat pooled in my belly; I sure as hell knew what I was thinking. It involved tackling him to the floor and dry humping.

Disturbing my fantasy, the office door swung open and

Mustache Guy stood in front of us. He coughed and Luke took a step back from me. "Thank you, Luke. I've got it from here."

The look that passed between Dean and Luke made it clear that Dean knew exactly what Luke had been doing before he opened the door. Neither man said anything for an awkward beat, their eyes searing into each other. "Thanks, Luke," I said to break the tension.

He was getting under my skin, and I really didn't like it. Okay. Maybe I did. A little.

I stepped inside the office, while Dean held the door open for me. Freshly baked scones and coffee filled the room with divine smells. My stomach rumbled.

"Good morning, Miss Andrews. Please have a seat wherever you like. I'm Dean Bogrov, the President of Fear University."

So Dean wasn't just an important guy at Fear University, he was *the* important guy. But I still stared him down with narrowed eyes and suspicion. "How do you know my last name?"

My *real* last name. That I never used.

Dean closed the office door and crossed over to his mahogany desk, which he took a seat behind. Reluctantly, I perched on the edge of a plush leather wingback chair facing his desk. I scraped the toe of my slipper on the Oriental rug beneath me, a nervous habit.

"Don't be alarmed. We pulled your file." My file. I fought hard not to cringe at his words. If they had my file, they had everything. "This is as unusual for us as it is for you, Miss

Andrews." Dean smiled a warm, fatherly smile, and I hated myself for relaxing a teeny bit.

"If you pulled my file, then you have to be government affiliated. And you know . . ." I took a deep breath. "You know about my warrant."

"Miss Andrews—"

"It's Ollie. Just Ollie."

"I see." There was that smile again. "You're a smart girl, Ollie. We are government affiliated, but only a very small committee of officials know we exist. This school, this place, is a legitimate effort to hunt and kill aswangs. Thank you for meeting with me."

I snorted. "Did I have a choice?"

"Of course! Would you like some orange juice or water?" Dean waved a hand toward a small breakfast cart sitting in his office. The ice in the water was still frozen, drops of condensation rolling down the sides of the crystal carafe. Orange juice and coffee filled the other pitchers. I eyed the bagels and scones, my stomach rolling with hunger, but I shook my head. "No, thank you."

I never took food from strangers.

While Dean poured himself some more coffee, I took the chance to examine his bookshelves, which lined every wall in his office but the one full of windows. I spotted a dagger, human skull, and a statue of an eagle amongst the books. A large map of the university hung on the wall behind Dean's desk, covering a patch of the window. The desk itself was a vision of disaster: papers were strewn all over, held down by coffee mugs and opened books.

"I trust Sunny took good care of you last night?" Dean asked, smiling. He sipped on a large mug of coffee. When he picked it up, I noticed it had left a damp circular stain on the paper beneath it.

"She did."

"You took quite a beating. How do your hands and elbow feel?"

"Fine."

Dean smiled even broader, leaning forward and resting his elbows on the desk. "You don't talk much do you?"

"Not to people I don't trust."

He laughed, though it was more like a bellowing guffaw than a laugh. Loud and unrestrained. His hand rested on his slightly round belly, his mustache twitching. "I like that," he managed, still laughing. "It's good to not trust many people. That's how you get hurt."

"Or how you get thrown in the back of vans and drugged."

My flat expression turned Dean serious. "You're right. I apologize for our behavior. Finding you . . ." He shook his head, making me think he wanted to add more. "Well, let's say that we've never dealt with something like this before."

"I'm something to be dealt with?"

"Not at all." When I merely glared, Dean leaned forward on his desk. Normally, I made people nervous, but I only intrigued this man. I didn't know if that should worry me more or not. "You could help us, Ollie."

I sat back in my chair and crossed my legs. "I'm not helping anybody until I get some straight answers."

Dean mimicked my position in his own chair and took a long sip of coffee. "By all means, fire away," he said, smiling once again. I waited a moment to see if he was serious, but he merely waited patiently. I took my chance.

"I want to know what you people are doing here and what these *things* are."

"They're called aswangs, but we call them 'swangs around here. Since the beginning of time, man and 'swangs have walked this earth together. They originated in the Philippines but many migrated north to Russia, then to Alaska, Canada, and Greenland. They walk among us, going mostly unnoticed in the daytime and nighttime, feeding off our fear, making the attacks look like a rabid animal. But since the beginning of man, there's always been a group of people who fight the 'swangs to keep the world in balance, and when the 'swangs came north, so did select hunter families from the Philippines. They joined up with the Alaskan native tribes, and over time, the families started intermingling and marrying outside of the original groups, which is how we have the amount of hunter families we have now. *Next*."

He was playing along with the notion I was in control of the meeting and asking the questions, so I continued while my luck held, even as I processed the fact that Sunny's superstitious remedies now made sense. "How does no one else know about this war? If you're government affiliated, why doesn't the United States drop a nuke on a 'swang den or something?"

"The war is a secret for humanity's own well-being, and because it isn't going well. The balance is tipping toward the 'swangs. They're reproducing faster than we can kill them. If we lose control . . ." Dean's humor faded away, his eyes searching the depth of his coffee like he wished there was a glug of whiskey mixed in. "If we lose control, this entire world would become one big fear concentration camp, where humans live in terror and the 'swangs lap it up like honey. Humanity would be lost."

I'd never cared much for humanity, which sounded awful but it was true. People didn't treat me well, and, in return, I never treated them well. But I thought about Sunny and the young man lying down in the ward with his throat nearly ripped out. "What about you and Luke and all those kids out there training?"

"This place isn't a prison, as you can see. It's a school, a university. We teach the college-age children of the hunter families to kill aswangs. These people live and die by this war. They send their children here to fight and bear this burden. And their children will do the same, and their children after that."

"So what's the big deal? It sounds like you have an endless supply of fresh blood."

Dean shook his head. "We don't, Ollie. This life is hard. People are afraid, and our numbers are dwindling. The 'swangs, for the first time in history, have the upper hand on us."

I sat forward in my seat. "What are they so afraid of? What can these 'swangs do?"

Dean took a long sip of coffee and set the mug down. Rolling back his chair, he stood and flipped the map of the grounds back to reveal an old drawing of a black dog with elongated, skinny legs and paws eerily familiar to a human hand. The proportions of its body alluded to the appearance of a dog, but looked almost as if a human had been stuffed inside its jagged ribs and was straining to get loose.

"That's what I killed," I said, my eyes glued to the creature's weird, human-like eyes and startlingly white teeth.

"This is an aswang," Dean said. "These creatures have two forms: a night-form where they become black dogs, and a day-form where they return to their human form."

"Human?" A hazy memory from the flight over here surfaced, and I remembered a body lying next to me. A man with a broken jaw and neck. But I'd likely been dreaming.

"Their human forms are simple husks, like a paper envelope holding in the 'swang until it can come out at night. During the day, 'swangs are harmless. That's when they are easiest to kill, but it's impossible to know a 'swang in its human form."

"They sound like werewolves."

"The concept of werewolves and even vampires evolved from the lore of aswangs, but aswangs are very much real. And far more dangerous. When 'swangs hunt at night, they don't just kill you. They don't drink your blood or eat you. They kill you with your own fear of pain manifested inside your brain."

A chill crept down my spine, like when I was younger and used to hear really good ghost stories. My heart fluttered with excitement. I stood and crossed behind Dean's desk to study the drawing of the 'swang. In its pencil-drawn eyes, I almost made out a weird reflection, like the artist had caught the inverted image. "How? Are they telepathic?" I asked, thinking of how the 'swang had spoken to me.

"A 'swang manipulates the parts of your brain that process fear. These creatures turn your mind against you and make you experience a pain unlike any other. They make you think you're dying, and then they feed off the fear that's coursing through your body alongside the pain and adrenaline as they eat you."

The eating me part didn't bother me; the manipulation did. I didn't like that some creature could crawl into my mind and take control, even if I couldn't feel the pain they were inflicting on me. "Is it like magic?"

Dean made a noise in the back of his throat. "That's a big debate here at Fear University. We don't know if the 'swangs use magic or some kind of supernatural power against us, or if it's mere evolution."

I wanted to laugh but I stopped myself. "Magic versus evolution? What do you think these things evolved from that they can be so much more advanced than we are?"

"I don't believe they're more advanced. 'Swangs are primal beasts driven by basic desires. They just have a cool hat trick up their sleeves."

"A hat trick that kills a shit-ton of people."

"True. But aside from the debate, we really don't know how they came to be or what they came from. A lot of what we know about these creatures is theoretical."

"So they can't *speak* to you or anything?" I said the words carefully, like they didn't mean anything.

"No."

I frowned and stepped back from the picture, putting the desk between Dean and me again. "So however they do it, they mess with your brain and make you think you're experiencing pain. But I didn't feel pain that night. Or ever. So whatever they use to screw with people, they can't screw with me."

Dean smiled, and, for the first time, he relaxed. We took our seats again, as if this was a negotiation or a board meeting. "I believe it's because your brain processes pain differently due to your mutation of congenital analgesia. The 'swang couldn't affect your brain, which meant it couldn't feed off your fear."

"I wasn't afraid."

"I know," Dean said, laughing, and I knew he believed me. "That's why you're special, Ollie. You have a power hunters can only dream of. These monsters can't touch you. Do you know what that means?"

Dean turned serious again, leaning across his desk like I was a piece of lemon meringue pie with whipped cream on top. He meant every word with every last ounce of truth in his body, and what's more, I knew he needed me. This whole place needed me. Because I was special.

I'd never been special my whole life.

"It means I would be a good hunter," I said, keeping my voice carefully under control. I didn't want him to see how excited I was. Excited at the hope I could possibly belong somewhere.

Dean shook his head. "No. It means you would be the

best hunter that ever lived."

"That's why you made Luke bring me here. You want me to stay and learn to kill them."

"To kill *monsters*. To help us obliterate these vile creations and take back our world."

I frowned at his words. From the back of my mind, I recalled the 'swang's horrible, painful whimper as I'd broken its jaw. "What if I say no?"

"You can," Dean said quickly. "You're not a prisoner here, but I think I can offer you something that might make you want to stay."

I knew what he meant. I'd been expecting it. "The murder warrant," I said evenly. "And Maxwell Taber."

"Yes. Our work here is sanctioned by a very select group of individuals in the United States government, like I said before. They have the power to pardon you. And my hunters, well, my hunters have the power to take care of your brother."

"He's not my brother." I bit off each word with force, clenching my fists.

Dean's mustache stretched above a soft smile full of understanding and sympathy. "We could do that for you, Ollie. You could start over here. You'd be safe. We would become your family."

I looked away at his words. How many times had I wished for a family? A real family that actually wanted me. A place where I belonged and felt special. Where I wasn't a neat party trick drunk men showed their drunk buddies. Where my condition, my curse, could be a gift. When I was hurt, someone besides myself would take care of me. It sounded so much like Heaven, my knees went a little weak.

Sensing I needed a moment to collect myself, Dean changed the subject. "What do you think of the estate?"

"I think it's a prison."

Dean held up his hands. "No one is trapped here. The fence and a few other security measures are used for the pretense of the university being a prison, but they are also for protection against the 'swangs."

"They know about this place?" I asked, my fingertips turning cold.

"They do, but they've never been organized enough to mount a decent attack. Normally, it's two or three rushing the fence. We have alarms and motion detectors, so it doesn't take much to subdue them. There are plenty of emergency procedures in place. You're safe here, Ollie."

"I don't put much stock in *procedures*."

Dean smiled warmly. "I think you and I could get along quite well."

I shrugged without responding. I'd heard that a lot in my life. Never worked out well.

"Now, Ollie. We need to talk about the other night."

I sighed. "Okay."

"You were walking home from work. You're a waitress, right?" He smiled again when I nodded. "My wife was a waitress. She hated it. Said too many people got off on commanding other people."

I smirked. "She's right. Does she still waitress?"

Dean's smile slipped ever so slightly. "I'm afraid she's not with us anymore."

The way he said it made me think one thing: *'swang.* I saw a flash of teeth and hungry eyes, and I blinked the memory away. "I'm sorry," I said.

"Thank you." He quickly brushed over the subject. "Can you start from the beginning? What did you hear or see before the 'swang appeared?"

I thought back to last night, trying to remember the details. Details to share and the ones to keep to myself. Like hearing the 'swang. Something told me I should keep that card close to my chest. When I was ready, I launched into my story, telling him about the dark street, walking home alone, and the ticking sound.

Dean nodded like he expected this. "It started loud at first, right? Then got quieter?"

I blinked in surprise. "How did you know?"

"That's how the 'swangs hunt. To trick their prey, they make it sound like they are moving away from them, not drawing closer. The nearer they are, the quieter the night."

"Oh," I said, unnerved by that. "Okay. So that's what I noticed right before I saw the dog—'swang. I knew it wasn't normal right away. It just stood there, staring at me like it . . . was human or something."

"What did you see, Ollie?" Dean prompted.

"My reflection," I said, deciding to tell the truth.

Dean leaned forward. "What about it?"

"It was upside down."

Dean smiled suddenly like I'd aced a pop quiz. "Not a lot of people notice that. Their fear controls what they see."

"I wasn't afraid."

"I can tell. What happened then?"

Damn if his approval didn't bolster my confidence. I launched back into my story about fighting the 'swang. When I finished, he leaned forward on his desk again, hands clenched together in front of him like he was praying. "We could use *your* help, Ollie. Your gift could make you almost invincible against 'swangs. You could kill thousands with the proper training. We would take you in, make you family. You would live and train here. This would be your new home, but you'd have to leave your old life behind. No contact. All your friends and family would think you're dead—"

"There's no one."

Dean paused, sadness deepening the wrinkles around his mouth. "Another gift, I guess. This lifestyle isn't conducive to connections to the outside world. It gets too hard. But it's a big commitment. You would be giving up everything. You would be in for life. And in the end, you might even die for the cause. All our hunters accept this. If you choose—"

"I do."

And I did. For me. For a home. For a family. For belonging. But I also agreed because I knew I was a certain type of person. A bad kind. A killing kind. I would be good at hunting monsters, because I was a monster myself. Why run from something that felt so right?

"You do?" he asked, taken aback. "You're sure? This is serious, Ollie."

I made myself wait, so he knew I understood how serious this was. I didn't want to play too much into Dean's hands, but he already knew he had me hook, line, and sinker. He'd seen my reaction when he talked about family. He knew that was what I wanted, even more than the pardon and Max's death. But I still told myself to wait, to make it seem like I at least cared about my freedom.

But in the face of all this . . . my freedom was the last thing on my mind. I longed to be special. To belong. I wanted it more than I'd ever wanted anything. The decision was one I'd been waiting my entire life to make. I didn't need to think about it.

"I want the murder charge taken care of. If you can make that go away, I'll stay. But I take care of Max Taber. No one touches him but me. Got it?"

I would finish the job I'd started two years ago. The justice wouldn't be for me but for the other little girl who had been in the basement that night.

"We can do that. But before we do, I want to make sure you're a good fit. You will go to classes at the first-year level and train in the evenings with a tutor. You will have final exams and the Field Testing this semester like all the other first-years, but you will also have an extra evaluation from me in two weeks from now. If you pass, you can stay at Fear University, and if you make it through this semester, I will get your pardon."

My future here would be riding on this evaluation. No matter what, I needed to pass. "Fine. The evaluation then. And you'll clear my name at the end of the semester."

Dean waited a long moment, like he was examining me again, looking for any lies. I waited while he searched. When he sat back in his chair, I knew I was in. "We're glad to have you, Ollie," he said, sighing like a heavy burden was lifted off his shoulders. "You don't know how relieved we are." He shuffled out some papers from underneath his coffee mug. He held up a folder. "This has your temporary schedule, student card, which Sunny will explain, and a map of the grounds. I want to talk to some professors and get their opinions, but I'm putting you straight into all the first-year's classes. You've missed about a month of school, but you won't have too much catching up to do."

"Great." I took the folder he offered me. "I'm ready."

"If you have any trouble with anyone, you come straight to me, okay?"

"What kind of trouble would I have?" I narrowed my eyes, wary again.

"Ollie, you're an outsider here. Until you prove yourself, and until people have time to forget how you came here . . . you might be caught in the crosshairs. All these people have ever known is their duty. We were born into this. You weren't. It will take time, but I'm afraid you might catch some grief for it."

I gritted my teeth. Always the outsider. Always the foster kid. "I can handle myself just fine."

"I know you can, but I don't want you to hurt any of the other students when they piss you off." He grinned at me, and I couldn't help but grin back. This guy understood me; I liked it. It felt nice to be respected.

A knock rapped against the office door. Dean smiled. "That must be Sunny now. I told her to drop by and show you around. This is your home now, Ollie. You're not a prisoner, but if you want to go outside of the fences, please talk to a professor or me first. We will have to ensure your safety. If you need something other than what the university's general store provides, a professor goes out once a week. You can leave a list with her."

"Okay," I said, sensing that our meeting was over.

We rose from our chairs. Dean stretched out his hand. It took me a moment to realize he wanted me to shake it. Carefully, I grasped his hand. If he noticed my reluctance at touching him, he didn't comment. "Can I ask you something?"

I glanced at him before quickly pulling my hand back. I didn't like those words; they sounded like a test. "What?"

"Why did you kill that man?"

My mouth parted in surprise, and, for once, I didn't know what to say.

"He was Max's father right? His biological father? That's why Max has been stalking you?"

I swallowed, the act feeling impossible in my dry mouth. Images flashed through my mind. Blood. Not mine. Screams. Not mine. Max's hands. His father's hands. Rope and darkness and a bleak basement that smelled of fresh earth. A little girl with pretty hair and bright-blue eyes begging me to save her. I gritted my teeth. "I didn't do anything that he didn't deserve."

"So it wasn't an accident then?"

"No." I ground out the word. "And I would have killed Max too if he hadn't gotten away."

I didn't know if that was the answer Dean expected, but I took his silence as my cue to leave. I crossed the cozy room to the door, and, with the doorknob in hand, I turned back around. Dean was already sitting back in his chair, sipping his coffee. "You said I would have a tutor. Who is it?"

Dean smiled. It looked almost apologetic. "We want you trained by the best, Ollie. I know he's a little rough, but he's the greatest hunter we've seen in a long time. Luke Aultstriver will be your tutor."

I nodded and opened the door, trying to hide my smile. That's who I'd hoped he would say.

FOUR

Keeping up with Sunny, who resembled a child's doll more than an eighteen-year-old young woman, turned out to be harder than it sounded. She bounced down the hall, springs engineered into her little heels. This part of the school was mostly empty since it was the weekend, but we passed a few students wearing the same gauzy pants as us. Sunny smiled and waved at each of them, calling their names in greeting, though they were too busy staring at me and the bandages on my hands to wave back. I kept my face carefully blank, one brow cocked in a "back off or die" manner I'd perfected over the years. It seriously surprised me how a mere facial expression kept people back at a safe distance.

Between cheerful waves, Sunny showed me all the classrooms I'd passed on my walk over with Luke, pointing out where my classes would be as she consulted my schedule.

"The third floor in both wings is for classrooms and professors' offices. Your schedule will say east or west for what wing your classroom is in, and then you can follow the numbers to the right room. Easy peasy, lemon squeezy."

I couldn't hold back my smile at her cheerful tone. If I looked past the fact that this place was a prison, it actually felt kind of nice, like an old university full of happy students and the smell of leather books. "Will we have any classes together?"

Sunny squished up her nose, making her glasses touch her eyebrows. "No. Some of the students, like me, are in accelerated classes."

"You must be really smart, then." I didn't know how normal friends acted around each other, but it seemed like a nice enough thing to say.

"Oh, it's not like that. It's like," Sunny hesitated, "like, the students who were marked to be good hunters go straight into the advanced classes. Not that I'm going to be a good hunter or anything, but they didn't know that until my schedule was already set this year. They put us in accelerated classes because we're from the older families."

I was hearing a lot about these families. All this blood heritage talk and old prisons made me feel like I was in an mafia movie or something. "Dean mentioned some families came over from the Philippines when the 'swangs migrated here forever ago. Was your family one of them?"

"On my mom's side. My dad is Russian." Her tone changed slightly when she talked about her family. I understood. I didn't like talking about family either.

"Are students allowed to go outside of this building?" I asked to change the subject.

"Yeah, totally! We can go anywhere within the fence. Going outside the fences requires special permission, and normally only the fourth and fifth-years are allowed to go. They want to keep us safe, you know."

A group of students approached us from the other end of the hall. They were pretty girls dressed in a uniform of workout clothes: tight black shorts and brightly colored tank tops. The girl in the middle had perfectly tanned skin, dark mahogany hair, and a mean smirk on her face. "Well, look who it is. The Cowardly Lyon and a dirty old civvie."

I drew to a stop, ready to face off. But the group of girls passed by us, laughing at the joke. "Who was that?"

Sunny swallowed, her face looking slightly green. "Jolene and Allison and their posse of mean girls. You should avoid them."

"Why?" I glared down the hallway, watching as the girls pranced into the gym, swinging their long, shining ponytails against their backs.

"Because they're mean," Sunny said like it should be obvious to me. I turned my attention back to her. She really did look scared of them.

"I'm mean too."

Another scream echoed down the hall. My head snapped back in that direction, thinking maybe Jolene or one of her friends had slipped and broken their face on the floor. But I didn't see anything.

"Fear sim," Sunny said. "Students like to practice on the

weekends."

"Doesn't it bother you?"

"The screams?"

I nodded.

"Not really, I guess. You get used to it. The sim is the best tool we have to prepare for the 'swangs. We can fight them in the sim and not actually be in danger of being fed on."

"Do hunters get fed on a lot?"

"Not the good ones," Sunny said with a laugh, like it was an inside joke or something. "But in all seriousness, the university spends a lot, and I mean *a lot*, of time conditioning the third-year students who specialize in hunting. After two semesters of training in the sim, students are ready for a little fear feeding on occasion, you know?"

We continued toward the bank of elevators at the end of hall, which was actually the center of the building. We'd been walking for a while, and I had a pretty good idea of the building's layout with the east and west wings. Enough of an idea to know that there was something big positioned in the middle of the building that separated the structure into two wings.

"Training in the sim sounds like fun," I said, meaning it.

Sunny shuddered. "It's impossible to remember you're actually not about to die in the simulations. They're good."

"Have you been inside it?" I couldn't imagine her fighting 'swangs with her cute, nerdy glasses and quick smile. Sunny pushed the button for the elevator, and the door immediately dinged open.

"It's part of the university's application test. They use the fear simulator to create an encounter with a 'swang. You feel everything the 'swang would make you feel, and then, if it kills you, you feel that too. I, ah, I broke the record."

"That's cool!"

"Um." Sunny pushed her glasses farther up her nose and hit the button for the second floor. "Not really. I broke the record for dying the fastest. I was terrified, like, a total coward. The only reason they let me enroll is because my parents were doctors for the university and they bought the school a brand-new CT scanner. So the university trains me to be a doctor." She shrugged, flushing with embarrassment. "That's why Jolene and her friends call me the Cowardly Lyon. My last name is Lyons."

"That's bullshit. You should tell them to stop." There were a lot of things I hated in this world, but bullies were close to the top.

Sunny snorted. "I highly doubt telling Jolene to stop would do anything."

"Then beat her face in."

Sunny glanced at me in surprise, her dark brows high above her glasses. A nervous giggle escaped her lips. "I could never do that."

"I can," I offered, meaning it. This was the kind of friendship I understood: the violence barter system. It came in handy during my foster kid time.

"Um, that's okay." Sunny shot me a grin before turning serious again. "It's terrible to say, but I'm kind of relieved that I didn't do well on my entrance test. I came here thinking I would be a hunter, but I was naive. My grandmother always told me that the true hunters are called to kill aswangs, like, in their hearts and stuff, you know? But that's why everyone is talking about you. Most of the younger students have never even seen a 'swang, much less killed one. You're the real deal. My grandmother would say you were called."

I didn't like how her words made my heart flutter, so I joked, "Yeah or kidnapped. So you haven't seen a 'swang either?"

"Thankfully, not in real life. I'd probably curl up in the fetal position right there on the spot."

I decided not to voice my surprise. But how could these students fight an enemy they'd never seen before? Killing the 'swang in Kodiak hadn't been all that hard, but clearly I had a distinct advantage. I had no clue what it would be like for someone like Sunny or Luke.

The elevator arrived on the second floor, and Sunny marched me along more halls, groups of gaping students scattered throughout. The second floor contained the cafeteria, more classrooms, and some crowded rec rooms where students hung out and watched movies during their free periods or in the evenings.

"Will I have to do the fear sim?" I asked, returning to our previous conversation.

Sunny laughed, the sound dancing down the hall. "I really doubt it. I mean, you've, like, already killed one. So putting you in the sim would be a little overkill, you know? But Dean wants me to do a few tests on you later."

"Tests?" I was already nervous enough about the evaluation I would have in a couple of weeks. The thought of more tests on top of that one made me sick.

"Blood and marrow tests. Don't worry. I've done lots before, so you'll be safe with me. My parents sent me to loads of medical summer camps during high school. Anyway, after that you'll meet up with Luke and do a few physical tests."

"What is Luke's deal anyway?" I asked cautiously. I'd learned my lesson about showing interest in something or someone during my foster care years, when toys or food had been ripped out of my hands the moment my eyes lit up with joy. Pretending not to care was *always* the best policy.

"I don't really know much about him," Sunny confessed. "But he's the best hunter the university has. He's killed, like, five hundred 'swangs or something. It's almost triple what any other hunter has killed at his age. He's totally lethal and obviously deliciously good-looking. That's all I really know about him. The rest are rumors."

"Rumors?"

"I don't really like to gossip . . ."

"Oh, come on," I huffed, my heart beating with excitement.

Sunny glanced around like she was about to give me nuclear launch codes. She lowered her voice and whispered, "They say he drinks a 'swang's blood after he kills it."

"Why?" I asked, breathless. Sunny seemed surprised at my lack of repulsion, but frankly, after meeting Luke, I found it kind of . . . hot. Call me crazy.

"A 'swang's blood has certain powers. My mom always said it can make you fearless." At this, Sunny looked at me closely.

"I didn't drink blood," I said quickly. "Are there any other rumors?"

"Well . . . kind of. But I really doubt this one is true. Jolene and Allison, who are, like, super-duper skanky," Sunny said with a cute, totally not-vicious snarl, "say he's celibate."

I snorted. "No wonder he's so grumpy. Why is he celibate?"

"Uh." Sunny blushed. She suddenly busied herself brushing off lint from her pants. "They say he kind of likes it too rough or something," she mumbled.

I choked. "What?"

A blush spread from Sunny's cheeks to the tips of her ears. She lowered her voice even more. "You know how 'swang saliva affects hunters when they're bit?" I nodded quickly, stomach fluttering. "Well, rumor is that the saliva makes Luke, like, oh God, I can't say it."

"Say it!"

"They say it makes him super sexually aggressive!" Sunny said the words fast, like if she spilled them out quick enough no one would hear. I felt my eyes bugging out of my head.

"It can do that?"

"Yeah. Saliva reacts differently for everyone. Rumor has it that there was a young pretty hunter here once who spent a lot of time with Luke, but she left because Luke was so rough with her after a hunt that he hurt her real bad. I mean it was, like, consensual, but, well, you know what I mean."

"Holy shit," I said, totally floored. But totally, completely intrigued. Luke Aultstriver just got a hell of a lot more interesting.

"But it's not uncommon for hunters to abstain, especially if they follow the old ways of the earliest hunters," Sunny hurried to add. "They say it's a distraction. But with Luke, it's a little different."

More like a lot different. Luke was the first guy in years who actually caught my attention. I'm not a nun by any means, but after the life I've lived, it takes a lot to interest me.

"Is Hatter celibate?" I smirked at Sunny, who was blushing too furiously to manage a response. I elbowed her softly in the ribs, which made her burst out into hysterical giggles. The sound made me smile.

Made me feel at home.

She gave me a tour of the first floor next, which held even more classrooms, although these looked dusty and mostly out of use, and administration offices. By the bank of elevators, there was a gleaming entry with busts of past university presidents and old paintings lining the walls. The front doors into the university were no joke. I wondered how we would get them open, because they were thick iron with numerous locks and bolts. There was nothing pretty about these doors, just pure mean, clean "stay the hell out."

Sunny swiped her card, and the iron doors easily swooshed open. Squinting and shielding my eyes against the sun, I followed her out to a bright courtyard, where little round tables complete with red-and-white-checkered umbrellas filled the space and provided a cozy gathering place. Students clustered about with their laptops and textbooks, laughing and joking with each other. Music played from different sources, mingling together to make an entirely new sound that felt alive and vivid in my heart. The day was warm for fall on Kodiak Island, and the students soaked up the sun in their different groups. The courtyard buzzed with youth and promise. A tremble of excitement swept down my spine; this was my place now.

Remembering the building behind me, I glanced back. But just a glance wouldn't do. I slowly turned around, my mouth hanging slightly open, my eyes straining to take it all in.

From the inside, I struggled to remember the place had originally been a prison, a fortress. But now I understood. The building—comprised of two long, three-story wings and a hulking dome structure in the middle—resembled a snarling beast with jagged limbs of turrets that swept up toward the brutal arch of the dome, a thick fur of snarling vines and moss grown from the gutters' dripping moisture, and rows upon rows of windows that looked like gleaming fangs. The dome's roof glinted in the sun, a pretty blue metal—the first and only pretty thing about the building. Blocks of giant stone made up the structure, giving it a speckled quality from the hodge-podge of colors. Some stones had faded gray with age, while others gleamed bright red with newness. It could have been ugly, probably should have been, but to me, it was wicked. Completely, utterly, *wicked*.

This was Fear University.

"It's something, isn't it?" Sunny said quietly, reverently, from beside me.

"What's in that dome thing?"

"Uh." She cleared her throat. "The dorms."

"Are we going there?"

"Not yet."

I didn't let Sunny see my frown, but I kept looking back, watching as the domed structure rose into the day's sunlight behind me.

"Want to see something cool?" Sunny asked, growing excited, and clearly trying to distract me.

I looked where she pointed. Beyond the edge of the humming courtyard stood the university's front entrance. Like the school, the main gate showed its teeth with pride. It must have weighed a ton with so much tight twisting and lethal-looking metal. In the middle of the gate was Fear University's crest, a filigreed oval depicting snow-capped mountains beneath a sky full of stars. Along either side of the entrance, the main fence spread out farther than my eye could see. Off to the side, where Sunny pointed, a very tall ladder led up to a small hut-like structure atop the fence's ledge.

"What's that?" I asked, my eyes scanning up nearly thirty-feet to the top of the fence.

"A rook's nest. The guards use them for patrols. Each corner and middle point of the perimeter fence have huge watch towers, but they put up these rook nests in between, so guards can drink some water or something during their perimeter walks."

I raised my brows. Sunny hurried over to the ladder, but I followed at a more sedate pace as I studied the fence. It was thick, likely concrete, with a large landing along the top for patrolling guards. The railing consisted of protruding iron bars, as if they were there to keep the dogs from climbing up onto the landing. I wondered if the bars were overkill. A dog couldn't climb thirty feet into the air. Or maybe the professors and guards were worried about something else reaching the top of the fence.

Sunny had already climbed halfway up the ladder by the time I put my foot on the first rung. The fence stood tall, and when we reached the top, Sunny shook out her legs and groaned from the exertion. My breathing came fast as I crossed the rook's nest, which felt like a well-supplied tree house, and looked out beyond the fence.

The sight stole my breath.

"Tick Tock Bay," Sunny said quietly, reverently.

My eyes swept down the scraggy, rocky incline toward the bay, where the ocean, a deep sapphire blue, swept in, beating white spray against rock pillars and crashing against a stony-gray shore far below the rook's nest. Naked trees, stripped bare, tilted in the briny sea air. My hair wiped around my face, catching in my eyelashes. Somehow, the desolate place was peaceful, comforting even. Energy seemed to infiltrate the wind, making it sound like whispers as it blew through the trees. The cliffs surrounding the bay felt like arms holding the prison close. The tightness in my chest released, and for the first time since I'd arrived, I breathed.

"It's beautiful," I said, still looking out across the water. The fence was built atop the shore's stone. A road wound its way along the bottom of the wall and toward a dock that led out to the bay, likely for when boats came in with supplies.

"Beautiful?" At Sunny's shocked tone, I turned to face her. "It's terrifying!"

"Why?"

"The Tick Tock Massacre! The reason this bay is nicknamed after the ticking of a clock." I remembered how the 'swang had ticked when it attacked me, and I began to understand Sunny's wide-eyed reverence. "Nearly seventy years ago, on Halloween, the students and professors went out to the bay for a party. It wasn't dark yet, but it was twilight, and darkness comes fast up here." Her voice trembled with nervous excitement as she fell into the rhythm of the story, one she'd clearly memorized long ago. "The professors carefully watched the time, and when nightfall came, they called the students and told them to go back to the school. But the students were having a good time, and, for a night, they'd forgotten the war, their enemy, the night's monsters. When the students finally listened to the professors, the sun's light had nearly sank into the bay's churning water.

"They say the night suddenly turned very still, very quiet-like. And only when the students heard the beating of their hearts did a great noise build. From the edges of the trees and the cliffs surrounding the bay, came the tick-tocking of a clock. The sound surrounded them and the students remembered. Remembered the war, their enemy, the night's monsters.

"The tick-tocking echoed so loudly the students all fell to their knees and screamed, covering their ears. The professors had their weapons drawn, but no one could hear each other to coordinate a defense. Not that a defense mattered anyway, because by the time the ticking had faded enough to hear each other, the professors and few hunters present knew they were doomed. There was nothing they could do but fight. It was a bloodbath; there were too many 'swangs. Nearly everyone died."

Gooseflesh prickled along my skin, and the breeze picked up, threading through my hair, like an answer to Sunny's story.

"They say that the bay turned red with blood." Sunny and I both jumped at the sound of the voice coming from behind us. We whirled around and found Hatter had crossed to the platform behind us, an assault rifle casually laid across his chest, his finger mere inches from the trigger. His wide grin made his scars twitch and pull along his face. "And when the ocean carried the bloodied waves back out to sea, the fishing ships' captains thought a sea monster had been slaughtered and they cheered and drank lots of beer. Lucky bastards."

"A sea monster? Really?" I asked, trying not to smile.

"The other version is that the captains thought the sea had gotten her period. Which would you prefer?"

Sunny giggled. "Definitely sea monsters."

Hatter's grin softened when he looked at her. I doubt she even noticed, too caught up in her own admiring. "I agree. Much less gruesome."

"Because," I said, "a massacre isn't gruesome enough."

"Eh." Hatter shrugged.

"Sorry to interrupt your patrol, Hatter," Sunny said, the corners of her smile shaking slightly. "I wanted to show Ollie the bay."

"Be careful, don't want to scare her off," Hatter warned, winking at Sunny.

As soon as he finished speaking, heavy treads landed on the rook's nest beside us. Sunny gasped, but I turned to find Luke standing next to me. I hadn't heard him come up the ladder and I was the one standing closest to it. With him up here, the rather large rook's nest felt stiflingly small and my spine tingled at his nearness. I couldn't help but think of the rumors.

"Cause we would hate for that to happen," he said. He nodded at Hatter. "Your patrol's over. Want to go hunting?"

"Sure thing, L-man."

"For 'swangs?" I asked. I crossed my arms and studied Luke. A gun was slung across his back and knives were cinched in his belt.

"No," Luke drawled, letting Hatter descend the ladder first. He put his hand on the ladder's grip and looked back at me. He sucked on a caramel candy. "For Santa Claus."

As he started down, sexy rumors or not, I fought the urge to kick him in the face.

Sunny showed me a map of the estate, which was too big to walk in one day, with each fence line being around one mile long. I didn't know why I expected to see gas lanterns and outhouses, but the prison estate had its own power plant, water and waste treatment facilities, and an entire field of turbines that powered a margin of the energy a place like this took to operate. The university even had its own small airport and runways, which I supposed was how I'd arrived. Not that I would know since Luke had drugged me.

Sunny told me that when the estate had operated as an

actual prison, it had been for the most violent criminals in the United States. They brought all the murderers and terrorists up to this small, isolated patch of Kodiak Island where the criminals would be cut off from society. The estate had to be self-sufficient, because they had almost no outside contact with the world.

But there'd been a few new additions to the crumbling stone prison to make it more hospitable for the students. The courtyard where we'd first emerged was a hub of activity for young people, who wanted to study outside before the Alaskan winter crept in. Here, Sunny and I had an early lunch since I'd missed breakfast, and she showed me the general store, which basically looked like some rich kid's wet dream with designer clothes and super-techie devices. Not that I minded; Dean had put some credits on my student card, and I used them to buy all the pretty clothes and supplies I needed to get through my first couple of weeks at the university.

Sunny did a good job of keeping me away from the dorms, and when twilight came and it was time to go back inside, her voice was cheerful and bright as we ate dinner with Dean in his office. The conversation felt a little too forced as he asked about my day and everything Sunny had shown me. When a bell chimed through the building, Sunny met Dean's eyes. He nodded.

"Okay! Time to go see the dorms."

Dean stayed behind as Sunny led the way back to the prison's entry. I kept quiet, my guard way the hell up. "So, she said, clearing her throat. "At twilight, all students must report back to the main building. You check in with your student card."

"What happens if you don't?" I liked knowing what punishments I was up against.

"If you don't check in? You have to. Like, no one can be outside when the sun sets. That's when, you know . . . the 'swangs are out there."

"But they can't get in here, so what's the big deal?"

"It's a precaution to keep us safe."

"Right." Sunny didn't notice my sarcasm.

"So students are free to be in whatever part of the main building until nine o'clock—"

"What happens at nine?"

"Curfew. You have to be in your rooms, checked in, by then. That means you have to swipe your card again. Nine is lockdown. There's one thirty-minute warning bell before curfew, which we heard up in Dean's office, and then a final ten-minute bell."

Lockdown sounded interesting. Interesting enough to set my teeth on edge.

I asked a few more questions that Sunny artfully dodged around, her maneuvering so smooth I wondered if someone—perhaps Dean—had told her what to say.

Once we were back in the entry and standing by another heavy iron door, Sunny took a deep breath. "This is where we sleep. Where our rooms are. They might feel a little . . . oppressive at first, but, trust me, it's for our own safety."

Wrong thing to say. My spine stiffened. Sunny noticed my reaction and bumbled on, but I ignored her as I swiped my card and pushed through the door into the dome.

I looked up. And up. And up some more. Inside the structure, the dome was much larger than I'd imagined. It had no windows, but my eyes eventually adjusted to the darkness. The only exit was the door I stood in now. Behind me, tension rolled off Sunny in waves.

Then I saw the cells.

They lined the outer walls of the dome, one stacked on top of the next until I had to squint to see the curving ceiling far above me. A gangway encircled each level, allowing for walking space in front of the rooms. In the middle of the gigantic space stood a tall tower stretching halfway up the dome's height. Atop the tower was a booth made purely of glass. Guards stared down at me from inside. Another watch tower.

A watch tower for prison cells.

And the rooms were definitely cells. In the front, along each walkway, were sliding doors made of an impenetrable material resembling plastic. At least they weren't bars, and there would be some privacy inside the rooms when the doors were closed. I shook my head. Was I really trying to justify this?

This was what Sunny had been hiding from me all day, the bad thing her and Dean were so worried about. I looked back at Sunny. I'm not certain about my expression, but it had the once smiling, bright girl looking worried enough to step away from me with her hands up.

"Prison cells?" The words ground out through my clenched teeth. "Are you serious?"

"She is serious," Dean said, stepping through the door. He put his hand on Sunny's shoulder and gave it a reassuring squeeze. "We knew how you would feel about this given your past. That's why we waited until now to show you. This way, you could see the other parts of the estate and know that this is anything but a prison."

"If it's not a prison," I growled, "then why do you have cells?"

"It's for your—"

"My own protection," I finished. "Why do they lock then? Why have a watch tower? Why no windows and only one door?"

Dean smiled. "You counted the exits. Smart. But all those things exist so we can protect the students from 'swangs. Night is the dangerous time. We lock you inside to lock out the monsters, and the watch tower is so we can watch over you while you sleep. Ollie, you have to understand. This is a war, and these students are our future. We protect our future. Without them and without you, the world would be nothing but a fear concentration camp run by vicious dogs."

I gritted my teeth. I would feel better if I were on the other side of the door and not blocked off inside here. But they had me cornered, and I assumed Dean knew that.

"You really think I'm going to buy this whole safety bullshit? You have a huge-ass wall out there. Why do you need all this in here if the 'swangs never coordinate a real attack?"

"If it helps any," Sunny said, her voice quiet, "the doors locking at night really makes you feel safer. I mean, sure, you're locked inside, but nothing can get to you."

"Unless someone opens the doors during an attack," I said, directing this at Dean.

"The 'swangs can't do that. They're hardly more than rabid animals."

Rabid animals who need to be kept out with thirty-foot-tall fences, numerous huge watch towers, rook's nests, a prison security system with key cards, and a dome of locking cells with another huge watch tower. I called bullshit. Bullshit a hundred times over. Dean was lying to me about something.

Maybe lying to all these students too. I wondered if Luke knew what it was.

A beeping noise grew throughout the building, like the one I'd heard in Dean's office. Not quite an alarm, but not that soothing either. It echoed over the intercom system and boomed in my ears.

"Ten-minute warning to lock down. What's your choice, Ollie? You're not a hostage here, and this isn't your prison. Remember that we can help you if you help us."

I stared at Dean for a solid minute as I thought through my options. There weren't many. Staying on the run and buying black market medical supplies was expensive, and I was tired of living like a bum. I shifted back on my heels and studied the cells. This was how I'd expected my life to go after all. Most murderers don't count on freedom their whole lives. So why did it freak me out so bad now?

"Let me show you to your room. Maybe that will help you decide." Sunny stepped forward and took my arm, aiming me toward a set of stairs. We went up to the third floor, our footsteps ringing off the metal landing. We were well out of Dean's earshot, though I still felt his eyes on my back.

"Seeing my room won't help," I said back to her.

Most students were already inside their cells. Some had numerous people inside one cell, friends catching up on last-minute gossip. Others were alone, studying. Some played music or watched television. It looked like a normal college dorm, except for the thick sliding doors I kept passing.

Sunny leaned over and whispered in my ear, "If it helps, these rooms are really easy to sneak out of. You swipe your card and then leave right before lockdown. No problem."

"They have all this security and they don't crack down on curfew?" I asked.

Sunny shook her head, making her silky dark hair bounce against her shoulders. We were still walking, curving around slightly toward the other side of the dome. "They have checks sometimes, but not very often. Besides, we're inside the building, it's not like 'swangs can get to us. Most of the time, it's just horny guys sneaking down to the girls' levels to sleep with their girlfriends. The guards normally look the other way."

I didn't like that either. I'd heard too much shit about safety and doing all this to protect the students. No way were guards looking the other way when valuable future soldiers snuck out. Maybe Dean and the adults wanted the students to feel like they had some amount of freedom, of control. But I wasn't going to be fooled.

"Here we are. This is where you'll stay. I'm down the

walkway a bit."

I looked into my room, not expecting much, but I was surprised. The bed was built for the slight curve of the outside wall, but it looked deliciously comfortable with a white down comforter and cream-colored fluffy pillows. More than I'd ever had. There was a television, radio, and desk, where a sleek white laptop sat beside a curving metal lamp. A plush gray and black fur rug covered the bare, cold concrete. In the back corner stood a small bathroom.

I stepped inside, walking until I came to the middle. With my back to Sunny, I closed my eyes and imagined myself locked inside here. Locked. Inside. My breathing turned shaky.

I've killed a guy. I'm a murderer. Landing myself in prison was inevitable, but I believed I had a few more years of freedom left in me. But if I could swallow sleeping in a jail cell, I might be able to secure my freedom for life. Thinking of it that way made the decision easier.

I turned back to Sunny. She watched me patiently, her eyes understanding. "Two minutes," she said. "You have a toilet and sink in your private bathroom, and there are showers on each level."

I ignored her, lost in my own thoughts, which turned to basements and locked doors. Little girls and bad men. Blood and screams. Pain that can't be felt, only wedged into a deep, unforgettable part of the brain. I swallowed. "What if I say no right now?"

"Dean will take you to an empty apartment in the barracks. All the professors and hunters who live here, like

Luke and Hatter, stay in apartments over there, but there's always some left open for hunters or parents passing through."

Hunters and professors had apartments. Students had cells. Bullshit. Bullshit. Bullshit. This was all about control. Not safety. I would have to sacrifice a part of my pride to stay in here. I would have to give them some control over me. I hated that. Hated it down to my cellular level.

"Thirty seconds."

But this was a place where I could belong. Where I was wanted, at least by some. Where I could be special and powerful if I passed the evaluation with Dean. But I had a choice.

I glanced at Sunny. She shifted on her feet as her eyes darted down the row toward her cell. She would be late if I kept this up. I gave her a tight nod. "I'll see how tonight goes."

"Great!" She jumped in my cell and gave me a quick hug before careening back outside, her slippers slapping down the row as she ran toward her room. The beeping got louder. I watched as the doors started to slide closed.

When they locked, they locked with a deafening bang. I was glad no one saw me flinch at the sound.

FIVE

The doors unlocked at five the next morning. I know, because I sat on the rug in the middle of the floor all night and watched the lock until it released. Moving quickly, I slid open the door enough to slip out. My steps were silent along the walkway, everyone else still asleep behind thick doors. One guard in the watch tower gave me a nod as I descended the stairs. I expected someone to at least try to stop me, but the main door's handle easily turned beneath my clammy hand.

No one stopped me on the way out the front door, either. Not that I saw anyone anyway. Apparently I was the only one who couldn't sleep well inside a prison cell. Interesting.

I needed to get outside to breathe. I slapped my card against the reader and waited for the front door's release. When I heard the click a moment later, I shoved my way out and gulped down the cool, dewy morning air. I hadn't put on a jacket. Or shoes. But I breathed.

My legs made their way to the rook's nest overlooking Tick Tock Bay of their own accord. I climbed the ladder, thankful that the nest was empty, and sat down. I let the chilly morning air and the beautifully cruel view wake me up, clear my head. I needed to decide if the prison cells were enough reason for me to run. Over the years, I'd run away for a lot less.

Footsteps crunched behind me, and I looked out over the edge of the nest's landing. Far below me, Luke passed by on his morning run.

He didn't look up, but I kept to the shadows in case as he approached the rook's nest. His tan skin was slick with sweat, his shirt clinging to his muscular chest. A loose piece of black hair flopped into his eyes with each stride. Every inhale and exhale looked carefully regulated, each stride perfectly measured and executed. Corded muscles roped up his legs, bulging with every footstep.

He moved the way he looked: dangerous and menacing.

I might have drooled a little as he passed below the nest and continued on. It wasn't bad enough that I actually needed to wipe my mouth or anything, but there was definitely drool. Fear University had hot hunters. Point for the "stay" category. Not to mention Luke didn't seem to be that bad. Or that brainwashed. He was grouchy and a little worked up over me being a civvie, but he didn't seem like a total asshole.

Famous last words.

"There you are!" Sunny climbed up the rook's nest ladder later that morning. Her cheeks flushed pink, the tip of her nose red. "How was last night?"

I stood and dusted myself off. "Pretty good for my first night in jail."

"Ollie—"

"Yeah, yeah. I get it. For our own safety. What's on the agenda for today?"

Sunny quickly recovered from her worry and grinned. "So you're staying?"

"Until I decide I'm not." I wiggled my toes against the cold and hoped the blood still flowed down there.

I would figure out how to deal with the prison cell issue. The promise of this place was too great to pass up because one little cell bothered me so much. Bothered, not scared, I told myself. I wanted to lock myself inside that damned cell until I didn't panic, didn't see basements, didn't want to tear my fingernails off on the doors as I tried to claw my way free.

Sunny noticed my bare toes wiggling. "Goodness, Ollie! You must be freezing! Let's get you inside then we can grab some breakfast before we start the testing."

She clapped her hands and turned back toward the ladder, her motions hurried, like she really was worried for my toes. I followed at more sedate pace, but my long legs easily kept up with her as we traversed the rungs.

"So do you have any family back in the real world?" she asked.

It made sense everyone in here would think of the outside as the "real world." To them, Fear University and their war with the 'swangs was their entire world. They were isolated and separate, fighting in a war no one else knew existed. "No," I answered.

"Really?" Her surprise was cute.

"Really." My voice came off a little harsh, and Sunny fell silent below me. Our footsteps rang off the metal later as we climbed down. I scowled at the concrete fence and tried again. "Lone wolf and all that, you know?"

"Must get lonely."

The morning breeze blew across my shoulders and into the loose strands of my hair until I shivered. "It's not too bad once you get used to it." Wanting to avoid any more talk about my life, I said, "So you have a crush on Hatter, huh?"

I shot a grin down to her so she would know I was joking. She saw my face and laughed some more. Her laughter, like church bells I remembered from a time long ago, made my heart ache until I shoved the memory back in its lock box full of other forgotten things. "I don't have a crush on him!" Sunny resumed her descent. "Okay maybe. But I'm trying really hard not to. Dating hunters is an awful idea. Anyway, Luke is way worse than Hatter. And Hatter is pretty bad."

"You mean pretty crazy?"

Sunny snorted with laughter and jumped off the ladder, hitting the ground with a thump. I followed from higher up, bending my knees to soften my fall. Sunny's eyes widened. "Ready?" I asked her, striding off toward the main building.

The courtyard was empty; the general store still closed. I'd never been on a college campus, but I imagined most were ghost towns this early too. Students sleeping in on Sunday mornings had a safe feel to it that I liked. Like I was one among the masses, camouflaged. *Safe as houses*, I told myself, but I'd never had a safe home, so I corrected myself. *Safe as colleges on Sunday mornings.* I tilted my head back and breathed in the fresh, cottonwood-scented air as Sunny hurried to catch up to me.

We went back to the Death Dome, as I'd dubbed it during my long night last night, and I quickly changed into some workout clothes I'd picked up yesterday with Sunny. When we left again to head down to the ward, the dome was still silent with the occasional bout of snores and soft music playing from forgotten headphones.

"So," I asked, returning to our earlier conversation, "why is Luke worse than Hatter?"

"Oh, well, Luke comes from one of the oldest hunter families—the Aultstrivers. His mother and father take all this very seriously. I mean," Sunny said, correcting herself as she breezed down the stairs to the ward, "we all take this seriously. But they take it to a whole other level. Luke's father started training him before he even learned to talk. He could have skipped Fear University and gone straight to hunting. He's that good."

I raised my brows as I thought over Sunny's answer. We'd arrived down in the main ward. Sunny waved to the exhausted night nurse still on duty before heading into the communal area, which looked the same as when I'd arrived the other night. Throat bite guy was gone. Dead or moved to another room.

"Should parents do that?" I asked. "Train their kids so

early?"

Sunny pulled out supplies from the shelves. I sat down on a nearby stool and watched her work. "It's not recommended," she answered. "The university wants to be the primary teacher, but Killian Aultstriver follows his own set of rules."

"That must have been hard on Luke."

"He's hard to read, Ollie. Hatter wears his scars on his sleeves. We all know what the 'swang saliva does to him when he's bit: it makes him manic. But with Luke . . . no one really knows. Everyone guesses based on the rumors, but they're just that: rumors. He holds it all in, and he and Hatter fight more than any other hunters I know. So you know he has to be damaged from the saliva. But he doesn't let it show, and that's dangerous around here."

I examined my hands as I thought over her words. When the 'swang bit me the other night, I hadn't felt anything but a slight burn. But then, I hadn't really been bitten. I shoved my own hands into its mouth, so maybe that made the difference.

I still couldn't help but wonder how I would react to their saliva.

Sunny set out sterile packets of syringes and blood sampling tools, lining them up neatly on a tray. She worked without looking at me, which I preferred. "Have you always known about the 'swangs?"

"Pretty much. My mom told me stories about them since I was a little kid." She laughed softly, shaking her head. "My grandmother is even worse. She's constantly teaching me remedies for healing bites, about the usog, and everything else. I had a good childhood. Some aren't so lucky."

While I thought over her answer, Sunny arranged my arm on the counter before wrapping a tight tourniquet around my bicep. I looked away, licking my dry lips, as she picked up the needle, which met my skin with a cool, metal kiss. "Was it hard for you to believe in 'swangs?"

"Not really." I didn't know she was drawing blood until she slipped another vial into the syringe to fill. "They've always been a part of my reality. Like if you grow up knowing the monster under your bed is real, you don't understand a life where they aren't, you know? I always knew the night was bad."

Sunny released the tourniquet. I turned to look as a drop of blood welled in the crook of my arm. I'd heard about the night being bad a lot while I was here. Like these people lumped the night and 'swangs together as one big monster. But the night wasn't bad. Just the 'swangs. Why make everyone so afraid of the dark?

"Time for the marrow sample," Sunny said, startling me from my thoughts. She rolled over a padded table, and draped it with cloth. "Lie on your stomach, and I'll lift your shirt up over your back so I can see your hip bone." Sunny talked to me during every part of the process, even as she numbed the skin area, which we both knew I didn't need. She was kind and efficient as she worked, using her voice to soothe me. She would make a great doctor. The university was lucky to have her, even if she wouldn't be hunting.

I sensed her hand still above the scar on my back. She

didn't ask, and I didn't offer an explanation.

Thirty minutes later the test was done and Sunny used a liquid seal to stitch up the incision over my pelvic bone. "I'm going to keep some of this with me today in case this wound opens up after you work with Luke."

Before I nodded in agreement, Luke walked into the ward, the door swinging open with a bang. He nodded at Sunny, but didn't look at me. "Is she ready?"

"Oh," Sunny said, her voice cracking slightly. "She hasn't had breakfast yet."

"Too bad." Luke shrugged. "You're done?"

"She should eat." Sunny's sternness was lost on Luke. He just stared blankly at her until she sighed heavily and said, "She has a wound on her hip, so you might want to be careful. Her elbow and hands are still healing too."

Finally, Luke turned his attention to me, his eyes flat. "It shouldn't bother her if she can't feel pain."

"They're injuries and could be made worse. She might not be able to feel it, but it can still hurt her. Be careful with her blood sugar too since you won't let her eat first." Sunny lifted her chin. Seeing her square off against Luke made me grin as I hopped down from the table. Luke's gaze caught on my bare stomach, and I took my time lowering my shirt.

"Keep some of that liquid stuff close by, and I'll be good. Thanks, Sunny."

"No problem."

Luke didn't wait on me to follow him before he left the ward, the door swinging behind him. I rolled my eyes at Sunny and followed him out without a word. This was going

92

to be interesting.

I didn't have a hard time keeping up with him; he was tall, but I easily came up to his shoulders. He didn't check to make sure I'd stayed with him, not until we were in the courtyard. Finally, he stopped and fully looked at me, his eyes scanning the length of my body.

"What the hell are you wearing?"

I looked down at my clothes. So much for him checking me out. I'd dressed in a neon-pink baggy tank top over an electric-blue bra, gray galaxy stretchy pants, and blindingly bright yellow sneakers. I'd pulled my hair back in a tight ponytail, which I flicked over my shoulder, the long strands bouncing against the middle of my back. "Workout clothes," I said, grinning. Very nice, designer workout clothes I'd picked up yesterday with Sunny. I'd never worn anything so nice, and I liked it.

"That's not in uniform."

I checked out his pants and tight running shirt, the kind that wicks off sweat and leaves nothing to the imagination. "And you are?"

Luke clenched his jaw. I'd won. "Let's go."

I fell into step beside him as he jogged down the wide gravel road leading to the front gate I'd seen yesterday. He angled toward the fence's wall next to the entrance, where a guard in the watch tower waved down at Luke, who nodded in return.

"Where are we going?"

"Running."

I raised my brows, lengthening my stride to keep pace.

"How far?"

Luke grunted and ran faster, and I kicked it up a notch. No warm up then. I'd never gone for a run in my life. Not unless I counted running for my life, and I did.

The fall day warmed my skin enough that sweat spread across my brow and trickled down my temples. The scent of Luke's sweat mingled with the wet earth and brine in the air around me. All in all, it was a nice day. I'd definitely experienced worse.

We ran the first half of the front fence line winding along the bay, which was blocked from view because of the fence and front entrance. I expected us to turn around and head back when we came to the corner watchtower, but Luke hugged the corner, a trail worn into the ground beside the fence, and took off along the next fence line at a faster pace. This side of the estate grew thicker birch trees, casting the trail in cool shade, which I was grateful for. Spots of sunlight worked its way through the treetops and landed on the ground like puddles of golden lava. I sped up again and easily fell back into stride with him. I didn't miss his sideways glance, but I kept my eyes forward.

A mile later, at the second watchtower, Luke went into the corner again, shoes kicking up dirt, and sprinted out. I churned after him, noting the sweat dampening his shirt and making the material cling to the massive muscles of his back, but I didn't allow myself to enjoy the view for long. I wouldn't give him the satisfaction of having me behind. I drew level with him and shot him a grin.

The estate basically formed a rough square, and as we

barreled down the third fence line and almost the third mile, my breathing came in short, quick pants that left my tongue thick and the roof of my mouth dry. My heart banged about in my chest, but my legs stayed solid enough beneath me that I didn't fall flat on my face. No matter how good I thought I felt, I knew better; my body would pay the price for this tomorrow. My hip bone grew slick with what I assumed to be blood, which meant my cool pants were likely ruined. But if my evaluation with Dean had any running in it, I wanted to be ready, to be fast and strong. If running until my legs fell off helped me pass, then I'd run.

Along the back of the estate, we passed the bush plane runways and large hanger. Instead of trees back here, we ran under the massive, slowly turning wind turbines I'd seen yesterday. They whirred above our heads and cast crazy shadows at our feet that made me so dizzy I had to keep my eyes pinned on the horizon. A modestly sized water treatment facility and power plant took up as much space as the turbines. All the things that made Fear University run were hidden in the back, tucked away so young students didn't have to think about it.

I focused back on the run, having to think about each step so my lead feet didn't make me trip. Luke was pushing me, testing me, but when we came to the fourth corner and back along the front of the estate, I was ready. I stormed into the corner, passed Luke, and sprinted out, leaving him in the dust.

I cranked my legs and arms, urging myself faster and faster until my hair streamed like a jet's trail behind me. Luke cursed and surged after me, but I managed to stay in front, even as my heart lurched along in my chest. My breathing turned into one long gasp, and blood trickled down the back of my leg from the bone marrow test wound. I didn't care about any of it, though. I was beating Luke, and I would be damned if I let him pass me. A crazy grin spread across my face.

I felt alive and free for the first time in two years.

More people were in the courtyard, eating breakfast and hanging out as we came into view. I sensed the guards patrolling the fence above us, watching as we passed. I liked the attention. I liked that they saw me racing ahead of Luke, clearly beating him at his own game. His footsteps pounded behind me, but I crushed him. I didn't stop at the entrance; instead, I ran to the first corner, adding another half mile to our run.

"Stop," Luke growled from behind me, his breathing as battered as mine.

I slowly fumbled to a shaky stop, letting my legs unspool beneath me. Laughing, I turned around, ready to rub my win in his face, when he grabbed my shoulders and shoved me up against the fence.

"Hey!" I complained, but I couldn't move. He had me pinned with his hips, his grip crushing my upper arms.

I expected him to be angry, to lash out at me for turning the run into a race. Maybe a lecture about taking Fear University seriously. Instead, he leveled an icy cool gaze on me, his face so devoid of expression it looked creepy, especially since he was the one who had pinned me to the fence. My stomach flipped with nerves, and a lick of fear inched up my spine. I *loved* it.

"Is this some joke to you?"

He was inches from my face, but he acted completely unaffected. His voice sounded controlled, smooth and calm. Meanwhile, my heart flailed around somewhere in my throat, but I wouldn't let him know that.

"Actually," I said slowly, eyes lingering on his lips to piss him off, "I think it's very funny that I beat you."

Luke let go of one of my arms and reached behind him. He pulled out a knife from a holster under his shirt and flashed it in front of my eyes. If he'd been pissed at me, I might have thought he was trying to threaten me. But now, with his cold stare, I knew he was proving a point. "This isn't some joke. You will die here."

I rolled my eyes at him. "You should put that away before you hurt yourself."

He listened to me and lowered the knife. My legs wobbled like loose rubber beneath me, but my breathing slowly returned to normal. Although, my heart still thumped erratically from Luke's proximity. "You don't belong here," he said before stepping back and giving me some space.

"Really? That's not what I heard."

"It's true. You're going to get yourself hurt or someone else killed. There's a reason civvies aren't allowed here. We," he motioned to the school behind him, clearly excluding me, "have been born and raised for this. We can handle the pressure of hunting 'swangs. Civilians can't. You will never understand this life."

"Or maybe you're worried that I'll take your kill record. Be a better hunter than you. Are you that competitive?" I closed the distance between us until my breasts brushed against his chest. His jaw ticked wildly, rewarding me with some reaction from him; I knew I was pushing him too far, but I licked my lips. His fingertips started to dance across each other, nostrils flaring like he was scenting me. Slowly, I peeled away his cool exterior, his control. "I like a little competition, you know," I added, lacing my voice with a rough, husky rasp to jab at him a little more.

Something pressed against my thigh, making the muscle twitch with flashes of heat. A cool breeze brushed against my bare skin. Before I could look down, my leg gave out beneath me and I fell. Not bothering to catch me, Luke stepped out of the way and merely watched me collapse against the ground with a loud thump. A shocked hiss pressed between my teeth. Luke's knife was buried hilt deep into the muscle of my thigh.

My red murder haze descended on me like a fog that choked my breathing and made me lash out like a wounded animal.

"You fucking piece of shit. I'll kick your ass." I yanked the knife out and jerked to my feet. Swinging my arm, I aimed for Luke's heart, fully prepared to kill him. But my leg didn't hold me, and I went down again. When I tried to stand, I fell once more. Floundering on the ground in front of all the guards and students, I wanted to scream.

"If you stay here, you can't rely on your condition," Luke said above me.

I cursed at him, but to my horror, he let my words roll

right off him and bent to pick me up, plucking the knife from my grip and dropping it to the ground behind him. I tried to shove him away, but he ignored my fists and easily lifted me off the ground, blood running from my split running tights. He carried me all the way back to the prison building, passing in front of the students outside, who watched us like we were a twenty-car pile-up on the highway. I'd never felt so embarrassed, so small, in all my life. I wanted to melt into him, and not in a good way. I wanted to be acid that burned his arms off. I wanted to kill him.

SIX

On Monday morning, I limped into my first class. Not exactly the entrance I wanted to make on my first official day at Fear University. But I stepped into the classroom with the hope that not everyone had heard or cared about the little stabbing incident yesterday.

Luke had carried me all the way back to the ward, where Sunny, much to her dismay, had to sew my leg back up, reseal my bone marrow sample wound, and run me an IV for dehydration. Thanks to Luke's good aim, he'd only damaged my muscle, which, according to him, wouldn't be enough of an injury to slow down my training, even though Dean had apparently met with Luke in his office and given Luke a vicious talking to. I wished I'd seen it. He deserved it.

He was a total asshole.

As soon as I stepped into the classroom, the hope of going unnoticed dried up in my mind. Everyone, *every single person*, looked up as I walked in. The talking stopped abruptly, people's jaws still hanging open mid-word. I skidded to a stop, frozen in the doorway of the classroom, my stomach flipping over. In all my life, I'd never had that dream where I was naked in a crowd, but I was having it then.

So this was it then. Not only was I the freak outsider—the civvie—but now I was the girl Luke Aultstriver stabbed in the leg for the hell of it.

The professor stood at the front of the room next to a chalkboard, his hand hovering above the board. He was a gangly, skinny guy with milky white skin and black eyes. The awkward, silent moment stretched out until he scowled deeply, angry with the interruption, and waved a hand over his shoulder, which I took to mean I could take a seat.

Fear Theory. First period. Off to a great start.

I took a deep breath and started toward to an empty seat in the back. I tugged at the collar of my white shirt, the uniform's gauzy pants making my legs itch. I'd hoped wearing the uniform would help me blend it, but clearly that was a lost cause. I squared my shoulders and glared at anyone still staring at my bandaged leg or hands as I limped to the back of the classroom. I plopped my backpack onto the floor next to my desk and slid into the chair.

A few other students glanced back at me, but I ignored them and pulled out my Fear Theory textbook, which made my desk creak when I set it down. I seriously hoped I didn't have to learn all this in one semester. I'm smart, but I never graduated high school, and all that I've learned, I've learned on the streets, surviving day to day.

From the front of the room the professor turned around. "Miss Andrews, I'm Mr. Abbot, and hopefully you are aware that this is Fear Theory." The class snickered at his remark, which made him grin an oily little smile. "We will review today for you, but only today. From now on, you will be expected to be prepared and ready for lectures and all tests." He raised pencil-thin eyebrows and sniffed at me, like I smelled of day-old trash. "You will receive no special treatment in my classroom. Got it?"

Some of the students bowed their heads and coughed into their hands, masking the word "civvie" in the cough. I gritted my teeth, flexing my wounded thigh to remind myself that I felt no pain. I nodded toward Mr. Abbot with a single, violent twitch of my chin.

"Let's get started then." Mr. Abbot turned back to his chalkboard and began scrawling illegible words across the surface, the chalk clicking and scratching. Students scrambled for their pens and notebooks. "Fear is nothing but a reaction in our bodies, a release of chemicals, an autonomic response." He drew a rough sketch of the brain on the board and labeled parts and pieces that processed fear. I rolled my eyes. Did these people really think they could control fear by understanding how it happened in the brain?

"The stimuli initiate a release of chemicals that causes our bodies to react. Our hearts beating faster. Our palms sweating. Eyes dilating. Adrenaline. One frozen moment where we can do nothing but feel *everything*. Feel afraid. Human evolution is linked to those who feared the right things. But what's worse than fear itself?" Mr. Abbot asked the class, calling the question over his shoulder.

One girl up front said, "Anticipation."

"Correct. The fear of fear itself. For example, the fear of pain is worse than the pain itself. By allowing ourselves to feel fear, we are giving our power away. So, for the sake of Miss Andrews' ignorance, how do we best kill 'swangs, class?"

In robotic unison, the class said, "We teach ourselves to not be afraid."

Period Two. Aswang Psychology.

I was better this time. No stomach dropping. No hesitation. A kid like me didn't need long to learn appearing weak was way worse than actually being weak. The bottom of the food chain sucked. Trust me. If I was relegated to being the outsider here then I would be fierce.

Expecting the next professor to be as big an asshole as Mr. Abbot, I threw back my shoulders and frowned, waiting for the civvie mockery. But the professor looked up from her desk where she graded papers while the students settled in and smiled. Her straight, dark hair and tan skin with wide, round hazel eyes was exotic in a similar way to Sunny, but while Sunny was half Filipino, this professor was clearly descended from one of Alaska's native tribes. She was, quite simply, the most beautiful woman I'd ever seen.

She leveraged herself up from her desk and said, "You must be Ollie. Good to have you. I'm Peggy Coldcrow, but all my students call me Peg." She stuck out her lower left leg with a crooked grin, and sure enough, it was nothing but metal and a swiveling rubber foot. Only then did I notice the swelling bulge in her very pregnant belly.

"Morning," I said, feeling a tiny flicker of hope at her warm greeting.

"Take a seat wherever. We're going to continue with our scheduled lesson today, but you seem to be a smart girl. I'm sure you can get the gist."

From her, I took it as a compliment. She didn't study me or act like I was an alien. She treated me like anyone else, like I'd been in her class all semester. The rest of the class took her example and didn't mock me as I made my way to the back and took a seat. There were no snickering or darting glances, which made me wonder if Peg had warned the class or possibly threatened them, before I came in. After my first period with Mr. Abbot, I appreciated it.

"Let's pick back up with our discussion yesterday. Will someone remind me where we left off?"

"Immortality." A young guy spoke without raising his hand. Peg settled onto the edge of her desk with a sigh.

"That's right. Thank you, Liam. Pregnancy brain, you know." The class laughed warmly, and I relaxed farther into my seat. "Who wants to add to that?"

"We were discussing what we know about a 'swang's lifespan, and if their magic makes them immortal."

"Or if not magic," another student freely argued, "then they might have evolved to live out both the lives of their dog form and human form."

The magic versus evolution debate again. I raised my brows, listening as the class continued a rigorous debate for both sides. Peg moderated and took occasional notes on the board, but I realized this class was primarily dedicated to letting the students form their own opinions, which I appreciated, even though it sounded like a 'swang's lifespan was another gray area no one knew much about.

As the conversation continued, I thumbed through the pages of my textbook that I'd pulled out of my bag. My eye caught on one particular drawing of two tall aswangs on a cave's wall. From their mouths dripped red blood and black saliva. Their hands were human, but from the tips of their fingers grew long, slashing claws. They rose up on the back legs of a dog, but their chests were that of a man's. They were frozen in mid-lunge, snapping their jaws at each other's throats, their faces locked in vicious snarls.

I took a deep breath and forced my attention away from the image and to the board, where Peg wrote out more notes on 'swang mortality. I'd missed a lot of school when I was younger jumping from one foster home to another. The curriculum each school taught was always different and eventually I got so far behind that it didn't matter anymore. After all those years, finding myself in a classroom again terrified me. What if I was too stupid to keep up? My pen shook in my fingers as I began taking notes in my lopsided, illegible scrawl.

By the end of class, I'd filled so many pages of my notebook with words I didn't understand that my hand cramped continuously, and I had to jerk my fingers back into position. When the bell rang, I was the last one to leave.

"Ollie?" I looked up from gathering my books. Peg squeezed herself into the desk in front of me and stretched out her legs with a sigh. Her remaining ankle was the size of a cantaloupe. I grimaced; never, ever would I be pregnant. No way in hell would I have a kid, and possibly screw them up as badly as my mom had done me. "Standing up there the whole period makes my leg swell up like crazy."

"Were you a hunter?" I nodded toward her missing leg.

"I was. Had it bitten clean off." She tapped her metal kneecap and grinned at me.

"You killed it though?"

"Knife straight through the eye while he munched on his little snack."

A strange thing happened: I laughed. Like really laughed for the first time in a long time. Peg watched me with her grin still in place. I liked that her injury didn't bother her, that she could joke about it. I liked it a lot. If I stayed and became a hunter, I wanted to be like that, like my battle wounds were a mark of honor.

"So, Ollie."

"Yeah?"

"It's interesting, you being here. We've never had a civilian come to the university before."

"Trust me." I clenched my fists. "I've heard all about it."

"Let me guess . . . Luke?" I nodded, feeling my blood pressure rise, but Peg laughed. "The Aultstrivers are one of the Originals, and Luke believes in the purpose of the old families." She grew serious as she continued. "Maybe his ideas of honor and tradition would work if we had more children coming to the university, but we don't. We need fresh blood that hasn't been burdened by this war for centuries. If that means bringing in civvies then I think we should."

Her opinion put me further at ease. She was on my side. "Why are there fewer children? Are they dying?"

"Some of them, but that's going to happen. This is a dangerous world. We know there's going to be deaths. Mostly, families aren't having as many kids, or the kids they do have don't want to fight. You can hardly blame them." She frowned down at her belly, her hand working across the mound in soothing circles that almost put me to sleep just watching. My mom—before she left—used to rub my back like that. I told myself I hated the memory and shoved it down before it fully formed in my mind. "I can't imagine sending my child into a war where I knew he would most certainly die. Our lifespans are short, Ollie. Forty is old in this world if you're a hunter."

"Maybe he could teach, like you do."

The stress eased out of her face as she looked back at me. "Maybe. The point is, don't let all these old-school, old-family types scare you off. And if any of these spoiled little brats give you hell, you come to me, okay? Not Dean."

She caught my attention; my eyes narrowed. "Why not him?"

She studied my face, her pause stretching out. Finally she said, "He might not understand. Let's leave it at that." Peg stood, pressing the heel of her palm into her back and stretched. "You better hurry. You'll be late for your next class."

My third period class was more like a study hall in the library with tutors available to help first-years with the more normal "college" classes, like chemistry, history, economics. We were expected to pass basic competency exams in a range of topics, which worried me. Using my wits and fists didn't bother me; I could pass anything that included fighting if I was willing to sacrifice my body. But trying to understand opportunity costs or the paradox of value in economics scared the shit out of me. By the time I made it to the cafeteria after third period, the skin under my eye twitched like a meth-head five days out from a fix.

When I managed a thought that wasn't jumbled from the overload of information I'd received today, I returned to my conversation with Peg. She didn't want me telling Dean if I had any trouble with another student because she said he wouldn't understand, which told me she didn't completely trust him. Seeing her and Luke's reaction to Dean reminded me that I needed to keep my guard up around everyone. I couldn't let these people make me feel too comfortable. Just because Dean said the things I'd waited my entire life to hear didn't mean I should trust him completely.

Sunny met me outside the cafeteria with a startlingly wide smile and a high-five, which I half-heartedly participated in. "What's cookin', goodlookin'?"

"Are you always this happy?"

Sunny laughed. "I take it you're having a good first day?"

"Everyone has been very welcoming."

Sunny grimaced, but I knew she understood. "That bad, huh?"

"Definitely not that good."

With a shake of her head, Sunny opened the cafeteria door and we went inside. Walking into lunch was the culmination of walking into every first class on every first day all at once, and after the start to my day, feeling stupid and stressed out from all I'd have to learn, I wanted to sink into the floor, but I forced my chin up a fraction and told myself to get over it. The round tables teemed with students, all of whom abruptly stopped their chatter and stared at me. From a table in the middle, Jolene leaned into Allison and whispered something that caused the entire table to laugh.

"What is her problem anyway?" I jammed the heel of my hand into my eye socket and rubbed.

Sunny followed my dagger-like line of vision and said, "Oh. Jolene. She's like a bad STD you can't get rid of. Itchy in all the wrong places, if you know what I mean." Sunny's face contorted funny, like she was only just realizing what she'd said. I let out of snort of laughter at her discomfort. "I mean, not like I would know, and I'm totally not saying you know anything about STDs. Oh my gosh. Forget I said that. Whatever."

We made our way to the front of the room, where fresh, hot food steamed up the glass on numerous buffets. All-you-can-eat style. My stomach growled as we picked up little square plastic trays and slid them down the rails alongside a practical cornucopia of food. I'd never seen this much food in one place. Between it and Sunny, my day was infinitely better already.

"So she's always been like that?" I asked, nodding toward Jolene. I didn't care if she knew we were talking about her.

"I call it the 'only child syndrome.' The world's her oyster and all that jazz."

I reached for the fried chicken, piling a couple pieces onto my plate before I moved on to the mashed potatoes and macaroni. I added some steamed vegetables and salad to my plate, earning me an astonished look from Sunny, which I ignored. A girl's got to eat, and with my wicked metabolism, I kept my lanky, boyish figure with ease. Though if I wouldn't mind sacrificing my metabolism to have more of the soft, sweet curves that Sunny had.

"Do you have any siblings?" I asked once we found an empty table. I kicked a chair back from the table and set down, ready to dig into my food. I was starving.

"Two older brothers."

"Both hunters?" I asked around a mouthful of potatoes.

"They were." Sunny took a long drink of water. "Seth, my oldest brother, died last year. Killed by a 'swang."

I froze. "Christ, Sunny. I'm sorry."

She didn't look up from her lunch. "It happens, but Henry stopped hunting after that and became a doctor."

"And you still came here."

"My parents gave me the option," she said, which surprised me. "They're pretty progressive like that. But I wanted to come. It seemed like the best way to honor Seth. That was before I realized I was a coward."

"You're not a coward."

"I set the fudging fear sim death record, Ollie."

I stabbed some salad with my fork. "It's a stupid record."

"People call me the Cowardly Lyon."

Knowing exactly who called her that, I cut my eyes toward Jolene's table, where she held court like a queen. Her table was crowded and spilling over with zealous students, anxious to bask in Jolene's popular glow. "If an STD could have only child syndrome, she would be it."

Sunny snorted broccoli through her nose.

After lunch, my fourth period class was Weapons Theory. I had no clue there could be so many ways to kill a person, but by the size of my textbook, there were plenty. Looking around at all the swords, guns, and one drool-worthy stingray whip that practically sang my name as I walked by it, I grinned from the back of the classroom. I would like this class. I wanted to know how to use every single one.

After Weapons Theory, I wove my way across the prison, around the dome, and into the west wing for my fifth period class: Combat Theory. The classroom was a large amphitheater with all the students in first-year besides the advanced ones like Sunny. At the front of the room hung a large screen with notes and pictures projected.

Like in Weapons Theory, my Combat Theory professor didn't acknowledge me. He went on with his lesson while taking a few pointed jabs at civilians. Meanwhile, the students treated me with general disinterest and subtle disdain, but even they did little to dampen my enthusiasm for these classes. For the first time today, I didn't feel stupid because violence was a language I understood. Now, if they would let me hit someone, I would be the happiest girl in the world.

I didn't get to hit anyone.

Sixth period was the first-year's version of gym class, an introduction to fighting, which meant for once, I actually got a class with Sunny. But being with Sunny meant I was also in the same room as Jolene and all her cronies.

With the entire class in the glass gym, there were about eighty of us. I understood now why everyone acted so concerned about the war. From my seat in the bleachers— observing—I did the math. If each year of students consisted of this many people, from first-year to fifth, taking into account the fact some students wouldn't specialize or graduate to become hunters, the amount of actual fighting graduates would likely be dead in a single year. These were the people who would be protecting the world in a few years, and as I watched their clumsy, uncoordinated attacks, I understood the general concern.

No wonder they needed me.

I cringed as one gangly redheaded guy took a misplaced kick to the jaw. He spat out a bloody confetti of teeth and was quickly escorted to the ward.

They *really* needed me.

After sixth period, I headed to the girls' locker room crowded with blue lockers and communal showers. I changed into my workout clothes after I'd consulted my schedule for my locker number and combination. When I walked back, standing next to a large punching bag suspended from a beam in the vaulted ceiling, Luke waited with his back to me.

I seriously considered sneaking up on him and stabbing him in the ear. Considered it enough that I looked around for an impaling device.

"You won't find one."

I jumped at the sound of his deep, booming voice that filled the airy gym like he had a megaphone. He turned toward me with an impassive look on his face, arms crossed, toe of his sneaker tapping an impatient beat. Clearly, he couldn't read my mind, but I guess I wore my aggression on my sleeve. Shocker.

"Maybe I'll slam your head into the floor until your brains spill out like old, congealed ketchup."

If my graphic description alarmed him or amused him, he didn't show it. He uncrossed his arms and stretched out his neck. "Fine. I'll give you five minutes."

"For what?"

"Clearly, you have unresolved issues—"

"You *stabbed* me!"

"—with me. So I'll give you five minutes to work out your frustration. And then we start real training."

I narrowed my eyes. "You'll let me hit you?"

"If you can. No free shots."

"Fine." I closed the distance between us as he shrugged out of his hoodie and dropped it to the floor. His T-shirt's sleeves stretched tightly around his biceps, the material so worn and faded that I wondered if it was his favorite. The collar dipped low enough to reveal a series of corded, black claw marks that likely continued a thick trail down the middle of his chest.

"Anytime you're ready," he said dryly. I raked my eyes back up to his. The bastard totally caught me checking him out.

"Are *you* ready?" I asked him, raising my fists. He didn't move to match my stance. "Cause if I hurt you . . ."

I let my words trail off and ducked in, letting my fist fly. Luke sidestepped the blow, the muscles in his legs rippling in a really annoying, distracting way. I kicked, using the leg he *hadn't* stabbed, and aimed for his shin, but he caught my ankle and sent me stumbling back. With a growl, I righted myself and lunged at him, only to have him easily catch my wrist and swing me off balance, which wasn't hard to do with my banged up leg and hip that kept giving out beneath me.

And so it went for five minutes. Every time I tried to hit him, Luke parried the blow with a swat of his hand or a swift sidestep. When he checked his watch and held up his hand, sweat poured down my temples and off the tip of my nose. My breath came quick and fast, but Luke didn't even seem winded. I hadn't landed a single hit, which really pissed me off.

Though he'd signaled time was up, I ducked in, swinging my fist and aiming for his nose. I put all my strength behind the punch, grunting with the effort, but Luke merely grabbed my wrist and jerked my arm down like he'd been expecting the cheap shot. "I don't teach dirty fighting."

I pulled my hand free, still panting and out of breath, and

flipped my ponytail over my shoulder. "Do you have any fun then?"

He studied me for a moment, his face as unreadable as always. Finally, he handed me a piece of cloth. "You're out of shape. I want you running one lap around the fence lines for the next two weeks."

"What about my leg that you stabbed?"

His face remained unchanged, no guilt flashing through his eyes. "The pain shouldn't be a problem, should it?"

He was challenging me because he knew I wouldn't back down. Instead of answering, I took the strip of cloth from his hand. "What's this?"

"Every evening you run. If you miss your run you'll have double the laps the next day. And trust me, I'll know if you miss." He pointed to the cloth. "It's a blindfold. Tie it on."

"Why are you blindfolding me?"

"You're blindfolding you, and because we're training."

I offered the blindfold back, holding it by the corner's edge. "I don't like having my eyes covered. Let's start with something else."

"I figured." Luke crossed his arms, not taking it back. "You think you can fight your way out of anything even if you have to break every bone in your body to do it. But you can't always fight like that. So I'm blindfolding you. No more power. No more control. I'm in control."

"No." I shook my head, letting the blindfold fall on the floor.

"This is how we train today. It won't be every day, but you need to learn that I'm in control when we work together. I'm in control until I give you that control back. Now, pick up the blindfold."

"You sound positively delightful."

"Do you want to pass Dean's evaluation?"

My stomach twisted. I'd made it all day without thinking about the dreaded evaluation. "You know I do."

"No, I don't. The evaluation won't be easy. You'll need to be in shape and capable of keeping up with me. I won't go easy on you, and I'll use every weakness you have against you." His eyes flashed with a cool, cruel kind of sincerity.

I glowered at him. "Because you don't want a civvie here."

"Whether I want you here or not, you're here. If you want to stay, you have to be as good as the best first-year here. Otherwise I'll make sure you don't pass. Got it?"

"That's not exactly fair."

Luke shrugged, clearly unconcerned with fairness. My nervousness about the evaluation tripled. Not only would I have to get Dean's approval, but now I would need Luke's. "Fair or not," he said, "that's how it'll be. I won't have you getting someone killed if you graduate because I went easy on you during your training. So," he pointed to the blindfold on the mat, "do you want to pass the evaluation or not?"

"Will you let me pass?" I asked, glaring at him.

Luke crossed him arms and waited. I glanced at the blindfold and back to his face. Unreadable. Nothing. Blank. His face was the freaking Mojave Desert. I sighed and scooped up the cloth from the floor. Before I turned around and waited to be blinded, I handed the cloth to him, making certain our fingers didn't touch. He quickly tied the blindfold in place, tugging the ends tight enough that I saw nothing but blackness.

I hated it. The darkness and lack of control made me think of basements and screams. All my control went into keeping my hands at my sides and not jerking the blindfold off. I swallowed the whimper rising up my throat.

If I was going to pass the evaluation, I would have to be great. To get Dean's and Luke's approval, I would need to turn my weaknesses into my strengths. I wouldn't put it past Luke to blindfold me during the evaluation and make me look like a simpering fool in front of Dean if I didn't overcome this. So I gritted my teeth and shoved down my fear.

When Luke touched my shoulders to spin me back around, I tensed. I hated not being able to see him or my surroundings. But even more than that, I loathed the fact that he could touch me without me expecting it or being able to prepare myself for the contact. The training mat squeaked beneath Luke's feet when he leaned forward. "Let it go, Ollie," he said, his quiet words warm against my ear. I jumped back.

"Let what go?"

He didn't answer. I looked around even though it did no good. The smell of sweat-dried mats and over-circulated cool air gusting down from the air vents far above my head suddenly grew stronger. In the background, the air conditioner whirred quietly along, working hard to cool the prison, but closer to me, the mat gave beneath Luke's weight. There was a soft squelch of leather, and the clink of chains.

I threw my hands up right before the punching bag hit me in the ribs hard enough to knock me down.

I ripped the blindfold off in a flurry, spitting and sputtering as I scrambled to gather up my legs and lurch to my feet. "What the hell?" I shouted, advancing on Luke with every intention of breaking his face.

He stepped back, pulling the still-swinging punching bag with him, and swung it at me again. I quickly sidestepped it. "Put the blindfold back on," he commanded.

"Not if you're going to hit me."

"If you're good enough, you'll get out of the way before it hits you."

Luke kept the bag between us, making it impossible for me to reach him. Every time I got too close, he swung it at me. It was thick and heavy, but I managed to shove it back at him once. How he easily moved it around was a wonder.

"How am I supposed to move out of the way if I can't see it?"

In answer, Luke tapped his ears, meaning I should listen for it. I growled and yanked the blindfold back over my eyes.

Screw this evaluation. Screw Luke. Screw Dean. Screw these professors and students who hated me. I would show them all.

When I was ready, I waved him on with my lips twisted up in a snarl.

I hit the mat at least twenty times before Luke stopped an hour later. "Ollie, *listen*. You're not listening. You're not feeling. You can't always rely on taking the pain. You need to learn to avoid it."

I don't want to avoid it, I thought. But I didn't dare say it out loud. "Fine."

I imagined I heard Luke smile, but I doubted it. Probably too many punching bags to the temple. I wasn't paying attention. When the bag hit me again, I fell to the mats and didn't bother getting back up.

"Lis—"

"If you tell me to listen one more time," I threatened from the floor, directing my words up to the ceiling, "I'll shove this punching bag down your throat."

"That's not anatomically possible."

I rolled my eyes behind the mask and stood, holding up my hand for Luke to wait until I caught my breath. My breathing shook as I inhaled, but I shoved aside the bad memories. Luke couldn't know about the thoughts he'd triggered by blindfolding me, but I did and I had to get past them.

I knew I was safe here. This wasn't the house in Virginia. I wasn't in a basement. Max and his father weren't standing in front of me, laughing as I cried and begged them to let her go. I'd left that behind me. I focused on the smell of the mats and the clanking chain above the punching bag until my thoughts cleared of fear.

After a moment, my heart calmed, going from a manic flutter to a steady rhythm echoing down to the tips of my toes. I tuned out all the other sounds around me and waited until I felt *something*: the empty air in front of me, around me, behind me. A few feet ahead, I sensed a denser darkness where Luke stood behind the bag with it pulled back and ready to swing. The chains holding the bag clicked and clanked from the taunt weight. The air changed when he let the heavy bag go, not waiting for me to say I was ready, just as I'd expected. A cool breeze swept straight toward me, so I jumped to the left, and the bag swung by me without contact.

Luke grunted in approval before catching the bag and sending it crashing back toward me.

For another hour we kept up the dance. Like a ballet, we moved over the mats, dodging and ducking each other. Luke swung the bag harder each time as we moved in our demented circle. It came at me from all directions; sometimes I wasn't fast enough, but sometimes I was. When we finally stopped, sweat poured down my back and my knees wobbled, muscles twitching deep in my legs. I pulled off the blindfold and sank to the mats with a relived groan. Luke sat a few feet away.

"That wasn't bad," he said, stretching out his arms, his skin slick with sweat.

"Gee, thanks."

"You need to get over this no pain thing. It's your worst flaw."

"You keep saying that," I said, propping myself up on an elbow so to glower at him, "but everyone else thinks it's a gift."

"Who does?" Luke asked, dark brows raised. "Dean? The professors? When was the last time they were out fighting in the real world?"

"Worried you might have some competition?"

Luke didn't take the bait. "I'm serious, Ollie. You can't

rely on your condition. It'll get you killed."

"Or make me awesome."

"You're naive. Overconfident. Undertrained." Luke ticked off my flaws on his fingers like he was counting lemons. "You're brave because you don't understand the consequences that come with fear and pain, but that's the wrong kind of bravery we need around here. This medical condition you have makes you think you're invincible, but you bleed like everyone else."

Consequences? He didn't think I understood? My entire life had been on big consequence.

I quickly stood. I'd deal with being blindfolded and hit over and over with a punching bag, but I wouldn't sit here and listen to him talk down to me like he knew a damn thing about me or what I felt. "I'm not naive," I growled down at Luke, who made no effort to stand. "You have no clue what I've been through—"

"You're right." He held up his hands in surrender, but he'd already started a war with me. Wrong thing to say after the life I've lived. Way the hell wrong. "I don't know. But I do understand fear and you don't. You just know you can't feel pain. Everyone here thinks that's great, because you can walk out into the night and take down any 'swang because they can't affect you. But they're wrong. That won't happen. Those 'swangs will get in your head. Pain isn't only physical."

I couldn't say anything without revealing too much about my past and how well I understood pain. The Tabers' basement had taught me plenty about the true nature of pain, more than Luke could ever comprehend. Maybe I acted a little too fearless, but fear had nothing on pain. To me, the two weren't inherently linked like everyone at Fear University seemed to think. Fear was something I overcame *because* of my understanding of pain. I understood the inevitability of pain. Luke thought I was naive because I couldn't feel it, but I did—on the inside. Every breath cut razor sharp, memories of my childhood threatening to slice and dice me. Pain was a constant in my life. The only thing that had stuck by me. I didn't fear it.

I loved it.

Luke thought I would fall apart when I fought a 'swang, but he was wrong. I'd already faced down a worse monster that night in the Tabers' basement; I'd faced fear *and* pain head on and came out the other side a killer. But Luke had no clue about that night, and I sure as hell wouldn't be telling him. So I turned and left the gym, forcing myself not to look back.

I doubled my laps around the estate that evening to burn out the anger pumping in my blood.

SEVEN

L ater that night, in my cell, I sat at my desk, tap-tapping my new pencil against my new textbook in my new pajamas. My wet hair dripped down my back from the shower I'd taken earlier. A stiffness set into the muscles in my legs and back after practice with Luke and my run, but I ignored it for the most part. After a late dinner with Sunny, who'd waited on me to eat, I'd come back to my room with the intention of studying, but I could only marvel at how damn *normal* I felt.

I'd never felt normal my whole life. Maybe I had when I was little, before my mom left me in the closet, but I didn't let myself remember those times. The best policy was always to forget.

I propped my elbows on the edge of the desk and rubbed my temples. Of course, my "normal" had become a stab wound to the leg, a university of monster hunters, and a prison cell. That was messed up on so many levels.

But I was clean with a full belly. I had a space to call my own and a purpose to wake up to each day. I might have been any other student-athlete at any college, sore and studying, exhausted from a long day of classes. It was a drastic but welcomed change from my old life of cheap apartments and long nights filled with nightmares of Max finding me. Passing the evaluation in two weeks suddenly became more important than ever. Even if it meant training in a blindfold every day, I would do it if I could hold on to this feeling.

Thinking of the night my life had changed course so drastically, I flipped over my hands and studied the bandages. I'd peeked earlier in the shower; the skin was starting to close and form raised patches of thin, inky-black flesh. My first 'swang scars, the first of many more. As messed up as it sounded, the hope comforted me.

The ten-minute final warning chimed. I glanced at the lock on the sliding, solid, impenetrable material of my door. Hopefully tonight I would get more than an hour's sleep. I needed to get over this issue. I refused to let a little lock on a door freak me out so bad.

"Hiya!" Sunny slipped into my room, wearing pink pajamas with yellow ducks dancing on them, and slid the door closed. Before I'd recovered from my surprise at seeing her so close to lockdown, she bounced across the room and sat down on my bed with a thump that sent the springs popping. She shoved her glasses back up her nose, her hair in a floppy bun on top of her head, and grinned at me.

"What are you doing here?" I asked, shock turning my voice flat and mean. "The warning bells are going off."

"I know. I just thought . . ." Sunny's smile faltered and she looked at her hands. "I thought maybe you would want some company. I was pretty freaked out on my first day. Hearing about all that fighting stuff . . ."

Sunny's voice trailed off, and I was ready to tell her that I didn't need anyone's comfort. But the look in her eyes— bright and purposeful, like she was determined to keep me from being as scared as she was on her first night—stopped me. "That's, uh, sweet." I tried to say the right thing to show her I appreciated the gesture. "But aren't you worried about the rules?"

She grinned, looking almost as maniacal as Hatter that I wondered if she'd been staring at him too long. "This is the first time I've snuck out of my dorm. You're worth it, though."

Sure, I wasn't able to feel pain. But I damned sure felt when my heart broke as she told me I was worth it. It was like someone had lined up a hammer and slammed a nail right through my soft, beating tissue. The poor organ. It didn't stand a chance against this raven-haired, brown-eyed fiend. I swallowed to make sure my voice didn't sound funny and said, "Gee thanks. Maybe I won't pee the bed tonight."

The warning chimed from my lock, a sound that echoed hundreds of times over in the Death Dome. Sunny cringed a little, but laughed at my joke. "You better not pee the bed. I refuse to sleep on this floor." Her eyes found the textbook on my desk, and she scooted closer. "What are you studying?"

"Psychology. I really like Peg. She's a cool professor."

"Yeah. Everyone likes her a lot. Did she show you her leg?" I nodded. "How crazy was that? A 'swang fudging bit it clean off!"

"Pretty fudging crazy," I agreed, putting on a perky little drawl like Sunny's voice. She swatted at my arm, and I grinned at her.

"I have all my notes from the beginning of the semester. I could share them with you."

"That would be great—"

I didn't get to finish my sentence before hundreds of locks clanged shut. I glanced at Sunny, who stared back at me, wide white rings around her irises. "That's an awful sound," she whispered.

"Yeah. No shit."

The next morning, I shuffled along behind Sunny as we made our way to the cafeteria for breakfast before class. I'd gotten a few more hours of sleep last night, but that was it. Between my constant staring at the lock and Sunny's snoring and horrifying tendency to cuddle, I was beat. I rolled my neck again, hoping to get rid of the crick there, but it was as useless as trying to get my obviously sore legs to move right beneath me. I considered stopping to try and punch some life back into my tattered muscles. Running extra laps last night was a seriously bad idea.

Beside me, much too overly enthusiastic for what a morning warranted, Sunny practically skipped along, her cute little braid bouncing against her back. " . . . So then I was, like, 'well sir, if you wouldn't try to cut off chicken fat with a scythe, you wouldn't cut your blankety-blank thumb off—' "

"Are you supposed to tell me these things?" I asked, cutting her off during another one of her very gross, very detailed stories from the working in the ward. "Like HIPAA laws and all that?"

"Oh, please." Sunny snorted. "This is Fear University. HIPAA is for pus-o'lahs."

"Pus-o'lahs?"

"You know. Like, the p-word? For down there?" I didn't catch where Sunny pointed on her own body, but I got the gist. I shook my head, unable to keep the smile from my face.

"How do you come up with this stuff?" Thinking better of my question, I held up my hand before Sunny launched into another ten-minute conversation. "Never mind. I don't want to know."

Sunny laughed and swung through the cafeteria door. We were pretty late, since Sunny's perkiness had made me hide under the covers too long this morning. Luckily, it didn't take much time to pick out a new outfit from my very well-stocked closet, thanks to Dean's generous allotment of student credits and the well-supplied general store. No more Fear University uniform for me. If I was going to stand out, I was going to do it in style and comfort. I wore my new motorcycle boots, a new pair of black torn jeans, and a very cool, tattered, tank top that showed off my electric-orange bra underneath.

On cue, Sunny shot a side-long glance out my outfit, the

millionth skeptical look from her this morning. "What is it?" I asked as we wove through the students clustered in the cafeteria.

She cleared her throat. "Aren't you nervous about, um, not being in uniform?"

"Not really," I said with a shrug.

"What about getting demerits?"

I frowned. "What's a demerit?"

"Like a mark on your record?" Sunny's eyes widened behind her glasses. "If you get fifteen, you have to help the cleaning staff on the weekends."

I snorted. Yet another thing to not give a shit about. Who knew? "I'll risk it."

We got in line at the breakfast buffet, plastic trays in hand. I hadn't paid attention to who we stood behind until Jolene and Allison turned around, their faces stretching into suspiciously delighted grins. Sunny immediately tensed beside me, but I cocked my eyebrow and waited while I considered how much damage my tray could do if I was forced to cave in Jolene's pretty face with it.

I was picturing the destruction when Jolene said, "Well if it isn't a Little Goth Civvie and the Cowardly Lyon!"

"Did you two have a special night last night?" Allison's voice chirped like a bird that needed a bullet straight to its beak.

"Um," Sunny said, trying to smile, "sure?"

Sunny's gaze darted between me and the Douche Twins, but Jolene didn't let my silence deter her. "We saw that you two shared a room last night, and we think it's *great*."

"What do you mean?" I asked dryly, wanting to hurry the conversation along. Sweet-smelling bacon was calling my name from farther down the buffet.

"That you and Sunny can be so open about your relationship."

"Being lesbians and all," Allison chimed in.

My eyes peeled away from the bacon, and I gave Jolene and Allison my full, undivided, tray-wielding attention. Beside me, Sunny gargled her words like mouthwash, a blush spreading to her ears. Everyone in the cafeteria had gone quiet; clearly, word of our night together had spread, and I practically felt Sunny melting into the floor faster than the Wicked Witch of the West in a wet T-shirt contest. From the corner of my eye, I saw a group of hunters come into the cafeteria, Luke and Hatter among them. Like the rest of the cafeteria, they paused and watched the drama.

I didn't care about Luke being here, but I would be damned if Sunny was going to be embarrassed in front of Hatter. Okay, fine. Maybe I did care that Luke had walked in, but I still would've turned this bitch's face inside out anyway. The violence curled in my blood, ready and willing.

"We were just . . . It wasn't like that . . ." Sunny tried to explain, her eyes darting toward Hatter, who still stood with Luke at the other side of the long room.

"Oh, Sunny! Don't belittle your love like that. Really and truly, we think it's great," Allison gushed, her words ringing through the cafeteria. Jolene smirked beside her. *Really and truly*, her face would look a lot better when I stabbed it bloody with a quickly made lunch tray shiv.

"You think it's great, don't you, Ollie?" Jolene blinked at me innocently, waiting for any response she could pounce on to try and humiliate us.

My grip tightened on the tray and I closed the distance between us.

Jolene took a quick step back. Across the room, Luke and Hatter moved toward us, Luke's face grim. His advance snapped me back into a rational, less lethal frame of mind. If I beat the shit out of Jolene, I might get tossed out of Fear University before I proved my worth in the evaluation and gained my pardon at the end of the semester. I would have to play this safe.

I met Jolene's stare head-on and plastered a delightfully crazy grin on my face. Her mocking smirk faltered. Maybe she'd actually hoped to provoke me so I would be kicked out.

"Oh, Jolene!" I cooed. "You figured us out, you wonderful little homophobic heifer! Not that we want to keep our love a secret. Not that anyone should ever have to keep their love a secret. But I'm so glad that with the two of you syphilis-swindling sluts, people in this school will feel comfortable to share their equal love all over the place. Why," I said, spreading my arms wide and letting the tray dangle from my fingertips. I really imagined slamming it into Jolene's face. "I could kiss you!"

Sunny gasped. Allison's eyes bugged out of her head. Luke and Hatter came to a screeching stop. I swear, I think all the students' hearts in the cafeteria paused, waiting to see what would happen next, like the split second before a train wreck.

The moment passed. Hearts thundered. The train

wrecked.

I kissed her.

Right there. In the middle of the cafeteria. I wrapped my arms around Jolene's tall, skinny body and laid a big smacker on her overly lip-glossed lips. Her makeup, caked on, contoured, and likely spray-glued to her face, smelled like a musty doll pulled down from the attic. She was so stunned that she didn't push me away until I finished smashing my lips to hers in the wettest, loudest kiss I'd ever had the misfortune of participating in. I stepped back and swiped my hand across my lips.

There has never been such a complete, resounding silence as there was in that cafeteria right then.

I shifted back on the heels of my unlaced boots and waited, still grinning as I watched Jolene's face go from red, to purple, to white, and back to red. Incapable of anything else, Allison merely stared unblinking at Jolene's mouth, where smeared lip gloss colored all outside the lines.

A snort came from beside me, followed by Sunny doubling over in laughter. The noise broke the spell. All around us, students burst out laughing, hooting, and jeering. They pointed their fingers at Jolene's shocked face. Fists banged on the tables. Trays slammed against the backs of chairs.

Hatter clapped Luke on the shoulder like he was congratulating him, and Jolene's mouth opened and closed, the words to express my impending doom lost for the moment. I blew a kiss at her and moved up the line, aiming for some damn bacon to wash her taste out of my mouth.

The first five minutes of sixth period flew by. Not because the teacher allowed me to participate in the sparring today, which I was, and not because every single student insisted on re-living the breakfast kissing fiasco over and over, which they were, but because Jolene volunteered to be my partner.

And then promptly punched me in the face. Crouching beside me, she whispered, "Don't ever kiss me again!"

I puckered my quickly swelling, very split lips at her.

Her second punch straight to my nose was a cheap shot. Totally rude.

Our gym teacher sent us straight to Dean. My stomach flipped with nerves; hopefully this wasn't enough to get me kicked out of Fear University. It's not like I'd punched Jolene back, though I was sorely tempted. For the first time ever, I really had something to lose here.

Dean looked up from some paperwork as I walked in. From the poorly hidden grin on his face, someone must have already told him what happened. "Have a seat, Ollie," he said before taking a sip of coffee.

I sat in the same chair I had during our first meeting. "Sir, I—"

He waved off my explanation. "I know. This is what I was afraid of when I warned you about some of the students not being as welcoming. Although I will have to formerly make a mark on your records, and remind you to . . ." He coughed to hide his laugh. "Not kiss, uh, *unwilling* recipients."

"Oh." The tension in my shoulders released. "Thank you, sir. And I will. I mean, I won't. Kiss people, that is." I scowled down at my lap, feeling a blush spread up my neck as Luke's face flashed through my mind for some horrible reason. "Kiss unwilling people, anyway."

Dean smiled at me, his mustache twitching. Though I knew I should be keeping my guard up just in case, I couldn't help but feel a little tug in my chest when Dean's approval of me so clearly radiated off of him. I imagined this is what other people felt like with their dads.

"Also, I've had some teachers complain about your uniform or lack thereof today. Technically, we don't have an official uniform since all the students here are over eighteen, but the teachers are saying your style is causing some unease amongst the students."

"Seriously?" I scoffed.

Dean rubbed his temples, clearly thinking it was as ridiculous as I did. "Seriously. So I'm also going to give you a couple demerits for the lack of uniform."

"So I'm not in real trouble?"

"No. Just focus on preparing for your evaluation in a couple of weeks." My stomach flipped at the mention of it. "I'll deal with Jolene. Are you okay to train with your face like that?"

I rubbed my sore nose and mouth. "I'll live."

"All right. But I want you to go to the ward first and have a doctor examine you to make sure Jolene didn't break anything before you train with Luke today. Other than that, you're free to go."

By the time I made my way down to the ward and found a doctor to check my face, sixth period had ended and I was late to practice with Luke. Holding an ice pack to my face, I walked back into the gym.

"You're late," Luke called as soon as he saw me. He didn't bother to ask if I was okay. Ass.

"Been busy." Without comment, he handed me the blindfold again and I sighed, lowering the ice pack, which, I won't lie, I'd brought along only for sympathy points. "Really? I can't breathe."

"Do you think a 'swang will care if you've let a tiny girl sucker punch you in the face and mess up your nose?"

"First of all, she didn't mess up my nose. It still looks fine," I said with a sniff. "And secondly, Jolene is not tiny. She's stacked like an Amazon warrior or something."

"So you're saying you couldn't beat her in a fight?"

Well, shit. Time to change the subject. "I know you saw my kiss earlier. Did you like it?" I goaded, wagging my brows at him. He didn't react.

"Put on the blindfold and let's get started."

I smirked. It didn't escape me that he'd changed the subject just as quickly too. "What if I skip running this evening?"

"Nope. Got to get your ass in shape."

"I've never had any complaints about my ass before." Luke cocked a brow, muttering something I couldn't make out. "What was that? You like my ass?"

"That's not what I said." His jaw flexed, and I pounced like a shark smelling blood.

"I'll believe you if you let me skip running."

"Not happening, Ollie," Luke said, frustration thick

enough in his voice to make me smile so wide that my bruised nose hurt. "Put the blindfold on and let's get started."

"Fine. But try not to stare at my ass the entire time, okay? It makes me blush."

My first two days at Fear University were pretty hellish, but a change slowly happened over the next two weeks. The professors got used to me being there and eased off the hostility bus. First-year students stopped aligning with Jolene and actually talked to me after my kissing stunt in the cafeteria. A few even sat at the lunch table with Sunny and me, which was pretty cool. I made good headway in my classes, though Sunny still came to my room every night to study. Some nights, she slept over. I let her. The letting her got easier and easier with time.

Evening practices with Luke became less like a boxing match of stubborn wills and more like actual training for the evaluation. He barely spoke to me and did his best to ignore me the entire time, especially when I goaded him relentlessly. Pissing Luke off had become my number one source of entertainment. When my numerous wounds healed, he doubled my laps around the fence line.

He didn't stab me anymore, which I appreciated.

All in all, things were settling down. For the first time in my life, I had a place where I was safe. Where I belonged. Where I was wanted—for the most part.

EIGHT

I'd switched from working out in shorts and tanks to leggings and long-sleeved shirts. Though the gym stayed warm enough, the late September cooler air pressed against the thick prison walls enough that I didn't want to risk getting sick. And though I was getting better at sparring with Luke, he still left enough bruises on my arms and legs from his obnoxiously well-aimed kicks that I was embarrassed. After my tussle with Jolene, I had a new badass reputation to protect.

It was the day before my evaluation with Dean, and I intended to spend the entire evening in the gym practicing with Luke. Luckily, he was the type to not complain about missing dinner. At least, not out loud. He had his celibate, scowling hunter reputation to protect too.

When the gym emptied out after sixth period, tired students hauling their bruised carcasses back to their rooms before dinner, I slipped into the locker room to freshen up a bit. Not that I re-did my ponytail or put on another layer of deodorant for Luke. I really didn't care what he thought of me. But I sniff-checked my shirt before I slammed my now familiar blue locker shut, spun the lock, and headed out of the vaguely body-odor scented room.

Before I crossed into the glass gym, I paused. Voices— angry voices—sounded from the training mats only feet away from the girls' locker room. Quietly, I stepped closer and leaned my head out to see into the gym.

Luke stood with his arms crossed, making his shoulders look broader in his white workout shirt. He had his back to me, but I felt the tension rolling off of him in stinging, fizzling waves. His black hair curled over his neck, which was dotted with angry red splotches.

He faced a man who could only be his father, because they both had the same build, and the exact same hardened, sculpted jaw lines. But the familiar lethal violence in Mr. Aultstriver's eyes truly convinced me of his relation to Luke, who's eyes had held the very same look when I'd pissed him off in the van the first night I met him.

"You have no idea what you've done, do you?" his father asked and Luke lowered his arms, his fingertips dancing against each other in their deliberate fashion. I almost cringed, beyond thankful it wasn't me pissing him off this time.

"I do, actually." Luke's voice contained an edge of anger laced with a lethality that made my spine tingle. "I brought back a prospective hunter to help us fight. She's talented and smart."

Tingle officially gone. They were arguing about me, and it actually sounded like Luke had defended me, which shocked the complete hell out of me. We were cordial enough during practice, but I'd never thought of him as a friend until now.

Mr. Aultstriver clenched his fists, and I noticed the criss-crossing hatch marks of black scars across his hands. He wore expensive-looking pants and a crisp white button-down shirt tailored to his muscular form perfectly, seams nearly bursting when he leaned toward Luke. Both men looked ready to tear each other apart.

"Don't try to lie to me. You brought her back because you were thinking with your dick."

I blew a piece of hair out of my face, wishing *if only*. My thoughts startled me enough that I reprimanded myself, mentally slapping my cheeks. I didn't like Luke. Or his stupid dick. He'd *stabbed* me.

Luke went still. I wanted to see his face, his eyes. Why was he standing up for me? "I couldn't just leave her out there after she'd killed a 'swang and was injured. Besides, she could help us win this war if she's properly trained."

His father growled and jerked forward, grabbing Luke's shirt in his fist to yank him onto his toes. Luke didn't react. The position looked natural to them, like Luke had been in his father's grip his entire life and knew better than to struggle. It made me sick. "She's a fucking civvie. You're bringing down this entire establishment. This place is for the elite, not orphan murderers."

"Really, Dad? That's a little pretentious, even for you." At his words, Mr. Aultstriver shoved him backward, but Luke was built so solidly that he barely moved. He smoothed down his shirt.

"You're such a waste. Such a goddamned waste. All those years I spent training you." His father practically spat the words, his nostrils flaring. "All those years I spent teaching you, conditioning your fear. And look at you now. Nothing but a coward passing off *our* duty, *our* honor, to a civvie."

Luke's jaw clenched. "She's not a normal—"

"I don't give a damn what she is. Now, instead of killing 'swangs, you're here, teaching a murderer. Like you're some fucking professor coward."

"The professors here aren't cowards."

Mr. Aultstriver snorted with ugly laughter. "Yes, they are. They should be out there fighting. Dean Bogrov has made this school soft, ruined it with his stupid ideas for the 'future.' If I ran this place—"

"If you ran this place," Luke interjected, voice steady, "it would be an army base instead of a school. You would have twelve-year-olds out there fighting in the war before they'd learned what fear really was. You would kill us all."

Smiling cruelly, his father leaned into Luke's face and snarled, "Damn straight I would. And I would send you right to the front lines where you could get some sense into your head."

Luke didn't respond, which was obviously a tactical move

to further piss his father off. I had to give it to Luke. He had balls. Big, manly balls.

Stop thinking about his balls, Ollie!

"Such a waste." Mr. Aultstriver shook his head at Luke, disgust dripping from his eyes. "Such a complete, pathetic—"

I'd had enough. Honestly, if I never heard one more horrible comment from some piece-of-shit parent again, I would die a happy person. Some people were such wastes of space.

I stomped from the locker room as loud as possible, drawing their attention. With a warning in his eyes, Luke stepped forward like he wanted to intercept me before I reached his father, but I swerved around him and planted myself directly in front of Mr. Aultstriver. I smiled sweetly, smiled so big that my teeth dried in the stiff air of the gym.

"You must be Mr. Aultstriver! I'm Ollie, you know, the worthless orphan murderer. I would say it's real nice to meet you," I drawled, "but you sound like a real fucking asshole."

I surprised myself, but I wasn't going to cower in front of this guy. The silence after my introduction was so resounding that I imagined I heard the dust percolating up in the air-conditioning unit. Luke stared at me with complete shock; it was the most animated I'd seen his face in weeks. I couldn't help it; I felt a little flutter in my stomach that I'd gotten such a raw reaction from him. If I was going to get smacked down onto the mats for saying that to his father, it was worth it to see the look on Luke's face.

I wished he would let me see more of his true reactions. But then, that would mean we were friends, and I doubted

Luke wanted that, even if he had defended me moments ago.

Mr. Aultstriver's face turned redder and redder, but Luke recovered first from the shock. He snapped, "Do your laps, Ollie. We won't be practicing today."

"But tomorrow—"

"That's enough." Luke's harshness set me back on my heels, but when he cut his eyes to his father, who was still fuming mad, I realized he wanted me out of the line of fire. "Go run," he softly added, fingers skimming against my back to steer me forward and away.

That evening, a thick group of students clustered around our table to eat dinner. After my stunt with Jolene, Sunny and I had taken her spot as queen bee of the first-years. Not that I cared, but I was happy to see Sunny enjoying having more friends and not being called the Cowardly Lyon anymore.

The students around us chatted about their favorite topic of late: Fields, which was right before winter break, almost a month away. All the first-years had to pass the semester's final written exams in all their classes followed by a physical examination called Fields. No one knew exactly what Fields consisted of or how we would be tested during it because the older students liked to keep secrets from the first-years.

Rite of passage or some bullshit.

I didn't join in on the gossip about Fields. Once I got through my evaluation tomorrow, I would worry about Fields. Until then, I only thought about passing Dean's test and gaining Luke's approval.

My thoughts kept drifting back to the conversation I'd

overheard in the gym. Luckily, Sunny carried the constant chatter from the start of the dinner to the end, and when we finally headed back to the dorms, I sighed in relief, ready to be by myself.

An hour later, surrounded by silence and alone in my room, I hadn't gotten any studying done. And I wouldn't. Not until I talked to Luke. I didn't know what I wanted to say, but I knew I needed to say something. I needed, like really needed, him to understand I wasn't some naive brat with a super-hero complex, especially after he'd defended me to his father. I wanted him to see I was a real person with a past horribly similar to his own.

I needed his approval. And I hated that.

I slammed my Weapons textbook closed and checked the clock. I had plenty of time before curfew to make it to the hunters' barracks, which stood separate from the students' dorms, and tell him my side of the story.

The Death Dome thumped with talking, music, and general chaos. I made my way through the students shouting back and forth to each other on the third level and down the stairs to the entry, where I swiped my card and silently slipped outside. The silence was like a soothing balm after the cacophony of the Death Dome, and I picked my way across the courtyard in relative peace as I headed toward the row of apartments across from the general store.

The barracks' front door was similar to my cell door, but without a lock. The hunters were free to go and come as they pleased. Not wanting to be seen, I hurried down the cramped, narrow hall that smelled like sweaty men, checking the doors for any sign of the apartment that belonged to Luke. I got lucky. His running shoes—muddy from his morning run—sat outside his door.

I knocked. Nothing. Light streamed out from beneath his door. When I knocked again and got no answer, I tried the doorknob and found it unlocked. I twisted the knob, feeling nervous, which was almost as horrible as needing Luke's approval. Before I backed down, I swung the door open and stepped inside.

Luke sat on his bed, earphones in his ear, jamming out to screaming rock music. With a jolt of shock, he jerked to his feet, hand clenching around a slender, gleaming knife.

Blood ran thick down his left forearm from deep cuts he'd made in his flesh.

"What the ever-loving fuck?" I spat, feeling instantly sick to my stomach.

"Ollie!" He held his arm out to the side, where it dripped leaky tears of blood onto the floor, the knife like a bomb in his hand. "This isn't what it looks like."

I snarled in disgust. It couldn't be anything else. I backed out of his door and went to close it behind me, but he moved too quickly.

Luke grabbed me from behind, snagging my waist with one arm and pulling me back inside. He slammed the door shut. I turned around, forcing him to step back, and crossed my arms over my chest. "You have two seconds to let me out of here before I rip off your other arm."

Luke wasn't impressed by my threats. "Let me explain before you throw your tantrum."

"I wasn't going to throw a tantrum."

"It's not what you think."

"You've said that already."

"I'm . . ."

Luke obviously struggled to explain, and I had a horrible thought. When he'd sent me to go run before his father exploded, had he taken my place in the line of fire? Even as I thought it, I knew the answer: of course he had. But what had I abandoned him to? "This isn't about your father, is it? Because of the stuff he said? Luke—"

"No," he said quickly, cutting me off. He shook his head, jaw clenching. "It's not him. I don't care what he says."

I watched him closely, and he didn't shift under my gaze. He stared back at me, his green eyes so bright and lively in stark contrast to his perfectly schooled neutral expression.

"Then why?"

Luke took so long to answer, little lines forming between his thick, dark brows, that I answered my own question. A sound of disgust came up my throat. I backed to the door, my hand on the knob, which made Luke flinch, his hand twitching like he wanted to reach for me.

"Are you training?" The words were an accusation. "Cutting yourself to school your reaction to pain?"

My disgust quickly morphed to a slowly building panic. Did Fear University really encourage its students and hunters to cut? My stomach rolled and I had visions of basements and freshly dug graves.

"When I say that you're sort of right, don't freak out, okay?"

My jaw dropped open. I turned to open the door, ready to escape, but Luke closed his massive hand around mine and the doorknob. His chest pressed against my back. This was the closest we'd ever been aside from when he'd stabbed me. I growled in warning, just in case he was getting stabby ideas again.

"Not all the hunters cut, okay?" His breath warmed the back of my neck. "Only some of us do. It's an old method of teaching pain management. The school doesn't condone it anymore."

Slowly I turned back around, but Luke didn't back away this time like I'd expected. "You mean, this," I glared down at his arms, "was actually a thing once?"

"The cutting is an old-school method that my father taught—"

"You're father," I whispered, "is a jackass."

The corner of Luke's mouth twitched ever so slightly, and I wondered if he was about to smile. His chest brushed against mine with every exhale, making the hairs along my arms stand on end. "He is. But some families still use the cutting method to teach pain management. I've done it since I was eleven."

I flinched at his words. His father had taught Luke to cut, maybe even held the blade the first few times. "That's awful."

"Hatter had it worse. His parents gave him 'swang saliva when he screamed too loudly from the cuts." My jaw dropped open. Instantly, Luke looked like he wanted to rip his words out of the air. With a grimace, he continued. "It's how some of us learn, Ollie. I'm not trying to hurt myself."

"But you are hurting yourself! Shit, Luke. Look at your arms. You were bleeding all over the place."

Luke didn't look anywhere but my eyes. I'd come over here to explain myself to him, but he was the one trying to make me understand, as if he valued my opinion of him as much as I'd come to value his.

"We're not like you. We have to learn how to deal with pain, learn to condition our reaction to it, our fear of it. This way," he said, holding up his arm, "is an old-school method that I like to use every now and then to keep myself sharp."

"Christ, Luke. That's what I came to tell you. You the wrong idea about me. I'm not some unfeeling robot." I swallowed and looked away. This was what I came to tell him, I just didn't imagine it would be so hard. "Even as much as I would like to be sometimes."

"The foster brother?" Luke asked softly, understanding in his eyes. How much had Dean told him about my past?

I clenched my arms tighter until I knew I would have bruises. My head screamed at me to shut the hell up, but my mouth didn't listen. I wanted him to understand me, to understand the bad parts. I nodded.

Luke hesitated a moment, clearly thinking something over before he said, "I want to show you something. Will you come with me?"

"Okay," I said, not having to think that long on it.

After hastily bandaging his arm, he took us back into the main building and down the winding staircase to the ward, which was silent aside from the soft whirring and clicking of machines. Surprising me, we went another level below the school's hospital and subterranean garage. We came to a steel door with a large skull and cross-bone sign on it reading "Laboratory: Authorized Personnel Only." With a swipe of his card, Luke let us inside.

Instantly, the scent of disinfectant washed over me. Above us, power-saving lights flipped on as we walked inside. Tools of every type, sleek computers, vented booths, unnameable machines, and countless microscopes filled every inch of room, all if it white and clean and far more technologically advanced than the rest of the prison ever hoped to be.

"This way." Luke went into another room off to the side, which I assumed was a broom closet. Wrong. Inside, the sounds of a hundred scurrying feet accompanied the strong musky smell of animals. Luke flipped on the lights, and I gasped.

Cages upon cages of rats lined the back wall from floor to ceiling, spanning the entire length of the room, which stretched out much longer than I'd originally thought. A quick guess put the rats at a little over five hundred. They could only be down here for one reason.

Turning, I glared at Luke. "You really think that bringing me down here to show me the school's freaking animal testing lab will make me feel any better about what you do to yourself?"

"I want to explain why."

"And you're going to explain that using tortured rats?"

"Yes." Luke gave me a look that clearly meant to zip it. "These rats are constantly being taught to fear a stimuli and then conditioned to overcome that fear. Because of this lab and these rats, the school has learned much more progressive ways of teaching fear conditioning and pain management. We don't have to do the cutting techniques anymore."

I squinted at him, reluctantly curious. "How do the rats help teach people?"

"During testing, a bell is rung in the rat's cage. Right after the sound, the animals receive a small shock." At my narrowed eyes, Luke hurried on to explain. "It doesn't hurt them. Much. But they learn to fear the bell because they know they will be shocked right after. It's a fear stimulus. Once they are truly afraid, we slowly begin teaching them not to be afraid of the bell by not shocking them every time. They learn to overcome their fear. The techs down here monitor the rats' brain activity during the testing, and we use it to train the third-year students who specialize in hunting during their fear conditioning classes."

His father had mentioned fear conditioning. My eyes went back to the little rats scurrying around, their pink noses twitching at us. "Luke," I said quietly, "did your father do this to you?"

"Fear University does not do this to people. Nor do they practice cutting as a method for fear conditioning anymore."

He sounded like he was reading from a brochure and it scared me. "That doesn't answer my question. Did he shock you like you were some lab rat?"

"My father," Luke said, turning away from me, "and his training methods are not typical, but they're effective."

My stomach bottomed out, horror spreading through my bones and into the tips of my fingers. Had Hatter received the same kind of abuse too? "Luke," I whispered, wanting nothing more than to hug him.

He ignored me, half his face lost to shadow. "I brought you down here because I wanted you to see that a little bit of fear is good. Ollie, you could be a talented hunter. You're strong and smart and terrifyingly well equipped to handle this life for a civilian. But that's exactly what scares me the most. Dean would do anything to have an entire army like you, but this war isn't right for civvies. It takes a specially crafted hunter to kill 'swangs. Teaching civvies to not fear pain or death would create another kind of monster. Humans are meant to be afraid."

His words surprised me, but they gave me a shot of pleasure straight through to my stomach. He didn't hate me because I was a civvie, he was worried for me. "Would it be so bad if Dean had an army of hunters like me?"

Luke led me out of the rat hotel and closed the door tightly behind us. He spoke so quietly that I didn't know if I'd heard him right at first. "Yes. It would."

"You don't trust him." It wasn't a question, because Luke's eyes held answer enough for me. For some reason, he didn't like Dean. The blood between the Aultstrivers and Dean Bogrov was of the bad sort. "That's why you were scared when you brought me here. Why you tried to warn me away."

"I trust the man Dean used to be, but sometimes I don't trust how far he will go to win this war."

"You can go too far to win? But the guy lost his wife to a 'swang. Seems like a pretty good reason to be devoted."

"We've all lost people. It's so common and familiar it hardly affects us, much less drives us."

I blinked, surprised by his cold remark as he headed toward the lab's front door. I took a moment to look around the lab before we left. Now that I wasn't overwhelmed by all the equipment, I saw another large, steel door with a red 'x' across it on the opposite side of the room. "What's that?"

"That," Luke said, and I knew the distrusting look was back in his eyes by the sound of his voice, "is the west wing side of the lab. No one is allowed in there but very, very high-ranking members of the university. I've never been inside."

"Your father has?" I guessed.

Luke nodded. "Whatever is on the other side of that door worries me."

"Because you like fear."

"Because I think Dean is far too focused on making it easy for us to not be afraid or feel pain. It shouldn't be easy. Fighting 'swangs is meant to be hard."

"And I'm the easy way out," I said, drawing Luke's attention, which he leveled on me with all his dark, focused glory.

"War should never be easy."

"But you can go too far to win it."

"Of course," Luke said, completely convinced in his convictions of honor and duty. Peg had been right about him being the old-school, old-family type. I marveled at his ability to have that devout mindset after all his father had put him through.

"So where does that leave me?"

Luke held the lab door open for me, and I walked out with one more glance at the west side's door. "Don't worry," he said, sealing the door shut, "I don't intend on making it easy for you. When we're done training, no one will remember you can't feel pain. You'll just be a good, lethal hunter. You'll be so normal, Dean will forget all about you."

In the darkness of the stairwell, I sensed Luke beside me, his breathing slow and steady. I liked the way he felt, solid and reassuring, unyielding with a current of violence like electricity pulsing beneath his skin. "Will you forget about me if you're not training me anymore?"

Luke's breathing sounds stopped. My eyes adjusted enough that I saw the outline of his square jaw, saw the muscle there clenching as he leaned toward me. Caramel breath swirled across my face, making my mouth water. "I can find something else to teach you."

His husky, quiet voice nearly made my knees buckle. Suddenly, he was too close, too hot, too *Luke*. And this damn staircase was way the hell too dark. "Right. Well, I have to pass my evaluation tomorrow," I said, stuttering like a moron. For once, Ollie Andrews didn't have a snappy comeback.

"You're worried because we didn't practice today," Luke said, leaning back and giving me some space.

"No shit." I breathed a little easier now in this familiar territory.

I sensed Luke's smile in the change of his body, the corners of his mouth cracking with moisture from his teeth. I regretted the damned darkness for not being able to see him smile, anything but the stoic expression he normally sported.

His voice deepened when he responded, "Go back to your dorm, Ollie, and get some sleep. You'll do fine tomorrow."

NINE

The next morning, I sat in my Fear Theory class listening to Mr. Abbot talk about brains. Brains and rats. Rats and brains.

Apparently, some rats with damaged amygdalae will walk right up to a cat with no fear. Pretty cool, but not so smart. I wondered if I was like those stupid rats with the screwed-up brains. Luke had practically told me that he would do anything to keep Dean from creating an army of civilian soldiers like me. It didn't take a genius to figure out that I was the bad thing here, the monster to kill monsters.

Not that I minded. I'd always thought of myself as a monster anyway, but damn if it didn't bother me that Luke thought the same thing.

I copied Mr. Abbot's notes with little interest. Last night

had opened my eyes to many things, Luke's past being one of them. After our little field trip, I'd barely managed to make it back to the dorms before lockdown, but Luke had walked me the entire way, his eyes as watchful as they ever were. He never took a break, never relaxed. He seemed to be weirdly calm ninety-nine percent of the time, and the other percent was spent being incredibly angry and violent.

Almost as if he'd been conditioned all his life, which, I guessed, was true with a father like his. All Luke's work to control his anger and stay calm stemmed directly from his tumultuous upbringing. He worked so hard to be a different man than his father, to be better. To take the honorable ways of Fear University that his father had warped and make them right, even if it lost him the war.

It broke my heart to see him try so hard.

I sat back in my chair and rubbed my eyes. Mr. Abbot was giving us a lot of notes today, and I'd long ago tuned out his droning voice. Luckily, I didn't have to worry about him calling on me to answer a question, since he acted perfectly content to pretend I didn't exist, which didn't bother me. I was fine with just taking notes and spending the time figuring out Luke Aultstriver.

Which I was doing way too much of. Especially when I needed to be more concerned about my evaluation with Dean today.

"Christ," I muttered under my breath. I raked my hand through my tangled hair. My evaluation was today and I really didn't know if I was ready.

After class, I numbly packed up my notebook as a few

students tried to talk to me. I wasn't good for conversation today, and I barely managed single word replies to their endless chatter about Fields.

The rest of day fell into a similar rhythm: endless Luke thoughts, notes, lunch with Sunny, more notes, more Luke, stress about my evaluation. When the end of sixth period came, I was wrung out.

Sunny stood outside the gym with me while I waited on Luke to arrive. I took my chance to ask about the other thing that had bothered me all day. "Sunny, do you know anything about Hatter's childhood?"

She glanced at me, surprised by the question. Her smile faltered slightly. "No," she said, nibbling on her lip in thought. "His family isn't Original or even all that old. Just a few generations since they became a part of the hunters. Why?"

"Have you heard about how they treated him?"

Her face paled. "What are you saying?"

I took that as a no, which made sense if his family wasn't on anyone's radar. "You know how Luke was raised?" She nodded. "I think that happened to Hatter too."

"*Fudge.*" She looked away and took off her glasses to clean. "These families . . ." She took a deep breath, clearly pissed, her little doll-like hands shaking. "They just shouldn't do that. We have it hard enough here. Kids should get to be kids while they can."

I put my hand on her shoulder. I knew how much she cared for Hatter. "You had good parents. Not everyone is that lucky."

"I hate it," she said quietly, more venom in her voice than I'd ever heard. "It's not fair."

We waited for a while longer as Sunny's breathing slowly returned to normal. Students called out to us as they passed, waving and smiling. Eventually, Sunny asked, "Do you think you're ready?"

I knew she was talking about the evaluation without having to ask. "I hope so, or you'll have to find a new cuddle buddy."

In the hall, other students loitered, using the time to group together for gossip before dinner. They seemed to constantly group around us, even if we weren't talking to them. But it was nice during times like these, made me feel less alone.

"That's not funny," Sunny said. "I doubt Dean will make you leave if you don't pass."

I appreciated how hard Sunny tried to make me feel better, and I shot her a relieved smile for her effort. But I'd seen how committed Dean was to winning this war. Thinking about the rat cages still made me shudder. The fear conditioning, Luke's father, Hatter's family, and the cutting were too extreme. Of course Dean would cast me aside if I didn't prove important enough. I shoved my hands into my jacket's pockets to keep them from trembling.

"I guess we'll see," I said so that I didn't worry Sunny.

Suddenly, Sunny stood straighter next to me. "Thad's been released."

"Who?" Confused, I glanced at her, wondering what had distracted her.

"Thaddeus Booker." Sunny subtly nodded toward a group

of students walking toward us. Unfortunately Jolene and Allison were among them, holding court and fawning over a guy with light-blond hair and a tall, muscular form. I couldn't see his face, but I guessed he was older than us based on his sheer size. "You remember. The throat bite guy who was in the ward when you came in."

"Oh." I glanced at the guy with renewed interest, but he was already staring right at me and coming closer still, like he was aiming straight for me. Subtly, I glanced behind me to see if he was really staring at me. Unfortunately for me, no one stood behind me. I resigned myself to his attention with an unhappy scowl. Anyone who hung out with Jolene was not a friend of mine.

"You must be the new girl," Thad said, stopping in front of us. Jolene and Allison reluctantly drew to a stop, their lips curling into territorial snarls. Sunny shifted nervously beside me.

His face was beautiful, almost pretty with long lashes trimming weird lightly colored eyes. He still had a thick bandage wrapped around his neck, almost like a neck brace. I raised my eyes back up to his. "You must be the guy who almost got his throat ripped out."

His popular entourage gasped at my audacity, but Thad laughed, like *howled* so loudly we drew the attention of everyone else in the hall. "You're awfully bold for a girl I've seen naked."

That, more than his raucous laughter, definitely shut everybody up. I narrowed my eyes at his lie. I hated lies. They brought back memories of mothers and closets, and even more than I hated lies, I hated memories. "No, you haven't."

"Trust me. I wouldn't forget those." His eyes locked onto my chest and didn't move.

"Oh, come on, Thad," Jolene said, stepping forward. "She's a civvie."

"It's okay, Jo. Ollie and I know each other really well." Thad winked at me. *Winked.* I pictured peeling his face off with my nails.

"I've never met you before." Heat bloomed across my face, not from embarrassment but fury.

"Ollie. Ollie," Thad said. "It's okay. Don't be ashamed. Technically, we haven't met, but I would never forget a body like yours."

"You're lying," I growled. Sunny put a hand on my arm in warning; Thad noticed and grinned wider. I really think he wanted me to finish the job with his throat or something. Jolene's eyes roved between us, the hallway silent as a grave.

"Not at all! You remember, we were in the ward together. That morning, when you left, you changed clothes, and I got to see you in all your naked glory. Where did you get that scar on your back by the way? You know, the one that looks like an upside-down seahorse?"

Carefully, I sat my backpack down. I didn't want to get anything bloody, and this would certainly turn bloody. When I looked up, Sunny grabbed my arm harder. "Ollie, wait—"

"You're late." Only one voice could pull me out of my red murder haze. Luke walked up beside me, noting Sunny's death grip on my arm and Thad standing in front of me. "Thaddeus," he said, saying the name with the same amount of hate and damnation people used when they said "'swang."

"Hey, Luke. I was just telling Ollie here that she should give up this 'swang hunting business and go into porn or something. She has the body for it."

"Excuse me?" Luke spoke with such steely calm that I put *my* hand on *his* arm to hold him back. He wore long sleeves, but I felt the bandages from his cutting last night through the material. The tendons in his forearm twitched as he tapped his fingers together.

"Sure," Thad said, grinning. His obvious delight made me realize that it wasn't me who he wanted to pick a fight with; it was Luke. "Your girl here isn't very modest."

"I'm not his girl." I spat the words, my grip tightening on Luke.

"Leave it, Thad." Students, Jolene and Sunny included, stepped away from the confrontation, driven back by the threatening growl in Luke's voice. I stayed, but gooseflesh prickled along my arms.

"Don't be like that." Thad's grin stretched wider, making the bandages around his neck pull. "I heard your father was here yesterday. Little family reunion?"

Before I reacted, Thad reached over and grasped Luke's arm, the one I gripped. With my own hold on Luke's arm, I felt how hard Thad squeezed the bandages above Luke's cuts. A hiss of pain escaped his lips.

The sound undid me.

I let go of his arm and slammed my palms into Thad's chest, shoving him back as hard as possible, sending students scattering farther away from us. "You better fucking watch yourself," I said as Thad stumbled back, laughing.

"Feisty!" Thad's eyes flicked over my shoulder to Luke. "I hear that's what you want, right? For them to fight back a little in bed? I guess you really are your father's son." Thad threw back his head and laughed, outlining all the missing chunks in his neck.

A vibration began in Luke's throat. He'd gone much too still beside me, like he wasn't breathing.

I didn't know how much Thad knew about Luke's father, but I didn't want to risk anything else coming to light in front of all these students. With one last glare, I turned away from Thad and put my hand on Luke's chest. "Let's leave," I whispered to him.

"You better listen to her." Thad must have come closer to us, because Luke's head reared back, nostrils flaring. I pressed my hand harder against his chest. "Before Daddy's little monster comes out to play."

"Luke," I said, but he wouldn't look at me. "Don't let him get to you."

"I've always wondered something since you inherited your reaction to 'swang saliva from your father." Fear spread through my belly as Thad kept talking. "When Daddy Dearest went on all his little hunts, how did he work out his aggression when he got bit? Cause I heard your mom isn't much good for that kind of pounding anymore. Tell me, did he come for you—"

I was ready when Luke launched himself at Thad. I practically crawled up his chest, grabbing his chin in my hand. With all the strength I had, I forced him to look down at me, my fingers digging into his cheeks. I stared into his eyes long and hard until I knew I had his attention. "Luke, we're late for my evaluation, and I'm not failing because of this idiot."

Slowly, Luke's body relaxed as he stared at me. He nodded, an arm still around my waist from where I'd jumped on him to stop him from ripping Thad's head off. I didn't look around us at all the other students who were watching with their mouth's hanging open; I kept touching Luke, kept reminding him to keep looking at me. Slowly, Luke sat me back down on the ground.

Quickly, before Thad could taunt Luke again, I grabbed my backpack and eased Luke toward the gym. Sunny darted behind us, calling a hasty goodbye before she disappeared down the hall. The other students, Thad included, followed her lead and went to dinner.

When we were alone and inside the gym, Luke asked, "Did he really see you naked?"

His tone still worried me, but his eyes slowly returned to normal. Not so glinty and dangerous. "I guess he was awake when I changed the morning you brought me in. I didn't know." I shrugged like it was no big deal, but the asshole had seen my scar. Only two other people had seen it, and I'd killed one already. Max was next.

"I don't like him."

"Really? I hadn't noticed."

"I don't want you around him. He's dangerous. And he's not as good as he thinks he is."

"Why, Luke, are you jealous?" I swatted his uninjured arm, trying to lighten the mood. Anything to keep him from going over the edge.

"Hardly."

"I think you're supposed to kiss me now."

"What the hell are you talking about?" Luke's complete look of surprise told me I'd accomplished my goal of distracting him from the awful things Thad had said. Things that really worried me for Luke. I prayed Thad was just being a dick and none of it was true.

"You know, in the movies, the guy always kisses the girl after the big jealous blowup scene, where the guy makes himself look like an ass, but the girl deals with it anyway because she's settling and wants to get married and move to the suburbs and have babies and gain twenty pounds?"

Luke didn't laugh like I'd hoped he would. He blinked a couple of times at me before closing the distance between us. I was a tall girl, but he still loomed over me. I swear, some asshole was pumping carbon dioxide through the central heating unit in the gym because I suddenly couldn't breathe with Luke's dark stare bearing down on me. A piece of black hair fell over his eyes and I'm pretty sure my knees almost buckled for the second time in twenty-four hours.

The bastard wasn't playing fair.

"You wouldn't be settling for me."

With that Luke stalked off to the locker rooms to change, leaving me and my stomach, which had dropped to the floor, behind. Luke Aultstriver, flirting. I'd seen it all. And damned if it didn't get me a little fluttery, like my insides were humming. I glanced toward the glass wall of the gym, making certain no one else had witnessed my drool fest. Luckily, the hall was completely deserted.

I seriously had to get my shit together when it came to Luke.

Thanks to Thaddeus Freaking Booker, I didn't have much time to change. Not that I needed much, but I wouldn't have minded a little pick-me-up speech with myself in the mirror before I facing down this evaluation. I managed to shovel my hair up into a tight, no-bullshit ponytail before I hurried back out to the gym.

Dean was already there, standing with Luke. Both looked up as I walked out. They'd been talking about me, because now they grew silent, eyes serious, mouths pressed into a tight line. They leaned away from each other, arms crossed over their chests. Luke's jaw clenched and unclenched in a fury.

Something told me that they hadn't just been talking about me; they'd been fighting about me too. At the risk of sounding like a total pussy, after the fight with Thad, I really didn't want to deal with any more drama today. I wanted to pass my evaluation and go to bed.

When I was close enough, Dean uncrossed his arms and clapped me on the shoulder, his smile too broad to be natural. "You ready for this?"

"Sure." I glanced at Luke, who gave me a tight nod.

"Great," Dean said. "Let's get started then. Practice how you normally would. Try to forget I'm here."

Said the guy who held my fate in his hands. I watched as he took a seat on the bleachers. The flutter in my stomach had nothing to do with Luke's earlier flirting, and everything to do with the fact that I might puke at any moment.

"Calm down," Luke whispered, positioning himself between me and Dean to block my view. I craned my head back to see his face. "You can do this. Focus on me, okay? Just me."

Focusing on Luke that much wasn't going to help me at all, but I didn't tell him that. "Maybe you can go easy on me today," I joked, knowing if anything, Luke was going to lay it on harder.

"Don't be nervous."

"I'm not!" I lied.

"You say stupid things when you're nervous."

I gritted my teeth. "Asking you to go easy on me isn't that stupid," I said under my breath.

Luke ignored me, and I began my warm up. He led me through a series of exercises with his punching and kicking shields to get me loose. I lost myself to the rhythmic thwacking of my fists striking the thick pads. We moved in a circle, our dance perfected after weeks of practice. It was just warm up, but Luke hit back with the shield hard enough to send me rocking back on my heels. I gritted my teeth and dug in. He kept his eyes on me, and I focused on the shield, perfecting my punches and dodges, my kicks and parries. He came at me hard enough, harder than any warm up before, that I had to focus and forget about my nerves or else end up on my ass.

By the time he dropped the shield and got in position in front of me, sweat trickled down my back, but I raised my eyes, completely focused on him. For once, I didn't wait on him to throw the first jab. I darted in, caught him off guard, and landed a light hook on his jaw. I hit him hard enough to let him know to bring it on: I was ready. The hook surprised him but he rallied, and when he spun around me, he bared his teeth, his grin feral. I followed, unsmiling, my eyes locked with his.

He glided in, moving faster than a blink. I only managed to parry his jab, but I did hook his ankle with my foot. Sadly for myself, Luke knew all my dirty tricks, and he easily stayed balanced. We moved back out to our circle, dancing on the balls of our feet. He came in again, but I ducked and kicked out, my foot nicking his side.

Before I righted myself, Luke caught my foot as I tried to recover from the kick and jerked me forward. I forced myself not to grin. He was letting me show off; he'd taught me this move last week. Using our momentum, I stepped into his hand like a stirrup, and swung myself up and into his chest, hooking a knee over his shoulder. Together, we fell, hitting the mats hard enough to snap my teeth together. I tried for the choke-hold to finish him off, but he broke my grip.

Knowing my weakness, I scrambled away before Luke could get on top of me. He weighed too much, and I would be a goner if he got my back on the mat. Maybe a goner in more ways than one, but I was *not* thinking about that right now.

I sprang to my feet first, spun around him, and kicked again, my foot landing straight between his shoulder blades with enough force to leave a bruise. Luke flipped forward, over his head, and landed on his feet before spinning back around to me.

After three more minutes of parrying jabs, hooks, and his wicked crosses, I'd managed to land a few decent blows, though I took a few to the face and ribs as well. Sweat ran down my back and into my eyes, but Luke wasn't holding back. I danced around him, forcing my legs to stay light even though I knew my muscles were most likely screaming for relief. This time, I moved faster than Luke and caught him mid-step, using his weight to swipe his legs out from underneath him. He hit his back hard, and before he recovered, I launched myself on top of him and grabbed his jaw, forcing his neck back at an impossible angle.

He tapped the mat.

I released my grip on him, and for a moment, as I sat on his chest, a triumphant grin splitting across my face, I knew I was home. Not at home on his chest, although that felt pretty good too, but at home *here*: Fear University and its crazy students and crazier professors. Somehow, I'd made my place here, and when Luke returned my smile with a hint of pride, I knew he believed it too.

I became all too aware of his hand on my thigh, and my breath hitched in my throat. He gave my leg a soft little squeeze.

Dean's clapping jarred me from the moment, and I jumped off Luke, blushing but still grinning like a fool. My triumph returned as I realized this was the first time I'd ever bested Luke. Our sparring would look good to Dean, who descended the bleachers. He looked almost as happy as I did. Luke slowly got to his feet as Dean came over.

"Great work you two," Dean said. "You've done a good job of training her so far, Luke."

Luke dipped his chin in answer.

"Thank you," I said. I shook out my legs and arms to keep the lactic acid from building up.

"I'm impressed, Ollie. I didn't think you would be this good, this fast. Keep up the good work, and I believe you'll be ready for Fields at the end of the semester."

I'd passed, and I couldn't help but beam my triumph at Luke. Somehow, his approval of my test meant more than Dean's. When he smiled back at me again, I hoped the gesture meant he'd passed me too. If I'd been a weaker woman I would've melted right there on the mat beneath Luke's warm stare.

"Luke," Dean said, tearing my attention away from Luke's face, "are you still hunting tonight with Hatter?"

I glanced back at Luke quick enough to catch the warning in his eyes. "Yes."

Dean smiled, and it wasn't like the fatherly smiles he normally gave me. This one was sharp and jagged, like I might cut myself on it if I stared too long. Standing between them, it was like I wasn't there. "Why don't you take Ollie tonight? Let her experience a real hunt."

Dean's suggestion sure as hell shocked me, but Luke acted like he'd been expecting it. "She's not ready for a hunt like tonight's."

"What makes tonight's hunt different?" I interjected, feeling slightly offended, but still curious at why Luke was acting weird about this hunt specifically.

"Nothing," Luke snapped. "She's not going," he added to Dean.

"Fine. Your call." Dean shrugged, still smiling as he turned to leave. Luke didn't say goodbye, and I wondered if Dean had been taunting him.

When the gym's door was safely shut, and I knew Dean was out of earshot, I asked, "What was that all about?"

"You did good today." Luke's smile was gone from his mouth, but some warmth returned in his eyes as he watched me.

"I beat you." I let his avoidance of my question pass and enjoyed my victory.

Luke chuckled, and I'm pretty sure my stomach did that diving, swooping thing up my throat, and left my body from my mouth. He had a beautiful laugh, quiet and even, like him, mostly just little whooshes of air through his nose. I liked it so much I must have been staring, because Luke stopped and leveled a serious gaze on me.

"What?" I asked. My breathlessness should have bothered me, but it didn't.

"You did good," he repeated, quieter this time, like he didn't mean the sparring. "We're lucky to have you here."

The words were simple, easy, unimpressive words, but my heart soared, and my eyes moistened. Someplace deep in my heart, in a dark and spider-webbed corner, joy and hope rose up. No one had ever said something so nice to me, something that made me feel like I truly belonged. Not ever. And I think Luke knew the importance of his words, because he let them sink in, in his quiet way.

"Thank you," I whispered. His lips twitched into a soft grin again, and he turned to go.

I caught his hand and pulled him back. I stepped into him until the heat and sweat coming off his chest scorched me. Our joined hands fell beside us, and I wrapped my other around his neck. Before he could pull away, I kissed him.

When he kissed me back, I opened my mouth for him, feeling his tongue flick across my lips before he delved deeper inside. His instant, fiery response confirmed he'd been thinking about kissing me too. I pressed myself against him, and he pulled me in tighter, wrapping his arm around my waist.

Home, I thought. And damn if I didn't believe it.

The kiss itself lasted only a few seconds; we quickly stepped away from each other, too worried someone would walk by the gym's glass wall. But every spot in my mouth where he'd claimed me tingled. I licked my lips to taste him again.

When we stared at each other, close enough to hear our too-loud breathing, but not too close to attract attention, I knew I'd found my place here. With Sunny and the professors, who either loved me or hated me. With the cell doors that locked at night. With running laps around the fence perimeter in the evenings. With Dean, who Luke didn't trust. With Jolene and Allison and now Thad. But especially with Luke, who hopefully understood I wasn't any more fearless than him or felt any less pain than him. I just felt more on the inside instead of the outside.

"So why can't I go tonight?" I asked, ending the spell.

Luke sighed. "It's not safe, Ollie."

The way he said it aroused my suspicions again. "What makes tonight so different?"

"Nothing. It's a hunt."

"Bullshit."

"Ollie," Luke said, lowering his voice, "let it go, okay?"

"You won't tell me?"

"No," he said, but then added, "not yet, at least."

"Okay."

My easy yield surprised him. He watched me closely for a minute, as if he didn't trust me. Smart man. "Okay?"

I shrugged and walked away, ready to change out of my sweaty clothes. "Try not to dream about me tonight."

Luke didn't answer, but when I glanced back, he remained in the middle of the gym, dark brows lowered over his burning, tornado sky green eyes. I turned back with a smile. I would shower and change. Then it was time to get ready.

I was following Luke and Hatter tonight.

It was time to know what was so important that Luke, the university's golden hunter, would go toe to toe with Dean over.

TEN

Later that night when the sun had begun to set and curfew was moments away, I told myself the reason I was currently sneaking into the university's garage wasn't because I was worried about Luke and Hatter going on the hunt tonight. Or that it had anything to do with the kiss I couldn't stop thinking about. I let myself believe I was curious.

Rabidly curious.

The garage was beneath the ward level, and, to avoid swiping my card in the elevator, I took the stairs. Luke had gone to the barracks after my evaluation, and, unless Hatter was already down there, I assumed I would be the first to arrive at their van. The stairs wove down and down until I smelled the wet earth permeating through the thick layers of concrete around me. As I walked, the automatic lights flicked on above me, eventually illuminating a fleet of black vans and SUVs with tinted windows and all-terrain tires.

I hadn't been down here since my arrival a few weeks ago, but I instantly recognized Luke and Hatter's blacked-out industrial van amongst the throng of vehicles. I tested the handles and found the van locked, which didn't surprise me. I went around to the back and peered inside, cupping my hands against the glass and trying not to fog up the window with my breath.

Shadows swathed the inside, making it almost impossible to see, but movement caught my eye. At first I thought Hatter was asleep in the van, and my heart skipped a beat or two. But instead of Hatter's two-toned eyes, red ones blinked back at me and little white bodies scuttled back and forth, pink noses twitching. Lab rats.

Next to the rat cages lining the van sat piles of nets, coils of rope, chains, and a stack of heavy-duty padlocks. I pursed my lips and stepped away. I'd seen enough. The foolish idiots.

I certainly wasn't leaving now. So I waited. A moment passed before the motion lights went off, concealing me in a veil of darkness. I didn't move.

Five minutes later, the light beside the stairwell came on, and Luke and Hatter stepped into the garage. They both carried backpacks and wore their hunting gear, complete with vests and neck shields. Another light flipped on as they came closer, revealing the grim set of their mouths. Neither spoke, but I recognized a foreign look of seriousness on Hatter's face. Their bodies rippled with intensity as they stalked forward. This wasn't any other hunt for them. This was different. And I knew why.

Another light came on. Then another. And another. When the light above me and the van flipped on, they finally spotted me sitting on the hood of the van with my arms crossed.

Hatter yelped, the purple snapback sitting backward on his head nearly tumbling off. Luke didn't act that surprised. "What are you doing here?"

I picked at my nails. "Dean said I could go, so I'm going."

"Ollie-o," Hatter said, adjusting his hat, "I like you and everything but you can't sneak up on people like that."

"Sorry, Hatter." I shot him a grin, refusing to let my thoughts return to what I knew about his childhood, before turning my attention back to Luke.

"No, you're not. This is none of your business." Luke's words lashed against my skin. "Go back to the dorm and stay there."

"Really? You think you can send me away that easily? Come on, Luke."

"Leave," he growled.

"He's right," Hatter added. When I heard the fear in his voice, I became more convinced not to let Luke make me leave. "And you know I don't say that shit willingly, but Dean shouldn't have said you could go."

I leaned forward, my hands gripping the van's hood. "I'm not going anywhere. Want to know why? Because you two assholes are going to try and *catch* a 'swang. I saw all your gear back there: the rats and rope. So I want to know why. And after you've told me all the reasons, I'm going to come with you."

Hatter's brows rose and he let out a little whistle between his teeth. "I'm going to pack up while you two love birds chat. Try to make it a quickie though, we gotta split." He slapped Luke's ass, like a football player celebrating a good play, and walked to the back of the van.

"How did you know?" Luke asked, ignoring Hatter.

"It wasn't hard to figure out. The rats in the van are fear-conditioned lab rats, aren't they? The ones they train to be afraid of the bells. You're going to use their fear to lure in a 'swang." When Luke cast his eyes to the ceiling, his frustration evident, I knew I'd guessed right. "Won't the 'swang smell their rat scent?"

Luke sighed and rubbed his hands over his eyes. "We have human blood back there too, in the cooler. We'll pour it over the rats to mask their smell."

"Good plan." I jumped down from the van and wiped off my hands on my jeans. "Let's go."

"Ollie." Luke grabbed my arm, his hand sending waves of heat up to my collarbones, making them tingle. "It's too dangerous."

I stepped away from his hold as Hatter walked back up to the front. "That's exactly why I'm going."

"Shotgun, bitches," Hatter sing-songed as he hopped into the passenger seat. He rolled down the window and said to me, "You get the back. Try not to bother the rats. They're sensitive."

Not bothering to glance at Luke again, I walked around to the back of the van. The last time I'd been back here, I'd been a reluctant passenger, to say the least, but this time I didn't know what I was getting myself into.

Luke climbed into the driver's seat and settled his pack into the space between him and Hatter. The rats tittered and squeaked from the van's movement, and I had to make a little path through all of Luke's supplies so I could sit behind the console.

"So why are you trying to catch a 'swang?"

"Funny. I always ask that same thing." Hatter pulled a small device out of the van's console. It looked like a very sophisticated garage door opener. He punched in a short code on the small keypad that I made sure to memorize. Luke wove his way down the aisles of vans, trucks, and SUVs.

"You've done this more than once?"

"Just get the doors," Luke snapped at Hatter.

"It's a real wonder that you have any friends," I said. Hatter held up his hand for a high-five. Luke rolled his eyes when we slapped hands.

"I was in a great mood before I saw you."

I propped an elbow on the console and put my chin in my hand in an effort get comfortable. The rat cages were poking into my side. "Hmm. I wonder why you were in such a good mood?"

"Yeah," Hatter chirped. "I wonder why?"

"The doors," Luke growled, ignoring us both.

Hatter pressed the green arrow on the device, and a

massive bay door opened in front of us, letting the evening's setting sun stream through. Luke gunned the van up the ramp, squinting into the light of the setting sun. He followed the road around to the front of the estate, thick gravels popping and pinging below the van. When he pulled up to the front gates, they were already parting for us. They didn't open all the way, but Luke managed to squeeze the van through the narrow opening, twisting iron inches from the side mirrors.

"Where are we going?"

Luke sighed and raked his hand through his short hair, making it to stick up in the front. "A fishing village."

"Why a fishing village?"

"Increase in animal attacks."

"And you think the attacks are 'swangs?"

"Yes," Luke said through gritted teeth, knuckles turning white around the steering wheel.

"Does anyone ever survive an attack? Live to tell the tale and all that?"

Luke sighed through his nose. "Sometimes. Though they're normally too rattled and drained from the feeding to report much."

"What does it look like when a 'swang feeds on someone's fear?" I couldn't help the questions. I also couldn't help the fact I enjoyed pissing Luke off. Call me petty.

"It ain't pretty," Hatter said cheerily from the passenger seat. He turned around and grinned at me, two-tones eyes twinkling, his hat sitting crooked on his head. "Normally, they always kill their prey to make it look like an animal attack, but sometimes they're interrupted or the person manages to get away. Rare, but even a rainbow can shit a rainbow sometimes, you know?"

Luke rolled his eyes, and I held back a laugh. "No, I don't know."

Hatter waved us away like we were the crazy ones. "Those who get away often look haggard and sunken in, like all the good is gone out of them." His eyes brightened. "Like Luke when I kick his ass hunting!"

Luke and Hatter argued the point good-naturedly for a bit, and I grinned as I watched them hash it out. Hatter plugged his ears with his fingers and hummed along to a song on the radio, his feet propped up on the dashboard like we were going to the beach, and completely ignoring Luke, who raised his voice as he claimed he'd had the last three kills and not Hatter. It was fun to see them like this, like they hadn't been damaged by their families. As I watched them bicker, I felt a part of things even if I'd forced my way in. It was nice.

"So," I said when the debate had finally died down. "Are you going to tell me now or do you want me to ask a million more questions?"

"I think she wants to know why we're trying to catch a 'swang," Hatter offered.

"I know what she wants." Luke navigated the twisting road. The sun set quickly, evidence of the shortening days and coming solstice.

I scooted forward to see more of Luke's profile. The moon's silver light occasionally sliced through the tops of the trees around us and lit up his face, making him look like a supernatural creature with blue skin and dark, black eyes. I liked the look on him; I liked that he was dangerous and intimidating. And, damn, I really wanted to make out with him.

"We occasionally go out and catch one for testing," he said finally, distracting me from my thoughts.

"Like the lab rats?" I asked, completely and utterly surprised. This was not what I'd expected.

Luke sighed. "The lab techs need live subjects sometimes."

"I thought you didn't approve of Dean's methods?"

Hatter shot a careful glance toward Luke, who didn't pay him any attention. "I don't. But these tests are important. The more we understand about 'swangs, the better prepared we are."

"So you would torture an animal."

"Ollie, 'swangs are evil monsters."

"Are sharks evil monsters because they kill people sometimes too?" I fired back. I didn't doubt that 'swangs were bad, but I didn't like anything being called evil.

"We're losing this war," Luke said. "If we don't figure out some other way, we're going to get our asses kicked. Or worse."

Luke had spoken like this before the first time I'd seen the rats in the lab. I wanted to know why he thought like this, how his opinions of war fit in with the man I knew today. And he couldn't run from my questions now. "What could be worse than losing?"

"Losing what we've been fighting for this entire time.

Humanity."

"How would that happen?"

"Sweet Ollie, I know you're new to this," Hatter said, rolling his eyes to the roof of the van, "but don't get Luke started on his beliefs about humanity and why we fight this war. Unless you want to be bored to tears."

I swatted Hatter's hat down over his eyes and looked back at Luke. "So what could possibly be worse than the world turning into one big Fear Island?"

"That would be a good band name," Hatter mumbled, pulling out his phone to make a note of it.

"There's a wrong way to win a war." At Luke's words, Hatter snorted, but I let Luke continue. "If we win by losing ourselves, by losing what we were fighting for, then we never really win against the 'swangs. If we lose what makes us human then we haven't won anything at all."

"And what makes us human?"

"Our weaknesses: fear and pain. The very things that Dean would want to eradicate in an army."

Luke glanced up at the rearview mirror and met my eyes. His look conveyed all I needed to know. He meant an army of Ollies, fearless and unfeeling, making war too easy, would mean losing our humanity to win the war. Luke played along with Dean's game so Dean wouldn't take things a step further and start bringing in more civvies like me to train.

I carefully held his gaze until he looked away. He shouldn't have to apologize for his beliefs, for thinking if people were trained to be like me, we would lose our humanity. I understood why he thought this way after his childhood with a father like Killian Aultstriver, who would do anything, even abuse his own son, to win a war. I still didn't want him to see that he'd hurt me in ways with which I was all too familiar. Familiar being the bad monster everyone has to either abandon or try to break apart.

Reaching the fishing village didn't take long, which turned out to be kind of a bummer because I still needed time to wrap my head around this wild plan. By the time we pulled into the small town, which consisted of one street, no red lights, and a twenty-four-hour convenience store, the night's light came from the moon and a sputtering spotlight above the store's parking lot.

We were in 'swang territory now. I almost felt them singing to my bones.

Luke made a couple of passes through the town, which felt more and more like a ghost town. "Where is everyone?" I whispered.

"Brown bears."

"What?" I shot forward over the console, excited to see a bear. "Where?"

"Bear *curfew*." Luke's mouth twisted up like he was smirking at me. If he wasn't careful, he might risk actually looking human for a second.

I rolled my eyes at him. "What's that?"

"In remote areas like this, the curious bears get a little too bold and cause a lot of trouble, so everyone stays inside when it's dark. It's safer."

"And convenient for 'swang hunters," I added.

"What do you think about that alley?" Hatter asked Luke. He pointed toward a narrow, unlit alley between a closed grocery store and a dry cleaner.

I wrinkled my nose. "It looks sketchy."

"It's perfect," Luke corrected. He did a quick U-turn and parked the van on the other side of the road, in the convenience store's parking lot, which was completely empty. He turned off the engine and looked back at me. "You're staying in here."

"But—"

"I mean it, Ollie. Stay in here. Hatter and I have a method, and we need to focus. I can't be worried about where you are."

"What if something happens?"

"Then we will be running straight back to the van anyway. You have to promise me."

I didn't want to, but I knew I would be in their way. My training wasn't even close to being ready for this level of hunting. Luke had assured me countless times that my victory over the 'swang in Kodiak had been pure luck. I hated to admit it, but after all I'd learned about 'swangs, I kind of believed him, though I never told him that.

"Fine," I agreed. "I promise. But be careful."

"We will." Luke waved off my concern as he hopped out of the truck and joined Hatter at the back of the van, where they unloaded supplies. I climbed into the passenger seat to see things better and not be in their way.

As I watched, I found another level of respect for Luke and Hatter. Gone was his half-crazy, totally weird attitude;

Hatter worked with silent efficiency, handing back rope and netting without Luke having to ask. They both worked fast, communicated little, and handled their supplies with knowledge and a wary sense of battle. I wiped my sweaty palms on my pants as Luke slung a rope over his shoulder, strapped some knives to his thighs, and closed the van door.

He walked up to my side of the van and opened the door. Without asking, he lifted a small vest around me and guided my hands through the openings. He tugged on the zipper, his knuckles skimming up my chest. My breath caught in my throat as he leaned in closer, his eyes going to my lips. He lifted my hair from the back of my neck and, with his other hand, did up the throat guard. I let out a long breath to keep my hands from shaking.

"Stay put." Surprising me completely, he kissed me, lips skimming mine for a brief second before he stepped back and closed the door, sealing me in with my thrumming heart and flushed skin. He joined Hatter by the road.

Instead of going straight into the alley like I expected, they split off in different directions: Luke with the rope and net, Hatter with the rats and blood. In moments, the darkness had swallowed them whole. I checked the street constantly, looking for 'swangs and brown bears. Every shadow could be danger. My stomach twisted with nerves. I was scared for Luke, and the fear came as a complete and utter surprise to me.

I huddled down in my seat and tugged on the uncomfortable throat guard, squinting into the darkness and hoping to catch any glimpse of them. I didn't.

I estimated half an hour passed. I shifted in my seat, my legs and ass numb. I should have asked how long they thought this would take. Then I would've known how long was too long, how long was *dead* long. I wanted to poke my head out the door and whisper-shout for them, but I knew that would be a horrible idea. I sighed and told myself patience was a virtue.

A shout came from the dark alley.

I reared up in my seat, eyes wide, and a gasp lodged in my throat. I stared, unblinking, into the darkness of the alley. I didn't know if the shout had been one for help or because they were struggling to wrangle the creature. But I hadn't seen anything walk into the alley.

I strained, listening for anything else, but heard nothing.

One more minute, I told myself. I'd give them one more minute, and if they didn't come out by then, I was going in. One minute.

I looked in the back and grabbed a lethal-looking knife with a curving blade from Luke's stash. I didn't know how to use it, but I figured anything was better than nothing. I didn't have a clock to count down the time, but it felt long enough. With held breath, I opened the passenger door and slid out, my feet crunching quietly as they hit the pavement.

Not wanting to risk shutting the door all the way, I left it slightly ajar before creeping across the parking lot. My eyes took a moment to adjust to the darkness, but eventually, the street in front of me and the grocery store beyond came into focus. I crept closer, every step bringing me to the alley's dark mouth. No more shouts or scuffling or struggle sounded from the blackness.

Once I was in the middle of the street, I paused. Maybe they were okay, and the shout was normal. I'd ruin everything if I went in there now, but then again, Hatter and Luke could already be dead with all the time I'd wasted trying to decide what to do. I adjusted my grip on the knife and looked both ways down the street. No movement.

Luke would be so pissed if I messed this up, and he'd said they would run right back to the van if anything went wrong. Chewing on the inside of my lip, I tried to decide. If I waltzed into that alley, and screwed everything—

"Ollie!"

I flinched at the yell; it sounded like it was coming from right beside me. Without thinking, I shot across the street and dove into the alley's shadows.

It was darker in here, but I didn't wait for my eyes to adjust. I crashed down the alley, stumbling over trashcans and bags of garbage smelling like rotten fish. "Luke!" I shouted. "Hatter!"

"Over here!"

I ran to the end of the alley, which was blocked off with a brick wall and a large metal dumpster. Beside the dumpster, Hatter crouched.

Blood had splattered everywhere. On the ground. On the dumpster. It coated Hatter's arms up to his elbows. There was so much of it that I almost didn't see Luke. Almost.

He lay crumpled on the ground. His vest and throat shield ripped off. Jagged claw marks shredded his thermal shirt. His chest was ribbons. Red ribbons of blood. Next to him was a dead 'swang, a dagger shoved through its left eye. The metallic smell of blood hit me so hard that I almost doubled over and gagged.

"Is he okay?" I asked, frantic as I knelt next to Hatter, whose hand was a bloody mess as he tried to press a rag against Luke's chest.

Luke weakly ran his gaze over me, making certain I was intact. "Take her." His words scratched together, and he coughed, the sound thick and wet. "Get her out of here."

"That's really sweet, but you're not exactly in the position to make me." I set my knife aside and pressed my trembling hands against his chest, shoulder to shoulder with Hatter. I turned to him and asked, "What the hell happened?"

"The 'swang snuck up on us. We gotta get him to the van."

"Okay." I jumped over Luke's body and kicked away the 'swang's legs. I was ready to help Hatter lift Luke when I heard it.

Down the alleyway, at our only exit, claws scratched over the ragged pavement. Bright eyes stared back at us from twenty feet away. Breathing, heavy huffing in the cool night air, rumbled down the shadows of the alley. The air suddenly smelled of rank, wet dog.

I didn't want to count. The pack of 'swangs was too thick, too damning. Hatter leapt to his feet. He tried to hold up his knife, but it tumbled from his hand and clattered to the ground. He swore viciously and stooped to pick it up. Only then did I notice he was missing a finger, blood gushing down his forearm from the gaping hole.

"Hatter," I whispered, eyes returning to the 'swangs standing at the end of the alley. "What do we do?"

"Run." Luke's hand wrapped around my ankle, like he could push me to safety.

"Fuck!" Hatter shouted in frustration. I glanced down; he still hadn't picked up the dagger. His fingers wouldn't close around the hilt. "My hand won't . . ."

Understanding, I stooped down and grabbed both of our knives. Hatter took his back with his other hand. Luke and I hadn't trained with knives yet, but I would have to make due. I glanced around, my eyes falling on a ladder going up to the grocery store's roof.

I nodded toward it. "Can you get Luke up that ladder?"

"Maybe. But—"

"Then do it. Can they follow you up it?"

"They can't climb, but they could jump from the dumpster."

"Okay. I won't let them get to it. Just go. I'll meet you at the van."

"Ollie—"

"Just fucking go!"

I didn't wait for Hatter's answer. I kept picturing Luke's shredded chest when I turned to face the 'swangs once again. I adjusted my grip on the knife, turning the blade downward, like I'd seen in the movies. When I heard Hatter scuffling behind me with Luke, I took a step forward to put distance between the fight and Hatter's retreat.

I bounced on the balls of my feet and stretched out my neck. My skin prickled with excitement, my red murder haze settling like a fog around me. "Come on, you fuckers!" I shouted down the alley, craving blood and death. "Let's do this!"

She smells good . . . Her skin is like silk . . . Where is her fear . . . Why isn't she afraid . . . She's going to taste good.

Their thoughts hit me like a train, and I stumbled back with a hiss. *Shut up!* I needed to focus on the fight and that wouldn't happen if they kept talking about how good I smelled.

Did she hear us . . . That's impossible . . . But why isn't she reacting . . . Someone call for Hex.

"Yeah, I hear you. So either come on and fight or go chat elsewhere."

Their laughter vibrated across my mind. Inky black bodies undulated in the shadows, and I didn't know where one 'swang ended and the next began. But judging by the amount of thoughts running through my head, the alley was at capacity.

Hex will love this . . . Save him a piece . . . He'll want to know what she tastes like . . . Maybe he'll keep her as a pet.

I shifted and glanced over my shoulder without completely looking away from the 'swangs. Hatter and Luke were gone from the end of the alleyway, and I caught a glimpse of Hatter's boot disappearing over the ladder. I was tempted to follow, but if I did there would be no one between them and the 'swangs. I had to stay and fight.

I focused back on the 'swangs, forcing their endless thoughts out of my head. Spotting a rock at the toe of my boot, I kicked it at them with all my strength. It pinged off a 'swang's chest, but the massive dog didn't flinch.

I stood too far away to see my reflection in their eyes, but their gaping mouths grinned back at me as they took a collective step farther into the alley. Drool, long and thick as ropes, dripped from their teeth. Their eyes shone wide and unblinking, the slinking of their bodies lost to the deep shadows. I picked out the biggest one—he was twice the size of the 'swang I'd killed before coming to Fear University—and decided to attack him first.

As I was about to dart forward, I sensed a shift in the 'swangs' focus. At first I worried they'd heard Hatter on the roof, but the creatures shifted to the side, their heads twisted over their shoulders.

Hex . . . Hex . . . He's here.

From the cleared path down the middle of the alley prowled the biggest 'swang I'd ever seen. His paws— thudding over the pavement and sending vibrations up my shin bones—were the size of my head. Unlike the other 'swangs, his jaw stayed closed, his black fur blending with the shadows around him, so that he seemed to command the rippling, pulsing darkness. His bright, glowing eyes revealed his steady focus: me.

As he advanced farther into the alley, his thoughts thankfully blank, I realized a normal person would be scared. I should have gone for the ladder when I had the chance and tried to fight them off from up there. But I didn't. And I kind of relished the idea of fighting this monster.

I narrowed my eyes, staring deep into his, my inverted reflection unflinching. Remembering Luke's lessons to steady my breathing, I closed my mouth and breathed through my nose. With everything I had, I focused.

Let's go, motherfucker, I directed toward the 'swang.

Instead of pouncing like I expected, the 'swang jerked to a stop. He cocked his head and scented me, looking me straight in the eyes. Because I was staring back, matching him gaze for gaze, I saw when the recognition clicked and the hunger cleared from his eyes.

Olesya?

Fear, heady like a blast of adrenaline straight to my heart, jolted through me at hearing my name. My full name. The name only my mother had called me.

A shrill, endless honking sounded on the road. Behind the pack of 'swangs, the van careened into view, a mad Hatter behind the wheel. He screamed at me from the rolled-down passenger window, but the screeching in my ears blocked the sound.

What did you say? I asked Hex. My knees wobbled. *How do you know my name?*

Something human and warm flashed through the 'swang's eyes. The expression chilled me worse than anything I'd seen these creatures do before. From the back of my mind, I remembered Luke calling them evil monsters.

Go! Hex commanded his pack, sending his pack scattering with one word. As the van skidded to a stop outside the alley, clipping one 'swang on the hip, Hex looked at me as he backed out of the alley. Over his shoulder, Hatter raised a gun.

Be careful, Olesya. Don't trust them. I'll find you. I'll save you.

Before Hatter pulled off the shot, Hex twisted around, leapt down the alley, and bounded over the roof of the van, denting the metal, and landing on the other side.

"Ollie!" Hatter shouted through the open window. "We gotta go!"

I couldn't move. I couldn't. That 'swang had known my name—my full name, a name I hadn't spoken in eight years.

"Ollie! We have to get Luke back!"

His words finally spurred me into motion and I took off down the alley. Hatter flung the passenger door open for me and I jumped in, hauling myself inside as Hatter rocketed out of the little fishing village. I slammed the door shut and locked it for no good reason other than the fact that I was creeped the hell out.

"Is he okay?" I asked, craning around to look back at Luke. Even to my ears, my voice sounded breathless and terrified.

Fear, my first real and honest dosage of it that I'd felt since my time in the Tabers' basement, made my body shiver.

"He will be once we get him back. Lost a lot of blood."

I turned back around and looked at Hatter's hand, which he cradled against his chest. "Are you okay?"

"Lost a finger in that fucker's mouth. Had to get it off Luke though," Hatter mumbled, his words losing themselves around each other. His eyes shone with adrenaline and blood loss, a clammy sweat across his brow. As he drove, his hands bounced against the wheel, drumming to some mad beat only he heard. The saliva had to be in his system by now. Briefly, I wondered if I should have driven.

We were back on the main road outside the village, the van hitting its top speed, when Hatter looked over at me and asked, "Ollie, were you talking to those 'swangs?"

I didn't answer before crawling into the back with Luke.

I had talked to the 'swangs.

And one had answered, calling me by my name.

ELEVEN

Hatter radioed our emergency into the university, his words one big jumbled up mess.

When we arrived at the main entrance, the gate was already opened wide enough for us to pass through. Or at least it would have been if Hatter had gone in straight. Instead, in his manic, blood-loss state, he ripped off a side mirror on the unyielding iron gate.

I bounced around in the back with Luke, applying pressure to his chest, which was a mess of blood and jagged claw marks. He hadn't gained consciousness the entire trip back. His skin looked stark and clammy, and his body kept convulsing against the floor of the van so badly that I had to lie across him to keep him still.

Hatter hit the brakes hard enough to toss me against the

van's front seat. I bit my tongue, and my mouth filled with blood. Before I'd recovered, the back doors flung open and flashlight beams seared into my eyes. Orders were barked off as I shielded my eyes, blood pouring down the back of my throat. People pulled Luke out and secured him to a gurney before whisking him away. Someone reached inside for me, hand grasping my ankle, and jerked me forward.

As I was about to fall out of the back of the van, someone caught me. I looked up into Dean's face. "Are you okay?" he asked quickly as he hurried us toward the school's main building. Hatter and Luke were gone.

"I'm fine."

"Ollie, I had no idea this would happen. Otherwise I wouldn't have suggested it."

"Okay." I didn't know what else to say, because my gut told me Dean knew exactly what would happen. I shoved the thought aside, though, and kept searching for glimpses of Luke.

"Go to the ward. You can sleep down there, but don't tell anyone that you were out hunting, okay?"

That got my attention. "What?"

"The other students aren't privy to hunters' activities. You can't say anything about tonight, or that Fear University catches live 'swangs. Not even to Sunny. Tell them that you were worried you had a fever and checked into the ward."

I frowned. I didn't like it, but my thoughts kept skittering back to Luke bleeding out in the alley, and I couldn't focus on why Dean's words bothered me so much right then. When we were halfway down to the ward, I tried to pull myself free, but he didn't let go. I glanced down at his grip on my arm, and saw the bruises already forming beneath his fingertips.

"Let me go," I said through gritted teeth.

He ignored me. "Did you see anything out there, Ollie? Feel anything?" His question startled me, but I hid it well enough to keep my little secret. There was no way he knew about me hearing and speaking to the 'swangs. Or that Hex had known my name.

"No." I jerked my arm again and Dean finally released me. I hurried away, daring one last glance over my shoulder. He remained in the hall, staring down at his hand that had just been crushing my arm. I shuddered and picked up my pace.

Maybe Luke was right to not trust him, but if I couldn't trust the President of Fear University, who could I trust?

All the nurses and doctors had been called in to help. Luke and Hatter were placed in different operating rooms. I stood on tiptoes to see into Luke's room, but I was pushed back by nurses rushing inside. As the door swung open and closed, I made out Luke's bare chest, streaked with rivers of blood.

I was back to being the freak.

Except no one else knew. I retained my badass status, the girl who'd kissed Jolene and killed a 'swang. Students still sat at our lunch table and talked to me in the halls between classes. I had people to share notes with and chat with before classes started. But I was the freak. At least in my own head. The freak who talked to 'swangs.

Peg, my psychology professor, stopped me on the way out the door the morning after the hunting excursion. "Ollie," she called, one hand resting on her pregnant belly.

I paused at the door, weary and overly tired from today. I wanted to get through sixth period and then go check on Luke. I'd heard whispers and rumors about his condition, but I needed to see for myself. "Yeah?" I asked.

"The other hunters are saying you came in with Hatter and Luke last night. Is that true?"

I'd kept my word to Dean and not told anyone about last night, but, of course, all the hunters, professors, and doctors knew. I nodded, not wanting to really talk about it.

I'd tossed and turned all night thinking about it, hearing Hex say my name like he knew me. "Don't trust them," he'd said.

Peg smiled at me kindly, and I relaxed somewhat. "That must have been pretty intense," she said.

I shrugged. "I guess."

"Some of the doctors said that you fought off the 'swangs single-handedly. That you ran them off so Hatter could get Luke to the van."

"They're saying that?" I was shocked. I hadn't done that at all. The 'swangs had left because Hex told them to.

"That's what Hatter told people. But he was so delirious he needed to be sedated. Do you want to tell me what happened?"

To Hatter, seeing me in the alley facing down Hex right before the 'swangs ran off, it might have looked like I ran them off, but I wanted to talk to Luke first before I clarified the story to anyone else. Though it went against my better judgment, I was going to tell him about hearing the 'swangs and talking to them. About Hex calling me by my first name. I had to trust someone, and Luke was highest on my list besides Sunny. So until I talked to Luke, I wasn't going to share with anyone else.

"Honestly," I said, "I don't know what happened. I better go. Don't want to be late."

Peg nodded. "Sure thing, Ollie. Don't forget that you can always talk to me, okay? I'm on your side."

I glanced back at her and tried to smile. After last night, I doubted anyone was really on my side. Except me. Just like always.

Sixth period drug by. By the time I wound my way down the stairs to the ward, my teeth were on edge. Professors had studied me in every class or watched me walk by in the halls. Even the few hunters who came and went in the school during the day stared at me, wondered about me. It was ridiculous. It wasn't like I'd ripped a 'swang's head off with my teeth or anything. If they knew the real truth about last night, they would have thrown me in a real jail cell instead of letting me go to class.

The hall in the ward was quiet. I checked the private rooms until I found Hatter. He slept with his hand heavily bandaged, a large gap where his missing finger should be. I cringed. None of the rooms housed Luke.

The nurse on duty would know where he was, so I headed toward the main room in the ward, but Dean's voice drew me to a stop. The door was open, and I heard him clearly.

"—really fought off those 'swangs?" I recognized Mr.

Abbot's voice.

"If she did, this is better than we thought."

"You think she's that valuable?"

"I plan on finding out."

I frowned. They were obviously talking about me. What was better than they thought? And what the hell was my *value* based on? Something in Dean's voice really pissed me off. He was talking about me like I was some prized heifer.

"Killian will want to know," Mr. Abbot said. I leaned closer to the door to hear Dean's response. "It might help convince him of her worth."

"Killian will do what I tell him."

Footsteps sounded in the main room, and Dean's voice drew closer. I stepped away from the door, moving down the hall slowly so that I still heard Mr. Abbot's response before I had to run.

"He's worried about Luke spending so much time with her. The purity of their family line is his primary concern."

The door started to swing open, and I took off down the hall, my steps silent. I bounded halfway up the steps and paused, leaning back to hear more. I held my breath and forced myself to breathe deeply through my nose.

"If she is who I think she is—"

I couldn't risk waiting to hear anymore; Dean and Mr. Abbot were almost to the base of the stairs, their voices ringing up the stairwell to me. I spun and skipped the steps two at a time. When I was out of earshot, I took off out the front entrance's door, straight to the barracks.

The building was quiet during the day, except for the

sounds of vacuums coming from the apartments' open doors as the cleaning crew worked. Luke's room was the only one closed off, music seeping from beneath the door. This time, I knocked.

"Come in," Luke's muffled voice came from the other side of the door.

"Hey," I said softly as I opened the door and stepped into his room.

Surprised to see me, he shuffled up in his bed, wincing as he moved his chest, which was bare and wrapped tightly with bandages. Between the thick gauze and tape, I finally saw the extent of his battle scars. He was a mess, like he'd tangoed with a permanent marker and lost. A barrage of black, raised scars marked his chest and shoulders, so many I needed to look away. His hair stuck up in a disheveled manner and huge dark circles stained the skin beneath his eyes. "Hey," he said, clearing his raspy voice.

I closed the door behind me and locked it, which earned raised brows from Luke. "Why aren't you in the hospital?" I crossed the room and sat on the edge of his bed. His heat filled up the small room, his scent overpowering me. Caramel candy wrappers littered the bed.

"The nurses won't let me eat candy in there," he said, his lips pressing together in an expression that so closely resembled a pout I grinned. "And I can take care of myself."

"Right," I said. "How are you feeling?"

"Like I nearly had my heart clawed out of my chest."

"Yeah." I cringed slightly. "Last night didn't go so well, huh?"

Luke gritted his teeth. "You could say that. Has Dean talked to you yet?"

"No, but I overheard him down in the ward when I went looking for you. He and Mr. Abbot were talking about my *value*." I kept out the part about Luke's father, because I didn't know what it meant and I really didn't want to upset him when he was hurt.

Luke fisted the bed sheets, crumpling them and the down comforter into a wrinkled ball. "Dean talked to me this morning."

"Are you in trouble?"

Luke shrugged a shoulder, the movement minimal so he didn't tweak his stitches. "No. These hunts go sideways all the time. Everyone is freaking out about . . ." His eyes met mine. "You. How you fought off those 'swangs."

I took a deep breath. I'd never trusted anyone before, but look where that had gotten me. "Something else happened last night."

Deep lines formed between Luke's brows. He reached for my hand. "What?"

"I didn't fight those 'swangs off." At my words, Luke frowned, his worry clearly growing. Instead of looking in his eyes, I watched as he twined my fingers through his, my smooth skin scraping his calluses. "They ran off."

He squeezed my hand. "They wouldn't run off. You must have done something to scare them away."

"It wasn't me who scared them off. Do you know Hex?" I said his name in a whisper, like it was cursed. It tasted cursed on my tongue.

Luke gripped my hand, tight enough that I knew my bones were surely protesting. My fingertips turned red then white. When I met his eyes, he looked furious. "How do you know that name?"

"I heard the other 'swangs call him that." There. I'd said it. Part of it, at least. I still had to tell him that I spoke back. That Hex knew me.

"*Heard?*"

"In my head. I heard what they were saying to each other."

"What?" Luke shoved himself farther up on the bed, not bothering with his injury. I put my hand on his chest to keep him from surging out of bed, but touching him messed my head up more. "How?" he kept asking, over and over. "What?"

"It happened once before too. I heard the 'swang the first night you found me. When I was attacked."

"Why didn't you tell me?"

I swallowed, feeling like my tongue was going numb. "I thought it sounded bad."

"Jesus Christ, Ollie. It is bad. I've never heard of something like that." He raked his hand over the scruff along his jaw. "Why did they run off then? What did you hear?"

I shifted off the bed and smoothed the sheets back down. Luke watched me with narrowed eyes. "Hex called them back."

"Why?"

He fired the question off like it was a bullet, and I cringed. This wasn't going well. "He told them to leave because Hatter was coming, but he said he would be coming for me."

"Oh my God." Luke dropped his head into his hands, a gesture I'd never seen him do. Watching him freak out freaked me out.

"Who is Hex?" I asked quietly.

Luke shook his head, grinding his teeth. "He's their greatest warrior. Christ, Ollie. Hex has killed almost half of all the hunters who have ever died. He's a legend."

"I thought these things weren't immortal?"

"They're not. He's that good."

I shuddered. "Oh."

"Ollie . . ."

I met Luke's eyes. In that moment, I wanted to tell him everything else. About how I'd spoken back and how Hex had known me. But the words dried up in my mouth. What did it mean that I talked to aswangs? Or that one of them—their greatest warrior—knew me by name? Maybe, like Luke, Hex worried about Dean building an army like me. Maybe it was all coincidence.

Maybe I was the real monster they should be hunting.

"What should I say to Dean?"

Luke gripped my hand again. "Don't tell him, okay? Don't tell anyone else."

"Is this bad?"

"'Swang saliva affects people in all different ways, but if Dean knows about it, you'll become even more valuable."

Luke thought the 'swang saliva made me hear them. But it wasn't some reaction to their spit. The very first night the 'swang attacked me in Kodiak, I heard it long before its saliva got on my hands.

"Should I run?" I forced the words out of my mouth. I hated saying them with every ounce of my being. I didn't want to run anymore, but I also didn't want to die. "I'm good at being hunted."

Luke shifted and lifted his arm around my shoulders so he could pull me close. The gesture could have been friendly— and I counted him as a friend now—but I felt too much flipping action in my stomach to let myself put this in the friend zone. Besides, I liked tucking myself in Luke's nook. He gave good nook.

"I could take care of him. I could make it so that you would never have to worry about him again."

"Max?" Startled, I glanced up at Luke.

"I'm trained for it. We could get rid of him the same way we get rid of the 'swang bodies. No one would ever know."

Maybe it was twisted. Maybe it was wrong. But my heart soared. No one had ever offered me anything so kind as murdering my enemy for me before. Smiling, I leaned over to kiss his cheek. I had to tear my lips off his skin, but I managed to pull it off. "I appreciate that," I said and I meant it. But my voice turned dark, and I said, "But I'll be the one to kill him." I meant those words even more.

"What happened? What did he do to you? That scar on your back that Thad mentioned, was that Max too?"

I felt Luke's gaze on my face as he watched my reaction. But I kept my feelings pushed down tight. "When I have nightmares, they're not about dark nights or 'swangs. Instead, I dream of him and the things he and his father did to me.

They gave me all my scars. They made me this way."

"We can kill him together." His words were fierce, protective, perfect, but killing Max was one thing I couldn't consider too closely. The things he'd done to me were still too sharp, too fresh. I needed time to grow cold enough for revenge.

"Luke," I said quietly, our conversation about dark subjects making me wonder about his own, "what did Thad mean about your father?"

Luke tensed beside me. "What part?"

"All of it."

The silence between us stretched out so long that I thought he wouldn't respond. When he finally did, I almost jumped at the sound of his voice. "It's true." I reared up in bed, ready to start yelling, but Luke put his hand over my mouth and pulled me back down beside him. "About the sexual aggression. It runs in our family. When we get bit, the saliva gets us heated, aggressive, primal. It translates sexually."

"Did he . . ."

"No." The word hung between us for a long moment. "You have to be careful around me, Ollie. If I'm ever bit . . . I don't want to hurt you."

I snorted. "Like you could."

"Ollie—"

"Stop. Don't give me whatever shit was about to come out of your mouth. Maybe I like it rough. Maybe I want you to come for me when you've been bitten. Ever thought of that?" From his shocked silence, I guessed not. "So keep your little chivalrous comments to yourself because they piss me off."

Luke let the subject drop, but I knew he didn't like it. We sat on his bed for a while, not saying anything. Eventually, I broke the silence. I bumped my shoulder against his. "You scared me last night, you know. You were very bloody."

"Yeah, well, you're scaring me now, so we're even."

After a long moment of silence, I whispered, "Am I in trouble with Dean?"

"We have to be really careful." Luke kissed the side of my forehead. It was the softest, gentlest gesture I'd ever received. Normally people tried to break me to see if I would scream. But Luke was here to hold me together. In that moment, I realized I never wanted to leave this place, leave this man.

TWELVE

Fall break's rapid approach meant a sense of excitement and anticipation crackled in the air constantly. It was the last break before finals, the big Halloween party, and Fields, which was less than a month away. After Fields was the three month long winter break.

I knew from my classes and talking with students that winter break was a big deal. Nearly all the hunters went north to different bases across the northernmost parts of the United States, Canada, Greenland, and Russia. Only during this time would so many hunters cluster in concentrated areas, because the 'swangs also collectively migrated north to reproduce.

Reproduction with 'swangs was another hot topic in my

theory classes. They flocked north for the winter solstice, where they would experience almost constant darkness, which left them in their night-forms nearly continuously for their mating rituals, which had never been documented, though many scientists traveled north with the hunters to capture the phenomenon on film. The 'swangs were also hyper aggressive and extremely territorial. More hunters died during the winter solstice than any other time of the year. More 'swangs too.

Kill or be killed.

As the killing season quickly approached, I tracked its progress by the shortening days, longer nights, and earlier curfew. Even without the shorter days, I sensed the coming solstice by the increasing anxiety amongst the students, the tension in the professors, and the vigilance in the hunters. We were all entering into a time when the 'swangs had the edge, and we knew it.

For once, our lunch table was quiet enough that Sunny and I managed to carry on a conversation without having to shout. Most students were busy packing for fall break or had already left. Sunny and I had taken a quick reprieve from her packing to eat.

"Is Luke going north for winter break?" I asked. I knew it was just fall break right now, but my mind kept returning to the thought of him going north to Barrow during the elongated winter break, where most of the hunters based in this area went since it was the northernmost point in Alaska and a decent-sized town that would need protection. Seeing all the students leave for fall break left me wondering what I would do for winter break.

Sunny looked up at me in surprise. "I assume so. That's where his family lives."

I lowered my spoonful of mashed potatoes and stared at her. After Luke and his father had argued weeks ago, I'd wondered where Killian Aultstriver had disappeared to. "His family lives in Barrow? Isn't that extremely dangerous?"

"No more than anywhere else. Well, except during winter. Then it's basically our frontlines of the war." Sunny wrinkled her nose in thought, making her glasses inch up her face. "So, yeah, I guess it is pretty dangerous."

I couldn't imagine living at the front of a war with my family and small child. But then, this was Killian Aultstriver. He'd probably had Luke fighting up there since Luke could hold a knife.

"Who protects the school if all the hunters go north for winter break?"

"The older hunters and professors stay behind, but the university will be pretty safe because most of the 'swangs will be north. Almost all of the students leave for their family's safe house, so there isn't much to protect anyway." Sunny polished off her lunch and pushed the tray away. When she leveled her serious gaze at me, I knew what was coming.

Before she could launch into another sales pitch, I held up my hand. "Seriously, Sunny. I'm fine staying here."

"But are you sure you don't want to come home with me? It would be fun, I promise!"

She'd been begging me to come home with her during fall break for weeks now, but, honestly, I wanted to be alone. I needed the privacy to research my ability to chat up 'swangs. "I'm sure it would, but I don't want to infringe on your time with your family. I know you've missed them. Besides, I *have* to study for finals. I'm really behind in economics."

"Do you still want me to show you the genetics section in the library?"

"Yes!" I said a little too excitedly. Sunny had told me about a section in the library where extensive records were kept of each hunter's kills and bite reactions. All the genealogical records were stored there as well. If I had any hope of figuring this out, it would be in those books. "Want to go now?" I asked a little more calmly.

"Why do you need to do this genealogical research again?" Sunny asked for the hundredth time. We gathered up our trays and put them by the dishwashers before heading out the door.

"I want to learn more about all this. You don't get it because this has been your life since you were born. It's an outsider thing," I said, bumping shoulders with Sunny.

"You're not an outsider." She rolled her eyes, finally laughing with me. Keeping what had happened that night with Luke and Hatter a secret bothered me. I hated lies. But having her constant smiling, reassuring presence helped me deal more than she knew.

We walked through the quiet halls; classes were canceled the day before break so students could pack and get ready for their trips. The classroom doors were closed, the lights off inside. Above us, the power-saving fluorescents cast a dim luminance that made me feel like we were walking through a deserted building. When we got to the library on the second floor in the east wing, the place was just as empty. Even the librarians were getting ready to leave.

Sunny and I heaved the old wooden door open and turned on the lights. Immediately, the scent of old pages and leather hit me. The prison-vibe the school sported had been turned down a notch due to all the thick rugs and brown leather chairs spaced throughout the room. Rows upon rows of book shelves lined the walls with a separate maze of shelves filling the center of the room. Sunny bobbed and weaved through the library like she knew it better than the back of her hand. She led me to a forgotten corner where huge leather binders sat on the shelves, labeled with years and letters of the alphabet. All the binders took up five floor-to-ceiling shelves, which were positioned to form a little room of its own with thickly cushioned chairs covered in a fine layer of dust and a wobbly table in the middle.

I sighed as I looked along the numerous shelves. There were thousands of binders for me to go through. Figuring out my problem was going to be harder than I thought.

Big surprise.

"That's a lot of records," I said.

"And they're not even complete." Sunny heaved down one large binder and thumbed through the thick vellum pages. "We didn't record family history until the first European contact in Alaska during the 1700s. Those are the earliest binders you'll find. All the stuff from before then, when it was just the Alaskan native tribes and the migrated Filipino families keeping the 'swangs under control, is lost. So the ten families—the Originals—listed in the first binder are the ones we can date back the furthest." She shrugged, as if talking about centuries of families fighting monsters was no big deal.

"How did the families grow to be this big?" I eased one of the older binders off the shelf and carefully opened it, the leather creaking and cracking. The ink was dotted and washed out in spots, but filled pages and pages with names and family descriptions, all painstakingly written by hand.

"Russian settlements. Gold rush. Army bases. Oil. Anything that introduced new people to the Originals. Eventually they mingled, and you get to the number of families and descendants we have now."

I pointed to a small stack of binders marked with dates in the mid-Nineteenth Century. "Why are there so few binders here?"

"Smallpox outbreak on Kodiak from the Russians. The hunter families practically started over after that."

"When did you learn all this?"

"Middle and high school. We learn all the history of the families then, or if you have a mother and grandmother like mine, you know them before you can talk."

I groaned. "I'll never catch up."

"But it's good that you want to learn." Sunny smiled at me, and I didn't have the heart to tell her my real reason for wanting to learn about her history was a purely selfish one.

"Yeah." I mumbled the word, unable to look her in the eye.

"Do you want me to help you go through some of them?"

she asked, eyeing the huge stack already on the table in the genealogical section's nook.

"That's okay. Let's go finish your packing."

Sunny sneezed. "Okay good. Cause this place is really messing with my sinuses."

The next day was a flurry of activity amid the first snow of fall. The tiny flakes melted instantly on the unfrozen ground, but the nippy air added to the excitement buzzing through the school.

To avoid students scurrying around like rats on a wheel, I headed to the library after saying goodbye to Sunny. Luke's injuries kept him holed up in his room, and I didn't feel like talking to anyone else anyway. There was something about seeing parents embracing their kids with hugs and excited chatter about all their great plans that made my stomach feel like I'd eaten a boulder. Actually, there wasn't *something* about it. It was *everything* about it.

Everything I would never have.

Back in the library, I hauled out a binder from the oldest year and settled into a chair. The binder's spine creaked open, sending a wave of musty-smelling pages and dust into my face. The scent comforted me, like I was reaching into the past and really touching history. It wasn't my history, but if I closed my eyes and sat perfectly still, I almost imagined it was. Like if I wormed my way into this world, one day a binder like this would have my name in it. Maybe if I became a really good hunter, many books would contain my legacy.

I pulled the binder closer to my face and took a deep

breath, letting the history fill my lungs. I'd never let myself hope for a legacy before. But everything had changed now. I sat the binder back down in my lap and focused on the first page.

The page depicted a tree with a few thick branches. I counted ten, each with a family name on the branch. The Originals. I didn't recognize many of the names, but a few stood out to me. Luke's family—Aultstriver—perched on a branch near the top. The Lyons family sat on one of the other branches, which surprised me. Sunny certainly wouldn't brag about her family being one of the Originals, but I thought she would have at least told me, especially when she brought me back here. She knew I would find it.

Then it came to me. For all her smiling, laughing, cheeriness, Sunny was horrified by her fear sim testing. Everyone had called her the Cowardly Lyon before my stunt with Jolene. Of course she wouldn't tell me about her family. She would see herself as a disgrace to their name because she wasn't going to be a hunter.

Sadness for my friend enveloped me. I wished she was here for me to hug. Who cared about those assholes who called her that stupid name? She was going to be a great doctor, and that was needed more than the hunters. Who would repair the hunters when they came back hurt and broken from a hunt? She would.

People would never call her that again, and I didn't care who I needed to hurt to make it happen. I almost wished the students were still here; violence pulsed through my veins, making me lightheaded with its potency. I wanted to hurt them all for calling her that. And I wanted it *now*.

I stood and paced, working the violence out of my system, until I breathed normally again. When I'd recovered, I sat back down and picked up the binder again.

I recognized one other name on the tree—Bogrov. Dean's family. That surprised me. I hadn't pictured him as a hunter, but it would explain Luke's weariness of him. Dean wasn't trying to avenge his dead wife; he fought for an entire lineage of relatives who had died too young. I didn't get why he was taking it so personally. It was horrible to say, but everyone had lost family in this war. Like the school's freaking slogan should be about dying young. It was expected. So if Luke was right about Dean's fanaticism, why did Dean seek vengeance so strongly?

There was more to the story. There had to be.

I flipped to the next page and the next, finding them carefully marked with each name in the original family, their birth and death dates, who they married, what their skills were. I didn't stop until I got to Luke's family. While some families had other occupations besides hunter, each name on the Aultstriver page had "hunter" listed out beside them. It took me a moment to understand the large number next to the word was the person's 'swang kill count. I turned to the previous pages. Luke's family had over triple the kills as the other families, which I confirmed by quickly skimming through the rest of the binder. Their kill counts were insane. Each member numbering in the thousands, while other families achieved a hundred or two at most.

What made Luke's family so special? Did they train that

hard? Luke's cutting was certainly one sign of his family's violent tendencies. But after hearing about Hatter's upbringing, I knew other families employed the same strategies. Which meant Luke's family had some other ability to help them kill so many.

I turned back to the front of the binder and took my time going through it again. By the time I picked up my fifth binder, I'd started a list of all the families as more added to the Originals through marriages, which were carefully picked and planned. Each new family that came into the fold had a documented list of assets and abilities that were added into the binder, as if the marriage match was assigned based on worth, not love.

I found a lot of information about 'swang saliva reactions, but none of them had anything to do with communicating or hearing the 'swangs' thoughts. None of it boded well for figuring out my situation, or at least attributing it to their saliva. I let Luke believe I heard the 'swangs because of the saliva, but I knew the truth: I'd heard them before I was bitten.

What this said about me, I couldn't begin to imagine. I desperately needed to find someone in these binders who had heard aswangs because of the saliva. At least it gave me a starting point for figuring out why I could communicate without being bitten. Unless hearing them had something to do with my medical condition. At the moment, without tangible evidence, it was the only thing that made sense.

When my stomach wouldn't stop growling, I looked up. At my feet and on the small table beside me, stacks of binders towered up to wobbly, dusty heights. I checked my watch. It was dinner time, which explained the hungry gnawing in my stomach. I stood, dusted myself off, and left the library, leaving my pile of books behind. I doubted anyone would bother them, and I really didn't feel like hauling those heavy things off the shelves every day.

I turned the library's lights off as I left, tucking the history in for the night.

Beyond the library, the halls stretched out before me, empty and gloomy, like the whole world had disappeared while I was reading all day. My footsteps rang off the floor with each step. I was likely the only student on campus. Though the students were gone, the guards and hunters had remained, but they rarely ate in the cafeteria or wandered through the halls. So I really felt alone, and after being surrounded by so many people lately, I was surprisingly lonely.

That feeling disappeared when I arrived at the cafeteria and found that I wasn't alone at all.

I scowled toward the one table where two people sat eating their dinner: Jolene and Thaddeus. Great.

I loaded up my tray from the single operating buffet. The meal wasn't as elaborate as when school was in session, but it was enough to make me happy. I sat at the farthest table from Thad and Jolene, who ignored me as much as I ignored them. Fine by me.

Halfway through my meal, Jolene got up and dumped her tray with the dishwashers. She banged out of the cafeteria doors and disappeared down the hall. I watched her go with a scowl on my face as I munched on some asparagus, which was why I didn't see Thad sit down at my table until it was too late to run him off.

"This seat taken? Guess not. Don't mind if I do." He sprawled across a couple chairs, kicking his feet up on the table and spearing a piece of chicken with his fork.

"What are you doing?" I reached over and swatted his feet off the table.

"Eating. What are you doing?"

"I would prefer if you took you're eating elsewhere." I didn't want to be anywhere near Thad after all he'd said about Luke's father. It was totally my luck that the one hunter who actually ate in the cafeteria was Thad.

He shrugged and kept on chewing his chicken. "I don't want to eat alone."

As much as I disliked him, I kind of understood the feeling. "Why didn't you go home for break since you're injured?"

"This is my post. Hunters don't leave their posts. Besides, there's no home for me to go back to." He waved his fork at his throat. "Family died when I got hurt."

The disinterested tone in his voice while talking about his parents surprised me, but this was Thad. "Do hunters like being posted here? I imagine being surrounded by young students all the time would suck."

Thad didn't meet my eyes as he ate his food like it was the most interesting thing in the world. "The best hunters get posted here. Protecting the school is the only way to ensure our future."

I couldn't help but glance at his throat. He still wore a bandage, though I figured the wound had to be healed by now since my own hand wounds had scarred over pretty quickly. But no amount of gauze and tape could cover up the fact the bite had disfigured him. I wondered if it was turning black yet and why he didn't display his scars with pride like the other hunters did. I ran my fingertips over my own battle wounds. "Doesn't it feel hopeless sometimes?"

"Wouldn't be war if it didn't." For the first time, he glanced up at me, his brows furrowed. "I guess you're missing your family with Dean having to cut ties and all that."

Though he said the words like he felt sorry for me, I didn't like the sympathy. Especially from him. "I don't have any family."

Surprising me completely, Thad laughed. "Lucky."

The contempt in his voice took me aback, especially after his general disregard for his family earlier. After spending all day reading the evidence of the school's obsession with family, I struggled to swallow his heated disregard of his own. Unless his family was like Luke's and Hatter's, and Thad had been trained too early and too hard as well.

I was never one to justify asshole actions, but it might explain the issues between Luke and Thad.

I nodded toward the door Jolene had left through. "Why isn't she with her family? Are her parents hunting or something?"

Thad spewed his water back into the glass like I'd said the most hilarious thing in the world. "Jolene's parents hunting? That's hilarious! They're hiding in Europe."

"How can they hide?"

Thad was still laughing, his shoulders vibrating with repressed chuckles. He actually looked pretty handsome when he smiled, although his laughing made his bandaged throat bob in a way that emphasized the missing chunks. I forced myself not cringe at the sight. "They have hiding down to an art. During the fall and winter, they 'travel' to their home in Europe. But really they go there to avoid hunting in the north during the 'swangs' breeding time. There aren't many 'swangs in Europe."

"That's awful though. They just leave Jolene here?"

"Yep. Priceless family moment, right?"

"Dicks," I muttered under my breath, making Thad laugh again.

He stood, scraping his tray across the table. "If you get bored during break, come find me in the barracks. I know some ways to make the days pass faster."

So much for having a nice conversation. "Gross, Thad. Not in a million years."

He smirked. "I meant sparring. What did you mean?"

He had my attention with that. Luke was still healing, which meant he couldn't practice with me. Neither could Hatter with his hand. I would take any kind of training I got, even from Thad. "I would like to spar, if you have time."

Clearly, I'd surprised him with my agreement. "Sure," he managed. "I'll find you tomorrow."

"Great. I'll be in the library."

With a confused look, Thad nodded and walked off. No matter what made Thad tick, if he was good at fighting, I wanted to learn. Something told me he would teach me all the dirty tricks Luke deemed too unworthy to learn.

This break might not be so bad after all.

This break was going to be awful.

I needed all of two seconds to figure out sleeping in the dorms tonight, the first night of fall break, would be impossible: the Death Dome sounded more silent than a grave. I pictured doors slamming shut on empty cells, with no music or televisions or students shouting back and forth with each other. Somewhere in here, Jolene was sleeping, but I didn't picture myself calling over to her cell and asking for homework help.

Not going to happen.

I turned on my heel and walked out, not bothering to figure out a way to not swipe my card on the scanner. I didn't know where I was going until I was at the barracks and knocking softly on Luke's door.

I heard his heavy sigh on the other side and took it as my invitation to enter. "Nice to see you too," I commented, closing the door behind me and crossing the room to flop onto the bed beside him.

"You're supposed to be in the dorms, Ollie."

His chest was bare again except for the swath of bandages over the cuts, revealing the tangle of black scars across his body. I wanted to trace their awful, horrible lines and commit them to memory. He set aside the book he was reading, along with a cute pair of reading glasses I hadn't expected him to wear; they made him seem older, more studious and less like the raw killer image he normally exuded.

"The Death Dome is too quiet tonight. Besides, don't you miss me?"

"Let me guess. You're staying here tonight."

"You should be excited to have a hot girl in your bed." I kicked off my shoes and tucked my legs under the blankets, wishing I'd thought to bring some pajamas. The bed radiated heat from his warmth, and I snuggled deeper into the thick covers, savoring the smooth, expensive sheets.

"You should be in your dorm."

"So what?" I mumbled, blissed out and comfortable. "It's fall break. No one will care."

"Ollie—"

"Do you really care? Or are you complaining because you have a stick up your ass?" I sat up in the bed, staring at him. His chest rose and fell evenly, his bandages tugging tightly against his muscles with every inhale. His hair was mussed, and he hadn't shaved in a couple of days, making his face full of scruffy, dark shadows.

Luke frowned. "I do not."

"Not the point, Luke. Do you want me to leave?"

He checked the clock. "It's after curfew anyway. I guess you have to stay."

"I'm sure there's an empty room in here somewhere." I swung my legs off the bed and stood, ready to shove my feet into my boots. I don't know why Luke's rejection hurt me, but it did. And it was really annoying. "Or I bet Thad wouldn't mind if I stay with him."

"Ollie. Wait."

"It's no big deal," I said like it didn't bother me, like my heart wasn't panging with sharp aches. I shot him a grin over my shoulder to illustrate how much he didn't bother me. But his dark, serious look gave me pause.

"Damn it, Ollie. You're not going to Thad's room." Wincing, he rolled toward me and grabbed my hip. With a firm tug, he pulled me back into bed. "You're staying here."

Even when he let me go, the tingling heat from his touch scored through my skin. I liked it. A lot. I settled back into bed, noticing the distance between us all too well. "I'm not asking for you to make sweet passionate love to me. I just need somewhere to sleep that's not as creepy as the Death Dome."

Luke snorted at my nick-name for the dorms, his lips tugging up into a grin. I always felt like I'd won some prize when I made him smile. "You're so weird," he said, still smiling.

I spotted the television's remote on his bedside table, and, leaning over him, I grabbed it. For a moment, I paused and stared down at him, remembering when I beat him in my evaluation. I knew I was pushing my luck, but seeing how his brows lowered over his narrowed eyes, like he was simultaneously pissed at me and turned on, was worth it. I flopped back to my side, bouncing the bed and making Luke hiss in pain, and turned on the television. As I clicked through the channels, searching for some epic reality television, he picked up his book and glasses. Every shift of his weight tickled up my belly, and sent a fresh wave of his smell up my nose.

I might have gotten more sleep in the Death Dome.

Eventually, a new show came on, but I had no clue what I was watching, and Luke hadn't turned a page in his book for the last half hour. I played with the hem of my shirt to have something to do, all the while knowing I exposed a bit of my stomach as I fidgeted.

"Ollie," Luke said, his voice deeper than usual. I hid my smile. "This isn't working."

"What do you mean?" I shot him a grin because I knew exactly what he meant.

"I can't do this."

"You are doing this." I motioned to the bed between us. "See?"

"I can smell you."

Laughing, I sniffed my armpits. "I took a shower."

"You keep lifting your shirt up."

"If you want me to flash you, all you have to do is ask." I turned onto my side and propped my head up in my hand so I could watch him as I teasingly lifted my shirt a little. He resolutely ignored me and glared at the ceiling, his jaw flexing. The tendons in his arm flexed as his fingertips tapped against each other. He struggled for control, and I liked it.

"People are going to think something is happening between us if you stay here."

I bit my lip to keep from laughing. "Don't worry, Luke. I won't sully your honor. I'm sure I could rig up a chastity belt for you, though, if you're that worried."

"This isn't funny. Stop laughing."

"It's hilarious. You should see your face right now."

"Ollie, nothing can happen between us. You don't understand what that saliva does to me . . ."

Seeing him in bed, like this, trying so hard to be a gentleman, had me smirking. He might intimidate everyone else at this school, but not me. I welcomed his wrath. I even welcomed his sexual aggression. "You've already kissed me twice," I pointed out. I pulled the sheets from his clenched fist and smoothed them out, my hand brushing against his arm.

"Mistakes," he said. "I'm your trainer anyway. It's a conflict of interest."

"You can't train me right now." I poked his chest, making him wince. "Besides I've already asked Thaddeus to help me out tomorrow. He said he would spar with me."

"What?" Luke growled, fingers dancing faster. "You asked him?"

"Well," I drawled. "Technically, he offered and I agreed. I thought he might show me a thing or two that you won't." I blinked innocently at him, refusing to let my face crack into a grin.

An odd noise came from Luke's chest, like he was humming with anger or repressing a vicious growl. I flung the covers down my legs, practically sweating from the heat circulating in the room. I shrugged out of my sweatshirt, knowing Luke watched every movement as I undressed. I took too long to pull down my shirt when it rode up my ribs, and Luke reached over and yanked it down for me.

"You don't need to spar with him. He's dangerous."

"He's just a spoiled brat." I adjusted the pillow behind my

head and picked up the remote again.

"He's inept." Luke indicated his throat to illustrate his point.

"That's rude. Besides, you managed to get your chest all clawed up."

"His throat was nearly ripped out. That's inept, not rude. He has nothing to teach you."

"I haven't had to save his life," I said.

"You did *not* save me. I was fine."

"Right," I drew out the word. Let him believe what he wanted to protect his pride, but my smirk said otherwise.

Luke reared up in the bed and leveled his best glare in my direction. As if that scared me. When I didn't look at him, Luke grabbed my arm and pulled me against him. "What?" I asked, grinning. I knew it was coming, and I relished pushing Luke to that point.

"You shouldn't do this to me, Ollie." The words were a warning, a soft hiss against my cheek. He raked the scruff of his jaw along my face, the rumbling in his chest and throat vibrating through my bones. I groaned.

"I like doing this to you." My fingers splayed across his right pectoral, where a deep black scar resided. I traced its length, feeling Luke's skin jump beneath my fingertip.

Without another word, he dropped me back against the bed and covered my chest with his. His lips crashed against mine as I gasped, not from surprise but excitement. He crushed me into the bed, his arms like huge pillars braced on either side of my head. I felt the pressure of his weight against me just enough to make my skin dance with feverish excitement. I twisted my hips up against him, and he deepened the kiss until he consumed me whole.

I wrapped my arms around his neck and held on, my smiling lips keeping pace with his.

The next afternoon, Thad found me in the library. Together we walked to the gym in silence, which shocked the hell out of me. Even after I'd changed into my workout clothes and walked back out to the mats, he didn't say anything. I was struggling to figure out how to break the ice when Luke and Hatter stalked in, their expressions stormy.

I groaned. This wasn't going to be good. I'd taken a shower since last night, but I still smelled like Luke, as if he'd marked me with his scent. We'd only kissed, which disappointed me. I'd wanted more of him, but Luke stopped us before we got that far.

"Let's get to it then." Thad nodded stiffly because of his thick bandage and reached for some sparring gloves.

"She doesn't warm up like that," Hatter called from the bleachers, his hand still wrapped in a bandage. He bobbed his head in time to the music coming through his lime-green headphones, but his eyes narrowed at Thad, watching his every move. Luke didn't comment, just sprawled across the bleachers like he was a king presiding over his domain. I rolled my eyes at them.

"Shut up." I turned my back to them and looked at Thad. "I'll warm up however you want me to warm up."

At my words, Thad directed his attention over my shoulder and smiled slowly at Luke. Behind me, the bleachers squeaked, which meant Luke had taken the bait. I bristled beneath all this testosterone.

"Sounds good," Thad finally said, focusing on me again. He pulled on the sparring gloves after handing me a pair.

As I got ready, more hunters streamed in through the gym doors. I tried not to pay attention, but there were so many, I wondered who was left to guard the fence. Even Jolene came to watch me practice.

"No pressure," Thad whispered when he sensed my growing nerves.

"Did you invite the freaking President of the United States too?"

"Maybe." Thad threw the first punch, which I blocked easily. The footwork went faster than when I warmed up with Luke, and Thad was unpredictable, coming at me before I righted myself from his last attack. He was relentless, and he fought dirty like I'd expected. I relished it.

The practice lasted two hours. Two hours of sweating, grunting, and cursing. It was wild and rough, our audience captivated the entire time. The girl who'd run off the 'swangs was putting on a good show.

I hit my back more than a few times, Thad standing over me with a feral grin, and Luke surging to his feet, ready to rip off Thad's head if Hatter hadn't pulled him back every time. Thad barely gave me enough room to get to my feet, but I managed to land an elbow to his bandaged throat once.

It was a dirty move, one Luke would have admonished me for if he was training me. The blow to Thad's throat should have done him in, but he grinned wider at me. So his throat had healed, yet he wore the bandages anyway.

When the practice ended, I didn't get a chance to sit down and catch my breath. Luke came over and grabbed my arm, ignoring Thad completely, and marched me back to the barracks, where he backed me onto his bed and kissed the hell out of me for the next hour. Pretty good cool down, all in all.

The rest of break passed in blur of routine. Against my better judgment, I ate my meals with Jolene, who didn't speak to me, and Thaddeus, who spoke too much. I spent an hour in the morning and afternoon sparring with him. He mostly took his new responsibility seriously, though he made a few more snide comments and lewd suggestions as we practiced, much to Luke's dismay, who spent our practice sessions glowering in the bleachers with Hatter and a barrage of hunters, who all called out corrections as we sparred. For the most part, Thad and I ignored them.

In between my evening runs and sparring sessions, I researched in the library until my eyes burned, and though I'd made my way through most of the binders, I still found no mention of hearing 'swangs. At night, I went straight to Luke's room. Wonderfully enough, I found the more I pissed him off during the day by ignoring him while Thad and I practiced, the more rigorous he was while we made out for hours.

I seriously loved fall break.

THIRTEEN

On my way to Luke's room the day before students arrived back from fall break, a siren began to wail.

Sunny had warned me about the school practicing drills every now and then, but I'd never experienced one. I knew we were supposed to immediately go back to our dorms for the emergency lockdown, but as the siren blared, I stood in the middle of the courtyard, frowning and mildly annoyed. The only students here were Jolene and I. There was no point to having a drill with two students on a Saturday night. Unless this wasn't practice.

This was a real 'swang attack.

My first thought was Hex. He'd come for me, like he promised.

I surged forward and sprinted to the barracks, but the building and Luke's room were empty. Instead of turning back to the Death Dome and going for my cell, I sprinted toward the closest rook's nest and flung myself up the ladder.

Organized chaos reigned on top of the fence. Most of the guards ran toward the east side of the fence. "What's going on?" I practically shouted to be heard over the clamor around us.

A guard fired his rifle into the woods, the sound ringing in my ears. He instantly ejected the round and reloaded, squinting down the sight. "Organized attack against the east wall. Big group." He took a second to glance up at me. "You should report to your cell now."

"Is Luke up here?" I pressed.

He shot again at something in the woods. From the east side of the fence, I heard a howl. The sound was a mixture between a wolf and a human screaming that sent chills down my spine. "Go to your cell. Now."

I ignored him and ran down the fence, ducking around the other stationed guards. Gunshots went off all around me, people shouting back and forth to each other. Their efficiency, their cold calculated method of destruction, excited me.

When I skidded around to the east wall, I saw a line of guards. In the night, their shots blazed with a blinding fire for a second before dissolving into darkness. There were no lights on the fence top; everyone, including the 'swangs, relied on night vision. I couldn't see what the guards shot at, but the shadows moved too quickly on the ground outside of the fence to be shadows.

'Swangs.

At the next rook's nest I came to, I ran straight into Luke.

His face showed a split second of shock before he turned furious. He slung his rifle over his back and shoved me against the back of the rook's nest, guards streaming around us as they ran to get into position. Over the cacophony, he yelled into my ear, "What the hell are you doing up here?"

"Is it Hex?" I shouted back, trying to see around his shoulder.

He shoved me back again, and I bit my tongue. I spit out the blood and glared at him. "Go to your cell!"

"Movement!" a guard close to us shouted.

Guns blasted. Luke spun around and turned his attention to the front of the fence. I slipped up behind him and peered down into the darkness. All around us, people were shooting and shouting, calling out positions and number of 'swangs attacking. My eyes were glued to the pulsing, teeming shadows.

They swelled and surged toward the wall with howls and sharp barks. The sound of their claws on the fence ricocheted up to the rook's nest. Luke called down the line, and a series of guards dropped flashbangs that seared my eyes and ruined my night vision.

As I blinked down into the chaos, I heard him.

Olesya.

I spun toward the other side of the rook's nest, blinking furiously to clear my vision. Off to the side, away from the fight, stood Hex. Shadows concealed half his body, the other half standing out enough for me to see him. His eyes glowed a bright white in the darkness. No one else seemed to see him, their attention reserved solely for the attack on the fence, which was obviously a distraction orchestrated by Hex.

Olesya, come outside. Come to me.

His voice slipped down my spine and curled around my insides like smoke. Horrified, I realized part of me really did want to go to him. But the more rational part prevailed, and I wished I had a rifle.

What do you want? I asked, focusing my thoughts toward him.

I thought you were dead. I thought you died that night with her.

With who? And what night was he talking about? I shuddered. Honestly, I didn't think I wanted to know. *You need to leave,* I thought instead.

These people are dangerous. You have to come with me.

"Ollie!" Luke grabbed my arm. He flung me back against the rook's nest and shouted in my face, "You have to go now! Get to your cell!"

Hex's predatory growl echoed in my mind. Though I couldn't see him, I still asked, *Who are you?*

"Look at me!" Luke yelled, shaking me.

You need to leave that place.

I'm not going anywhere until you tell me what you want with me and who you are, I shot back.

"What's wrong?" Luke sat down his rifle and searched my body for wounds. "Ollie! Talk to me!"

I want to save you, Hex said. *These people will hurt you, especially that Aultstriver. They'll cut you apart to figure out what makes you different. You can't let them do that to you. If they know what makes you special, they'll kill us all.*

You mean my disease?

"Ollie," Luke whispered in my ear, his breath hot against my skin. "Are you hearing them now? Don't listen. Baby, look at me."

My body reacted to him, arching into his heat, but I wasn't aware of him as I focused on my inner conversation.

It's not a disease, he said, chilling me to the core.

What do you mean? I've had it my whole life.

You were born with it, but it's not a disease.

Luke stopped a nearby guard. "Get her to the ward! Take her now!" He shoved the guard toward me. "And stay with her. Don't let her out of your sight. You hear me?"

"Yes, sir!"

The guard tried to lead me away, but my feet wouldn't move. Hex's words repeated over and over in my mind: *it's not a disease*. My thoughts were so jumbled that I couldn't tell if he was repeating them to me or if I was. I couldn't tell my thoughts from his words or mine. I might have been speaking aloud given Luke's terrified expression and the guard's confused one.

"Carry her!" Luke instructed.

The guard hefted me up and slung me over his shoulder. Blood dripped from my nose and onto the rook's nest floor. My head pulsed with Hex's words, with the gunshots, with Luke's continued shouting for the guard to go.

Why? I asked Hex. The word swirled in my mind, chasing its tail until I was dizzy. *Why are you helping me? Why are you here?*

The guard moved slowly down the ladder with me over his shoulder. I couldn't struggle. I couldn't move. My view of Hex was blocked, and his words faded drastically in my mind, but I still managed to hear him when he said the words that made me black out.

I'm your father, Olesya.

FOURTEEN

I jolted awake, an acrid scent swirling up my nostrils. I gagged and shoved myself away from the horrible smell. Only then did I notice Dean sat beside me. I was in the ward, lying on a cot.

"Good, you're awake," Dean said as he capped a small bottle in his hand. The stench wafted out toward me again, and my stomach turned.

"What the hell is that?"

Dean smiled and set the bottle aside. "I couldn't exactly pinch you awake, could I? Call it drastic measures."

I rubbed the bridge of my nose, hoping it would alleviate the smell still churning in my sinuses. "What time is it?"

"Morning. You've slept a long time. Students are arriving

from break."

I'd slept like the dead and rested like them apparently. I felt rejuvenated, but I suddenly remembered that more had happened last night than my internal chat with Hex. I almost shuddered. "Is everyone okay? None of the 'swangs got in, right?"

"Do you think we would be here talking if they did?"

I bit my tongue to keep my smart-ass comment in check, but holding it in tasted worse than the smell in my nose. Between now and the hunting disaster with Luke and Hatter, I understood why Luke disliked this guy so much. I was seeing a completely different side to him lately. "No wounded?"

"No. Except for you, of course. Which is interesting, because you should have gone straight to your cell. Instead, multiple guards noted your presence during the incident in their reports. Care to explain?" Dean leaned forward on his stool, making the thing creak beneath his weight. I didn't like being on my back so close to him, so I shifted, scooting as far away from him as possible before sitting up and crossing my arms over my middle. It wasn't much, but it made me feel better.

"That was more than an incident."

"What were you doing out past curfew?" he countered.

Not wanting to answer that, I pretended I didn't understand what he was asking. "I've never been through an attack drill before." I shrugged, forcing a casualness into my words I didn't feel. "I didn't know where to go. My instincts said the fence."

After I'd finished, Dean studied me for a long, tense moment. I sensed him turning my words over and over. I knew he didn't believe me: his eyes flared with skepticism as he examined me.

Abruptly, he reached forward and slapped my shoulder, like he was rewarding me for a right answer. The blow made my teeth sing, meaning I would likely have another bruise tomorrow. I resisted the very strong urge to punch him back. "You'll be a great hunter, Ollie, with those *special* instincts. I knew I was right about you." Dean stood, wiping nonexistent dirt of his pressed khakis. Too casually, he said, "Remember our agreement. We have rules in place for a reason, and you, more than anyone else, are expected to follow them. Understand?"

"Yeah," I said through my teeth. Dean's smile disappeared and he cocked his head. I knew that look. "Yes, sir," I quickly corrected.

"Good. I'm glad we understand each other. Oh, one more thing. You're not to say a word about the attack. Not one. Not even to Sunny."

My hands dropped to my sides. "What?" I sputtered, though I shouldn't have been surprised.

"None of the students are to be informed of last night's events. You and the guards are the only ones who know. Even Jolene doesn't completely know what happened, because she actually went to her cell when the siren started. So if any information leaks, I'll know where it came from." Dean's smile turned sharp, dangerous, and I crossed my arms over my chest to shield myself from him. "And that's a disobedience I can't tolerate."

My throat was too dry to respond.

Dean took my silence as submission. He walked to the door, whistling under his breath. For the first time, I wondered if he was crazy. With his hand on the swinging door leading into the ward's hall, he paused and looked back at me. "I forgot to tell you. I found Max. He's in Alaska, did you know?"

His words processed slowly in my mind, but eventually my fingertips began to tremble. I pressed them into my ribs to hide them from Dean, who was watching my reaction with a dark gleam in his eye. I didn't trust myself to speak. I might scream instead.

"I wanted you to know," he continued. "All I'm saying is that he's close if we need him. Which, I hope we don't."

My vision slanted, hot vomit pulsing up my throat. Distantly, I heard him leave, the door swinging behind him. I fell back against the bed, shivering so badly I barely managed to pull the blanket up around my chin.

I knew I should be planning to escape. I had all the signs. I knew better than most when to leave, when everything pointed straight at danger. I freaking knew better. But I hated that, once again, one man was going to send me into hiding, force me to run away from where I belonged. I hated that. It disgusted me.

And Max was close. He was in Alaska. Too close. Too close for me to breathe. But in here, at Fear University, I stood a chance against him.

Eventually, the shivering passed, taking my fear with it.

Exhausted, I laid on my cot, and the thoughts I'd fought so hard to keep down, surfaced.

I'm your father, Olesya.

My father. I tested the words over and over in my mind, but they never fit. I had no one. Certainly no memories of a father. Much less a 'swang father. 'Swangs could only reproduce with other 'swangs. It was impossible for a 'swang to mate with a human. Not to mention the thought of being half 'swang revolted me. No, I didn't believe Hex. I didn't.

"No," I whispered. *No. No. No.* Shove it down. Push it away.

The ward's door swung open again, and I jumped, nearly screaming. My stomach flipped at the thought it was Dean returning with more threats.

"You're awake," Luke said, and I couldn't help my sigh of relief.

I rubbed a hand across my forehead, where a pounding headache grew. "Barely," I said, hearing how weak my voice was. "Could you get me some aspirin?"

Luke went to the cabinets and pulled open a drawer. He knew exactly where the right medicine was, almost as if he'd spent a lot of time in the ward. But given his battered body, he obviously had. "Here you go," he said once he'd filled a small glass with water and returned to my cot. He deposited the pills in my hand and waited.

"Thanks," I said after I'd swallowed the pills and downed the water.

Luke ignored the stool beside me and sat on the edge of the cot. It dipped beneath his weight, and my body slid toward his until our hips touched. He leaned over me and propped a hand on the other side of the bed. I looked up into his face. For once, I didn't hate being on my back around someone. I never minded Luke's proximity like I minded others.

"Ollie," Luke sighed, his breath whooshing over my face and fluttering the little hairs at my temples, "what happened last night? You lost it on me. It was like I was staring at a dead girl. Were you hearing them?"

I clenched my jaw and forced myself to look away from him. If I stared into his warm green eyes a moment longer, I would tell him everything. The real, horrible truth. Even Hex's lie. The worst lie. The lie that I had a father. The words were all right there, right on the tip of my tongue, waiting to spill out and become someone else's problem. But I held them in, forced them into submission. And when I looked back at him, I had myself under control.

"They were looking for me," I said, giving him the best version of the truth I could offer. "Like you said they would."

"Shit." Luke raked a hand down his face. Dark circles stained the skin beneath his eyes, and he wore the same clothes from last night.

"Yeah," I said quietly, wishing we were talking about the real truth.

"This is bad." I nodded in agreement at his words, but it was worse than he thought. Way worse. "If they're looking for you, that means more organized attacks."

"I know."

"Has Dean been here yet? Told you not to tell the

others?"

I let the anger bristle up my insides. The feeling was better than the bottomless loneliness that threatened to devour me. "He was. Why the hell can't I say anything? The students deserve to know. They—"

Luke put a hand on my arm to calm me down. Annoyingly enough, it worked. Either that or his intoxicating man-smell was messing with my fried brain. "They should know, but Dean has it on lockdown. He doesn't want to freak anyone out."

"They deserve to be a little freaked out."

"You're right, but Dean asked me a lot of questions about you last night. The guard who carried you here told him you were unconscious and had a bloody nose. Dean knows we aren't telling him something, and he knows it has something to do with the night we went to the fishing village."

"He told me Max was in Alaska," I said quietly. I refused to let the fear quell my voice. Or my heart. Not happening.

"Why did he tell you that? Was he threatening you?"

I shrugged, not wanting Luke to know how much Dean was getting to me. Luke jerked to his feet and paced away, cursing enough to impress even me. He was a powerful man, virile and intimidating, but I drank him up, his anger and violence, like it was the best thing I'd ever tasted.

"Do you think," I ventured, choosing my words carefully based on what Hex had said last night, "that Dean would use me to figure out a way to make other hunters not feel pain? Like, experiment on me or something?"

Luke spun around to face me. "Did he say something like

that?"

"No," I said quickly. "I was just wondering."

Luke's eyes bore into the floor, his eyelashes fluttering against his cheekbones like he was thinking too quickly. It took him too long to look back at me. Too long, and I knew Hex was right. It was another sign I should run. Escape. But I stayed sitting on the cot, waiting, praying that Luke would look up. When he finally did, I sighed with relief. "I won't let that happen. You know that, right? I won't."

"I know, Luke, but men like Dean don't stop."

"It's a medical condition. They aren't God. They can't *create* super soldiers."

My heart twisted at his words. Medical condition. *It's not a disease*, Hex had said. But it was. It had to be. By sheer will alone, I would make it so. "You said he would make an entire army out of soldiers like me."

"It won't come to that." Luke sat back down on the cot and took my hand. "I'm going to figure out what Dean is doing in the west wing of the lab. If he's going to try anything with you, we might find answers there."

It was a shot in the dark, and we knew it. Dean was coming for me, and I was a sitting duck. I didn't even know who I really was. Why could I hear the 'swangs? Talk to them? Was I Hex's daughter or a medical fluke? How deep did my ties run with Fear University? But more important than all those questions was one simple one: were the 'swangs the monster or was I?

"I don't want to stay in here," I said, because it was the only honest thing to say.

Luke stood and reached down for my hand. I wove my fingers through his before he helped me off the cot. Not that I needed the help, but he held my hand after I was righted, and that was worth it. "Where do you want to go?"

I thought about running into Sunny and seeing the other students, flushed and happy from spending the break with their families, and said, "Can we go to your room? I don't want to see anyone yet."

Luke nodded, though I saw the question in his eyes. He led me through the ward's main hallway and up the stairs. Instead of going to the main front door, he took me out a side entrance, directly in front of the barracks. Thankfully, none of the other hunters were in the hallway to see me go into Luke's room. I didn't think our friendship or whatever was something I needed to hide, but I didn't want to put Luke in a weird spot.

When we were settled on the bed, my head resting against Luke's battered chest, and the television turned on, I asked, "How can you stand it? All the lying that goes on here?"

Luke ran his hand down my back, fingers tracing the knobs of my spine. He followed a path: straight down, a few brushes across my lower back, and then back up the notches of my ribs. He made three passes before he answered. "It's something you get used to, I guess."

I bunched his shirt in my fist, feeling the hard contours of his abs beneath my hand. "It's not fair to ask these students to risk their lives, and not tell them the truth about what they're really going to face. It's like giving a scared little kid a sword and pointing him toward a dark cave as you tell him the Easter Bunny is in there."

"I know," Luke soothed as he kept his hand roving across my back.

"I hate lies." The words were quiet and muttered against Luke's skin, but he still heard me. His hand stilled.

"What happened to you?" he asked after a long moment of silence.

"What didn't?" I tried to joke, but my laugh sounded brittle, and the words hung in the air between us.

"Ollie—"

I heard the pity in his voice and I shut it down. "No. It wasn't bad. Well, it was, but I'm glad it happened to me. All of it. Even the . . ." I stopped myself. Not going there. Luke didn't need to know that.

"You shouldn't be happy it happened to you." Luke tried to shift away from me so he could look me in the eyes, but I hunkered down and kept my cheek pressed tightly against his chest.

"I am," I whispered fiercely. I was. "I'm happy for all of it, because it made me a killer. And I like being a killer."

Luke tried to shift away from me again, but I held on tightly. I didn't know if he was afraid of me, disgusted, or just wanted to reassure me, but I couldn't handle any of it. Eventually, he gave up and said, his voice defeated, "That's not who you have to be anymore."

"Don't be naive," I snapped.

Quietly, Luke resumed his path along my back, but his fingers dug into my skin with a little more pressure. It might have hurt if I knew what that felt like. Maybe he was trying to pull me back to the world. But I was lost to the past.

"When did you go into foster care?"

"I was ten. They found me in my mom's house nearly dead from starvation and cold." I lifted his shirt and skimmed my fingers down his muscles until his skin danced. "She told me to hide. To not come out no matter what. She was coming back for me. She would be right back. She didn't come back. But I waited, because I loved her and obeyed her. I stayed in the closet for nearly a week and a half. No food. No water but the bottle of Coke I found on a shelf. When the social workers came, because the neighbors had heard me crying, I was sitting in my own mess, half dead. But I didn't know I was half dead. I felt none of it but the waiting, the wanting her to come back. So I didn't understand why they took me away, and I cried harder.

"After that, it was foster care. Lots of homes. My condition didn't work well for most families. Or worked too well for some." Luke tensed beneath me at those words. I heard him open his mouth, felt the humming growl in his chest, but I went on before he could say what I expected him to say. "After the Tabers, I had to leave. I was sixteen."

"That's—"

"The past," I said, fixing his response so that it didn't piss me off. "I can't change it now, and besides, I like who those years made me into. I wouldn't want to be anything but tough and fearless. I like not feeling pain. I like it all."

At my words, Luke stopped rubbing my back. Like I'd held him to me a moment ago, he clenched me against his chest. I knew he thought my past was bad; I sensed the horrible pity and, even worse, the anger that radiated off of him in thick, hot waves. But he didn't say anything. And best of all, he didn't call me out on my lie, though I knew he'd heard it when I said I liked who I was.

The next day was a blur of classes. Final prep had started for exams, and teachers were cramming in as much as they could last minute. When it was time for lunch, my hand ached from taking notes, and my eyes were sore from squinting at the tiny letters scrawled across the chalk boards. By the time I crawled into the cafeteria and got my lunch, Sunny was already sitting at the table waiting for me.

"Ollie!" she squealed, pulling me into a tight hug. I balanced my tray in one hand and patted her awkwardly on the back while I waited out the bouncing, gleeful tirade of her excitement. I bore her touch because it was Sunny, and I would allow her anything.

When she finally released me, I said, "Hey, Sunny. Did you have a good break?"

She launched into her monologue about fall break, telling me everything from what she wore to what she ate to who she saw. I nodded and chimed in with the right words at the right times, but my thoughts kept circling around the attack. I wanted nothing more than to interrupt her and scream to the cafeteria and all the students in it that we'd been attacked, that we weren't safe, that nothing was okay. But I listened and ate, nodded and smiled, waiting until I could hide myself away from all the smiling, happy students who didn't have a clue, not one, about the real truth lurking beyond the fences.

I knew I needed to stop letting this bother me so much. The lying was a part of this world. On some level, I understood why they did it. If every young teenager knew the truth about the 'swangs, no one would want to come to Fear University. And the war would be in an even worse state than it already was.

Though I understood the reasoning to an extent, I couldn't justify it. Bad things happened when people lied. Maybe it was because it was so fresh in my mind from telling Luke, but the image of me sitting in my own filth, my hands quaking with a hunger I didn't feel, while I waited on my mother to come back filled my head. She'd lied. She'd told the worst lie ever. My mother was a liar, and she'd abandoned me to a life where I had to kill and run to stay alive.

Other memories threatened to surface too. I saw the glimmer of it before I shoved it away. A little blonde girl so similar to me. Another orphan from a lying parent. She was tied to a chair in a basement. Her screams. Her blood splattering my face. *Oh god. So much blood. She feels the pain. She screams. I have to watch. Watch and don't look away or she's cut again. Do you feel the pain yet, Ollie? Tell the truth. Never lie. Do you feel it yet? What if I cut her here—*

"Ollie?" Sunny's voice jolted me from the memory. "Are you okay? You're really pale."

"Um," I stuttered.

No. No, I'm not okay. I'm not okay and you're not okay and everyone in this place is not okay. The words clanged against the back of my teeth.

No, that was vomit. I slapped a hand over my mouth and

surged up from the table. Everyone stared as I ran from the cafeteria, steering toward the first restroom I came to.

I barely had time to make it through the door and to the sink before my lunch and breakfast splattered all across the porcelain. For a moment, I saw blood but then I blinked and it was gone. My hands trembled against the faucet as I tried to turn on the water. It took a couple tries, but eventually the water sputtered on and I splashed some across my face and in my mouth. I glanced up at my reflection and saw terror in my eyes. Sweat slicked across my brow. My entire body shuddered, convulsing. I dry-heaved again and again.

I was about to smash my fist into the glass mirror to make the scared girl in the reflection go away when the bathroom door opened and Sunny slipped in. Her eyes were wide and extremely worried, but she came straight to me and pulled my hair away from my sticky face. She didn't say anything as I heaved some more, her hand dipping into the stream of water and dropping cold drops on the back of my neck.

I needed to explain myself. Make the situation sound better. Hide my weakness under the rug. *Lie*. "I—"

"I understand," Sunny interrupted, still dropping water on the back of my neck. "You don't have to say anything."

I stared into the bottom of the sink. She knew I was weak. She'd already seen too much. "How?" I asked; I thought I'd shown nothing.

"I'm your best friend, Ollie. You haven't told me everything, but I can read between the lines. And I don't need to know. I'm here for you, okay?"

I looked up and met her eyes in the mirror. She really

didn't need to know, but she knew already. I straightened off the sink and turned around. Sunny wet a few paper towels and handed them to me. As I pressed them against my cheek, I wanted nothing more than to tell her. To tell her everything.

How I was a party trick, a cool thing to show friends. Break Ollie and she won't scream. I wanted to tell her about all the bad that had made me this way. About the Tabers. About the little girl who was buried in that basement. How I'd dug her grave, repeating over and over that I felt her pain. That I was a dead girl like her. Then I'd dug my grave too. And slept in it until the house fell quiet. How I'd crept up the stairs, broke the door handle with my hands and slipped down the hall. I dented Mr. Taber's skull with the shovel he'd made me use to dig our graves until blood dripped from my eyelashes and into my eyes, and then I went to Max's room. But he was gone. Someone had heard Mr. Taber's screams, and sirens were coming. I debated letting them take me or killing myself too. But I left instead, because I liked it. I liked the feeling of killing him. It made me feel powerful and in control for the first time in my life. Savoring it, I slipped away and started running. Always running. Always lying.

I wanted to let all my secrets out, let them spill across the floor like black diamonds. But I couldn't. I couldn't say a word.

And I swear it nearly killed me.

Every night after the awful day in the restroom, Sunny came to my room and we studied far past lockdown and curfew. I hadn't had time to return to the library, and I didn't plan to.

Studying for finals was my secondary focus. No matter what my future brought, I knew I would need to be strong and ready to fight. So I trained harder—running twice a day and adding an extra hour to my sessions with Thad. I got good enough in the two weeks that passed that I beat Thad regularly, and when I returned to sparring with Luke closer to finals, I almost beat him too. Dean and other hunters stopped by more and more to watch me practicing. Eventually, Luke added in some some small, blunt weapons for me to wield while I worked on my balance with them.

I was good, and they knew it.

Saturday was the last delivery day for supplies before winter, and some parents were coming in to see their kids before final exams and Fields. The sun shined bright that Saturday morning when I woke up and headed out for my run. Bush planes were landing and taking off on the airstrip, cars and vans coming and going so frequently that the gate opened and closed almost continuously. As I ran, I heard people laughing and calling to each other. Light snow flurries stuck to my face and hair, but it felt nice and brought everyone outside. It was a good day so far, and I almost forgot my problems.

Until the day turned bloody.

FIFTEEN

After my run, I went looking for Sunny. People inside the main building rushed to and fro, carrying supplies from the delivery, which had arrived while I was out racing along the fences. Most of the people were unfamiliar to me— delivery men and such—but I didn't look too closely at their faces. Once I started down the stairs to the ward, things grew quiet after the hustle and bustle upstairs.

When I stepped onto the ward's floor, I glanced around, confused. No one was down here, which was odd. Surely the doctors and nurses needed to unbox the supplies lining the hall. I walked toward the ward's communal room, thinking maybe they were all in there.

When I was halfway down the hall, I heard a sound that

made my stomach drop.

Tick tock tick tock

It was quiet, a whispered threat. But my skin prickled and my blood pulsed straight to my head. My first thought was a 'swang; my second thought was day-form 'swangs didn't hunt. The human form was a husk for the inner monster, which became weak and useless during the day. I didn't trust Dean or most of the professors, but Luke had even told me day-form 'swangs weren't dangerous. If he said they weren't, then I was safe.

Tick tock

But daytime or not, I knew that sound. I crept forward, my footsteps silent across the floor. I passed a pair of work gloves tossed onto the ward's floor. Then a baseball cap and sunglasses. A pair of coveralls and a thick sweatshirt lay a few feet from the main ward's door. I stepped over the clothes and paused at the door, listening.

Tick tock

I swung through the door, uncertain what I was going to find.

Peg stretched across a gurney, both arms twisted up behind her like loose dough. Her shirt was lifted, exposing her swollen belly. A man, tall and thin with pale skin, leaned over her with a slender hand clapped across her mouth. He wore only a tattered pair of thin pants hanging from his sharp, pointed hipbones. Staring in horror, I understood his need for the disguise he'd discarded outside. Hair, long and matted, hung down his back, which curved over in a permanent hunch. His other hand sat poised at Peg's stomach, a jagged, yellow nail that was more like a claw pressing into her tender flesh.

Peg saw me, her eyes wide, her agonized, terrified scream muffled against the man's hand. I smelled her fear, saw where she'd wet herself. He was ready to rip her open and eat her.

Tick

With a hiss, the man twisted his neck, looking much too far over his shoulder. His eyes met mine.

My reflection, bright against his black irises, was upside down.

Peg tried to scream again. The 'swang—in its day-form—smiled at me, his teeth as yellow as his nails. Maybe he'd looked like a normal person once, and I knew day-form 'swangs normally did, but this guy was seriously fucked up.

Tock

"Her baby," the 'swang hissed, his tongue smacking thickly across cracked lips, "has the sweetest smelling bones."

So much for being harmless. Peg jolted at the 'swang's voice, and I knew, at least this time, I wasn't the only one hearing it. The 'swang looked completely human, and it talked like one too.

The door behind me was still slapping closed. A fire alarm hung on the wall two paces away. A half-opened box with plastic-wrapped scalpels lay on the table, out of reach. Where was Sunny? The other nurses? If the 'swang had already killed them . . .

I couldn't think about that. I had to focus on the fight. I looked back at the 'swang in time to see him lunge for me.

I dove, hitting the alarm at the same time the 'swang

slammed into me, sending us both crashing into the wall. The alarm, rising to a screaming wail, dug into my back. I gave the creature a satisfied flash of teeth before I slammed my forehead into his nose, a nasty little move Thad had taught me. He stumbled back a few inches and gave me enough room to slap the box of scalpels off the counter. It hit the ground and broke apart, sending little razors in pristine packets scattering over the floor.

The 'swang slashed his claws, catching me in the abdomen. Almost immediately, my blood seeped, hot and river-like, down my stomach. A deep cut, then. Likely more scars. No problem.

"You will be nice to eat too, pretty girl."

I punched him in the mouth, my knuckles breaking against jagged teeth. As I twisted away, dodging the 'swang's reach as he bellowed in pain, I swiped out with my foot, catching his ankle and sending him stumbling into the wall. I dove around the creature and snatched a handful of scalpels. From the corner of my eye, I saw Peg pushing herself off the gurney and crawling toward a surgical room, where she could lock herself inside.

The 'swang didn't notice. He came at me full tilt, hitting me with enough impact to send my teeth clacking in my skull and our bodies into the other wall. The sheetrock dented and crumbled behind me, sending bits of plaster tumbling off the ceiling and into my hair. We fell to the floor, the 'swang landing on top of me. I pummeled my handful of scalpels into the side of the 'swang's face. A few blades made their way through the plastic and lodged into the side of his head.

The rest cut and dug into my hand, slicing my palm apart.

He bellowed his agony into my ear and heaved my back up off the floor. Before I got my leg between us, the 'swang slammed me down, my head cracking off the concrete floor with enough force to blur my vision and send a swell of metallic blood into my mouth. With a horrible roar that sent spit flying across my face, he buried his teeth into my shoulder, biting the tender flesh between my neck and shoulder.

Almost instantly, the 'swang raised his head, blinking dully at me. "You taste of 'swang," he said, astonished, with blood—my blood—trickling out of his mouth. Faster than a blink, he was back at my shoulder, yellow teeth locking around my collarbone, more frenzied than before.

I screamed, furious.

My thumbs found his eyes. I gripped his head with all my might, crushing his eyeballs until I felt them explode with a moist pop that sent fluids and thick mucus streaming down my arms. Sucking up my blood, blinded and screaming into my vein, the 'swang hefted me up again and slammed my head into the concrete. He didn't have as much force as the first time, but the hit was enough to send my vision scattering again with fireworks of dizzying light behind my eyelids.

Behind the 'swang, something ripped to life, a buzzing, chainsaw sound filling the room. Around the 'swang's body, Peg descended with a bone saw. Its whirring, flashing blades spun in a crisp, deadly blur inches from my face as she stabbed it into the back of the 'swang's head. Instantly, his bite on me released, and his body flailed. Blood and bone and thick drops of brain splattered back on Peg and down onto me, hitting the walls and floor and ceiling around us until all I saw was red. Even when the 'swang stilled on top of me, Peg screamed, cutting farther through the dead 'swang's skull.

The fire alarm turned off, leaving a silence more deafening than the wailing or Peg's screams when she finally stopped. She staggered back, hand to her belly, and dropped the still-buzzing saw. I heaved the 'swang off of me, his skull split down the middle, and slid across the floor, my traction lost with all the blood and brains.

The ward's door swung open and hunters and professors spilled in and came to a crashing halt at the scene in front of them. From their drawn weapons and vests, I knew instantly they'd known a 'swang was in the prison. Yet the only alarm that had sounded was the fire alarm I'd turned on. The thought clicked in my brain, but I didn't feel anything about it yet, because I had bigger problems.

My shoulder, where the 'swang had bitten me, was burning like Hell itself.

Burning as in pain.

As in I was feeling pain.

As in, *what the fuck?*

Horrible, searing flashes of white-hot blasts pulsed up my neck and into my spine, feeding through my entire body to alight every cell with crushing, brutal agony. Stunned, I stared down at my shoulder. It hurt so badly that my fingers on my right hand cramped and my eyes burned.

Motherfucker. I might actually cry. What the hell was happening to me? I couldn't move for the shock, or maybe it was from the pain. A tear tumbled down my cheek.

Was I dying? Is this what death felt like?

"Close off the ward!" Numbly I looked up as Dean strode into the ward with hardly a glance at Peg and me. "No one else gets down here. For God's sake, get them out of that shit, and get this room cleaned up!"

Hunters and professors alike jumped into action. A couple nurses pushed through from the back of the small crowd and carefully crossed over to Peg and me. As soon as the nurse touched Peg, she let out a wrenching sob, an arm wrapped tightly around her stomach. The nurse helping me pulled me up by my hurt arm and I would've yelped in pain if Dean hadn't looked my way right then.

He assessed me like a pig at a slaughter auction. Not dead. Not yet. Still his valuable prize. If he noticed how I trembled, he didn't comment or else wrote it off as a side-effect of killing a 'swang.

If he knew what was happening to his prize soldier right then, he would've been more nurturing. Or maybe he would have cut his losses and packed me off down to the lab, where he could test me over and over again.

A voice in my head said, *Do you feel it yet, Ollie? What if I cut her here?*

The basement. The young blonde girl with a pale round face and trembling lips. Me tied to a chair watching as Max and his father hurt the little girl until it was I who screamed, crying that *yes, yes I feel the pain.* The worst night of my life. My greatest fear. My greatest nightmare. It would happen all over again if Dean got his hands on me to test.

He would ask me, *Do you feel it yet, Ollie? What if I cut your brain here?*

Jolting me from my thoughts, Dean pointed to a nearby guard. "Get Peg cleaned up and on the first plane out." The barked order didn't sound like a compassionate one meant to send Peg back to her family after a traumatic event. He didn't want her around to shatter his precious control. She might have a hard time keeping quiet about a day-form 'swang trying to *eat her baby.*

A day-form 'swang who'd broken into the school. Who had walked amongst the teachers and students. No wonder the university needed those large iron spikes atop a thirty-foot fence. They weren't only worried about dogs. They were worried about 'swangs that could walk and talk just like us. Dean had lied to every young student here. Luke had lied to me.

I hissed.

"Are you okay?" the nurse asked, surprised to see me react.

"I'm fine," I snapped, still glaring at Dean, who instructed the discreet disposal of the 'swang's body.

The nurse led me into the hall, supporting half my weight as I leaned heavily into her, and sat me on a stool she pulled over. As she went to gather more supplies, I watched the other nurse and guard lead Peg into a private patient room at the far end of the hall. When the door closed, I couldn't hear her wails anymore. I wondered if I would ever see her again and if she'd heard what the 'swang had said about me tasting like an aswang.

The pain in my shoulder was enough to keep me from thinking about the 'swang's comment too much, which was good, because I would have cried. One thought did creep into my mind: I was having a reaction to 'swang saliva. But my reaction wasn't normal. The 'swang had bitten me and I was feeling it. All of it.

During all my research in the library, I'd never seen one saliva reaction listed as feeling more pain.

But then, I doubted any other hunters had been told they tasted of 'swang.

My nurse came back a moment later with a rolling tray of supplies to stitch me up and a bucket of water to clean me off. I stared at the ground, seething and trying not to scream from the pain cascading through me like fiery waves, while she sponged the gore off my head, chest, and stomach. When I was clean enough, she swabbed my wounds, each swipe making me dizzy enough I almost fell off the stool.

I tried to distract myself by thinking of something other than the pain, but I didn't have much practice at these kind of things. So I rocked to hide my dizziness and gritted my teeth. It took every ounce of control I had not to reach over and strangle the not-so-gentle nurse.

She didn't numb me before she started stitching up my shoulder and the deeper of my stomach wounds. Apparently, my reputation preceded me. I bore each stab of the needle and brutal tug with flared nostrils and hatred.

The pain stripped me bare and exposed all my damaged, ruined parts. I'd never felt so raw or vulnerable in all my life. The timing of feeling pain for the first time in my life was inconvenient to say the least. Monsters surrounded me. The pack of people who wanted me dead were circling closer and I could do nothing to stop them.

For the first time, I understood why Luke harped so much about my inability to feel pain being a weakness. It was. I finally understood. If I was in the woods right now fighting 'swangs, trying to defend my fellow hunters, I would get us all killed. I clamped my mouth around a whimper and prayed it was over soon. Every defense I'd built inside of me was because I couldn't feel pain. And feeling it now . . . it was like setting off a nuclear bomb in a glass house.

I was falling apart.

A growl rumbled low in my throat and I bared my teeth at anyone who passed. But when Dean walked over, his face crinkling up into a sickly sweet smile, the nurse had to hold me down in the stool, her stitching temporarily forgotten as she commanded me to hold still.

Dean crouched down in front of me like I was a child crying on the floor. "Ollie," he said, "I can't tell you how thankful we are that you saved Peg. That was a brave thing to do, but why were you down here?" The question was too pointed to fit into his fake gratitude. When it was clear I wasn't going to answer—words might break my loosely gripped murderous control—he added, "Whatever reason, I'm glad you were. Now, are you okay? You took a pretty good bite there."

The nurse ripped another needle pass through my skin and I hissed.

Dean's brows rose. I practically saw him taking in my

aggression and violence and accounting it to the 'swang saliva. Let him think what he wanted. I realized then, on that stool, as Dean's idiotic mustache curled above his widening smile as he categorized my vulnerabilities, that I would kill him. One day, he would die because of me. The violence— the beautiful siren call of it—curled through my blood and whispered to me, the first familiar thing I'd felt in the last few minutes. He'd lied to me and to all the other young students here. The day-form 'swangs weren't harmless. They were as bad as the night-form.

"Now, Ollie," he said, straightening and stretching out his back like he was the one who had fought a 'swang, "I think it goes without saying that you're not to mention this to anyone. Not Luke. Not Sunny. Not anyone. Got it?"

I couldn't hold it in any longer. "Their day-form is a sleeping husk, huh?" I jerked my chin toward the ward, where most of the hunters and professors were rapidly cleaning up. "Yeah, it was real fucking sleepy."

Dean blinked at me, and, for a moment, I thought he was about to hit me. But he didn't, and the disappointment was thick in the back of my throat. I could've ripped off his arm and let him bleed out if he'd hit me. When he threw back his head and howled with laughter, I glowered. "I like you, Ollie. You're funny."

He didn't wait for a response or my agreement not to say anything about yet another attack. As he left, he slapped my injured shoulder hard enough that the nurse squawked in indignation for me—a sentiment that didn't last long when I bent over and threw up on her white, thickly soled shoes.

Luke came to the now spotless ward to check on me. I didn't know how he'd heard I was down here, but he stormed into my private room with a growl and a slammed door. Seeing him stalk toward my bed, his gaze predatory, sent shivers down my spine. I tamped down the feeling and looked away.

He grabbed my chin and yanked my face toward him. My stomach fluttered and I almost moaned. I knew he hated when the uncontrolled side of him came out, but I couldn't resist this angry, unhinged Luke who made my blood sizzle and snap in my arteries. He didn't bother trying to control his rage. "What happened?" he snapped, leaning over my bed.

"I'm not allowed to say."

But those words told Luke all he needed to know. "You fought a 'swang in its day-form?" He released my face, his own paling.

Not answering, I sat up in bed, wincing as I moved. Luke honed in on my reaction and snarled. He yanked my blankets back and jerked up the hem of my new shirt. Nostrils flared, he took in the gashes across my belly and asked, voice tight with white-knuckled control, "Where else?"

Still not saying anything, I tilted my head back and pulled down the collar of my shirt. Luke leaned close and sniffed the wound. "It bit you?"

I nodded. He surged from the bed and paced away. Though he kept his back to me, I knew he was struggling to keep his anger under wraps. A long moment passed before he stalked back to the bed, his eyes unblinking and mouth set into a grim line. "How did you react to the saliva?"

With pain, I thought. But I didn't say it out loud. Luke wouldn't connect hearing the 'swangs and feeling pain when infected with their saliva, but he didn't have all the facts. I did, and I connected the dots. Especially after the day-form 'swang said I tasted familiar. Maybe Hex was right. Maybe I was part 'swang, an anomaly hybrid of some sort.

I admitted to myself it was the only thing that made sense.

"Ollie . . ." His voice snapped with warning.

His leash pulled taunt tonight, and I could cut straight through it with a look. Before, I might have done it just to see him go Hulk. But after today, after another lie—a lie Luke had participated in, after a baby almost died because Dean preferred sheep instead of smart students, I crossed my arms and blinked at the far wall. *I can't live with the lies. Yours and mine*, I wanted to say, but I didn't.

All the things I wanted to say to Luke, I held in. I couldn't allow any more. I had to separate us, give myself some distance. So that when I left, it wouldn't be so hard. And if he lied to me again, it wouldn't sting like this.

I would have to leave Fear University. That much was obvious. I couldn't swallow the lies like I'd thought, especially when they came from Luke. But beyond the lies, if I really was part 'swang, this was the most dangerous place to be. To live with people who would want my execution if they knew the truth . . . it wasn't a risk I was willing to take.

Not to mention Luke would hate me when he found out. Hate me and try to hurt me, kill me. Sunny too. Hatter. Thad. Jolene and her nasty friends. I wouldn't be able to bear that, to see the first real family I've had turn on me.

I was leaving. I just needed to figure out how.

"You're not going to talk to me?" I heard his silent threat: *I could make you.* And we both knew I would enjoy his making me. But I didn't give anything away.

He stepped back over to the bed, his hand reaching for me. Touching had always brought us together, and I never minded his hands on me. He'd always made me feel safe, but I pulled away from him and sank deeper in the bed, turning away and pulling the covers up underneath my chin. I clenched my eyes closed.

Luke's breathing went wild. His body heat filled the room and scorched me. He was ready to explode, but he held it in, stamped it down. I knew I'd hurt him, but it felt good to hurt him like he'd hurt me. He let loose a frustrated breath and left the room, softly closing the door behind him.

I wanted to know what he'd told himself to calm down. I wanted to know if he'd pictured his father and all the bad things he'd done to Luke over the years. I wanted to roll over and tell Luke to stop comparing himself to his nasty father. But I didn't. The first step I took toward distancing myself from him was letting him compare himself to that awful man.

And it broke my heart.

Later that night, another visitor slipped into my room.

I was dreaming of 'swangs who looked like walking skeletons when I heard my private room's door squeak open. A shadow appeared in the threshold—lumpy and misshapen. I surged up in bed, ready to fight, when the intruder said, "Ollie. It's me."

Peg.

I sighed and relaxed. "Are you okay? Is the baby fine?"

She crossed the little room to my bed and turned on the lamp. The warm light instantly filled the room and illuminated Peg's pale, cut face as she sat down beside me. "The baby's fine." Her eyes filled with tears. "I can't thank you enough. You saved our lives."

"You don't have to thank me." I couldn't bear her thanks. Not now. Not when I might be similar to the monster that almost killed her and her baby.

"Ollie, you don't understand." Peg shook her head, making the tears stream down her face, and took my hand. "I owe you everything."

"Peg, really it's fine—"

She clenched my hand tight enough my knuckles cracked in her grip. "I heard what it said."

My throat dried up. Whatever saliva was left in my shoulder gave a painful pulse. I cringed. "I don't know what you're talking about."

"You're different, Ollie. I know the truth." She glanced over her shoulder toward the door and the dark ward hall beyond. There was one night nurse on duty, and she was probably napping in some empty room. "I won't tell anyone. You can trust me."

I stayed very still in my bed.

"Somehow," she whispered, lowering her voice further and leaning closer to me, "you're part aswang. That's why that 'swang said that to you, right?"

She'd made the connection so easily. Even without

knowing all my other dirty secrets. But instead of feeling relief, it confirmed to me that if Luke ever knew, he would easily draw the same conclusion. And he didn't owe me any loyalty like Peg did.

But I'd trusted Peg from the beginning and she knew the dirty truth anyway. So I told her everything.

She listened and we talked, exchanging theories—hers from years of teaching and hunting. The hours slipped by, and Peg never wavered in her fervor to pay me back in whatever way she could. If she was disgusted by my alleged heritage, and we agreed there was a chance none of this was true, she didn't show it. Actually, she seemed excited, but not excited like Dean would have been. She genuinely thought I could serve the cause, that I wasn't a monster. But even she confirmed what had become my second greatest fear behind Max.

"You can't stay here, you know that right? If anyone finds out about you, you'll be dead. You can't trust anyone."

I nodded at her words, feeling heartbroken all over again. "I know," I whispered. "I'm leaving."

"You can't tell anyone." She glanced over her shoulder again. It was close to sunrise, and people would be stirring from their cells soon. "You could leave during winter break and come to my home. We could arrange it so that no one expects anything."

"What would your family say?"

"My husband would understand, and the only other family I have left is an uncle. But he stays up in Barrow year-round." She took my hands. "Ollie, you saved my life. It's the least we can do. I'm leaving today to go back home, but I'll arrange for a flight to bring you to Oregon, where I live. Okay?"

It was my only hope. If I passed finals and Fields, I could leave during winter break like a normal student. "Dean watches me like a hawk. I can't let him know something is up. We'll have to be careful."

"I'll be careful, and you need to be too. He's dangerous, Ollie. And if he knows about this," she hesitated, her eyes scanning my body, "he will never let you go."

A shiver crept down my spine and wrapped around my ribs, stealing my breath. "I know."

Peg glanced over her shoulder again. Any moment now, the ward would be full of nurses and doctors. She turned back to me and handed me a slip of paper with her address and phone number. "Don't hesitate to call me if anything urgent comes up. While I wait for you to arrive, I'm going to do some research on this. Maybe we can figure out if there's anyone else like you."

She straightened and stretched out her back. I noticed that her shoulders slumped, and her hands still shook. I stood next to her, careful with my thrumming shoulder, and we hugged. Allies, somehow. "Thank you," she said into my hair, her voice thick with tears.

"Thank you," I echoed back. She was saving me.

"Be careful, Ollie. Stay alive until break."

SIXTEEN

No matter what had happened on delivery day, I couldn't miss the study week before finals and Fields. The study week was supposed to be serious and wrought with anxiety that testing brought on. And it was, to some extent. But there was also excitement for the Halloween party and reenactment. The party would be at Tick Tock Bay until twilight, when the reenactment of the Tick Tock Massacre would take place. Afterward, the party would move inside, where it would likely get out of hand and too loud, but the professors would turn their heads so the students could let off steam, especially the first-years who wrung themselves out with anxiety for Fields, which, after an entire semester full of stressing out over it, was days away.

I wanted to scream that having a party in the bay, in the exact spot hundreds of students and professors had died before, was madness. The professors were flirting with disaster again so the students could feel normal. It didn't matter if the party moved inside at night, day-form 'swangs could kill the party-goers just as easily before nightfall.

It was insanity.

I shuffled from class to class during the study week, participating in the teacher-guided exam reviews, but I didn't listen. I knew I was ready to ace the exams, but I didn't care to pass anymore. Good grades wouldn't matter when I left this place. So when Sunny came to study Monday evening, looking for me when I didn't come to dinner, she found me in my bed, asleep.

Where I pretended to be every time she came looking for me after that. I slept a lot that week since Luke's training had been called off thanks to my injuries, and he didn't come looking for me. I'd pushed him away for good when he'd come to me in the ward after the attack.

As I lay in bed, my hand slipped under the pillow, fingers closing around the small razor blade. I pulled it out, careful not to prick my fingers. The edge of the blade was slightly dingy from use throughout the week, and, like I did every day before, I held the sharp edge to the skin on the underside of my arm and pressed until the metal bit into me.

And like it had every day before, pain washed over me until my eyes watered and my fingers trembled. I slid the blade back under my pillow and let the tears spill down my face and trickle into the corner of my mouth.

I didn't notice when my cell door slammed shut for lockdown.

Saturday rolled around quickly. Students set aside their books and took up the heavy mantle of party preparations. I kept to my bed, face turned to the wall. Sunny stopped by once, but I ignored her again.

It wasn't easy, trust me. Turning my back on Luke hadn't been that hard. He'd lied to me, and it had almost gotten me killed. We lied to each other more than we told the truth. But hearing Sunny's persistently hopeful voice calling my name from my door crushed me. Every. Time.

When the Death Dome fell silent, I told myself I wasn't going out there. I didn't support the stupid Halloween party and reenactment, even if it was done to honor the fallen. No way. But my eyes kept slinking to my cell door, and sleep remained impossible with the razor under my head and the pain claiming new territory in my body.

Mumbling a string of curses under my breath, I got out of bed and changed, pulling on my black jeans and knee-high, gray suede boots that hugged my calves like a dream. I layered after that to prepare for the cold outside. I pulled up the hood on my sweatshirt and slipped into my leather jacket before leaving.

The Death Dome was silent. Everyone was outside at the party, which was likely in full swing since it wasn't long before twilight. Even the ever-present guards in the tower were gone, their presence needed elsewhere, apparently.

I seriously hoped they had every single hunter, fifth-year,

and professor out there. The fools needed it.

As I walked outside, a brutally cold blast of air hit me in the face. With each day, Kodiak drew closer and closer to an Alaskan winter, and tonight was the coldest night of the year by far. I huddled deeper inside my jacket as I walked across the courtyard and down to the main gates.

Even if I didn't know where the bay was, I could have easily found it, along with every 'swang in the country, by sound alone. The fence blocked the bay but I knew exactly where it was from the blazing halo of lights. It was lit up like a neon homing beacon flashing "eat me" over the entire western seaboard. The music pulsed a steady electronic beat that reverberated in my heart. Underneath the pumping bass, laced through the melody so subtly it was an unconscious whisper in my ears, was the tick-tocking sound.

The music faded away as I focused on the sound, and all I heard was the tell-tale ticking of a clock. My mouth went dry.

These people were crazy. Would they know if real 'swangs approached?

I walked to the gates, and a pair of guards let me through with a warning about twilight and a swipe of my student card across their hand-held reader.

Before I headed to the party, I paused and turned back to the guards. They looked at me in surprise. "What's the security like tonight?"

They exchanged glances, clearly uncertain. "Um . . ."

I rolled my eyes. "What? You're not allowed to talk about that either?"

These guards knew me. They'd been on the fence wall

during the attack over break, and one of them had seen the bloody aftermath of the day-form's attack in the ward. He was the one who said, "No, it's not that. It's just . . . no other student has asked, and we weren't told it's a secret."

"Then there's not a problem."

"I guess not," he said with a shrug to the second guard. "Dean calls in nearby hunters. The woods are teeming with them. They also set up a temporary, highly charged electric fence. So don't wander too far from the party."

Keeping 'swangs out or containing the students who got too scared during the reenactment and ran? I raised a brow. "That's more than I expected."

The guard nodded. "It's a good tradition to keep up with, so we take all the precautions we can."

I almost let out a snort. A good tradition? Traditionally scaring the shit out of teenagers? "Thanks for the information."

With a salute, the guards hit the lever to close the gates. No going back now. I was a fool too, I guessed. Another bag of bones in the all-you-can-eat buffet.

The path was empty down to the bay. Everyone had arrived hours ago. Along the narrow path cutting through the dense birch trees hung hundreds of strings of twinkling lights wrapped through the branches to form a canopy of stars over my head. In any other circumstance, they might have been pretty. From up here, with the lapping of waves against the bay's stony beach and the crisp night air, I imagined nothing had happened and I was still the same girl hoping for a family and a purpose when I first came here.

I emerged into the clearing and stopped dead in my tracks. Over the bay, the sun was beginning its slow slog toward the horizon, sending oranges and deep purples, like a garish bruise, spilling over the cliff faces branching out along each side of the bay, creating a little divot of land carved out of the sea. It was beautifully horrifying and reminded me I wasn't the same girl who'd come here months ago.

Not even close.

Someone bumped into me, and I shot him a glare. Only then did I get a good look at who'd run into me, and I had to stop myself from gasping. The guy wore a mask of fur and a startlingly realistic gaping mouth with fangs, his eyes glowing through round holes beneath a sloping, hair-covered forehead. A headdress of thick, black fur covered his neck and back, trailing out behind him on the ground like a tail. He growled at me, making a claws with his hands before laughing and scampering off into the herd of bodies.

All around me, people wore 'swang masks. Others were dressed in the standard Halloween costumes: salt and pepper shakers, slutty cop, vampire, zombie, the guy from *Scream*, the guy from that other scary movie. But every costume, save for the ones who wore the tasteless masks, had wounds artfully painted on their face, throats, and arms. Blood splattered across their clothes, claw marks over their throats, intestines spilling from torn vests.

To watch them make a mockery out of their fear was almost too much for me to handle. They danced like idiots, grinding against each other on a raised wooden deck over the beach's rocks like their lives weren't on the line right this very moment. A table with a large fountain dispensed punch, where students kept returning for refills so often I wondered if it was spiked. I got my answer a second later.

"Hey! You're not in costume," a voice slurred in my ear. "No entry allowed without costume," he said, wagging his finger in my face. His breath reeked of rum.

I considered it great restraint on my part when I only told him what he could do with himself and gave him a look so mean that he held up his hands and backed away, as if I had a gun pointed at him.

I huffed a frustrated breath and turned to leave, having had my fill, when someone said, "I take it you don't approve of our sweet little traditions?"

Thad took a spot next to me. He had a scary monster mask resting on the top of his head and wore normal clothes. He'd scribbled a lopsided frowny face in red marker across the thick bandage around his neck. He took a long sip from his red cup.

"Nice costume."

"At least I tried. Where's your holiday spirit?" His grin stretched past the sides of his cup as he kept drinking. I rolled my eyes at him.

"Shouldn't you be patrolling the woods?" More lights wove around the trunks and limbs, making it impossible to see into the deeper, darker, possibly dangerous shadows. I felt like we were being watched. Hopefully we were. Hopefully we weren't.

He waved to his throat. "Still unfit for duty."

"You look fine to me." And he was; I knew for a fact

because I'd sparred with him for weeks and hit his throat on more than one occasion, not all of them accidents. He'd never flinched.

Thad lifted a shoulder in resigned disinterest. "Dean's rules."

I bit back a particularly nasty remark to that, and said, "I thought the whole point here was to not scare the younger students?"

He took another long sip from his cup. "They need some fear to help them transition into all they'll learn in the coming years, and if you dress up that fear with stupid costumes and alcohol and call it a party, then it's easier to swallow, I guess."

"Is that what you did the first time you came to this? Swallowed it like a good little boy?"

"If you want to talk about swallowing—"

"Cut the douchebag routine. I know you're not like that."

Thad raised his eyebrows in surprise but smiled. His eyes remained on the bodies swarming in front of the water. He scanned the party left to right and back again, on high alert. "I wasn't here for any of the parties."

"You didn't come to Fear University? I thought this was the only college that trained hunters?" I knew families were stationed all over the world, but there was only one Fear University.

Thad shrugged like it wasn't a big deal, his eyes on the dancing bodies across from us. "My parents taught me."

"I thought they were dead?"

"I didn't say they got to teach me for long."

"Is that allowed?" I asked, pressing him. "For hunters to

not learn here?"

"It's not exactly suggested."

I studied his face in profile. He was a hard guy to get a handle on. Sometimes he was an immature idiot, other times he was serious and brooding. In between, he was quiet and observant. It was odd. So were his non-answers. "So then why participate in this?" I waved to the party around us.

"Harmless fun?"

"You and I both know that's not the case at all. Do they bring in an electric fence for shits and giggles?"

"This is a rite of passage for these kids. They've been waiting for it since the day they started grade school and heard the ghost tales of Tick Tock Bay. They know they're going to be scared, but it's like a roller coaster clicking up the hill, you can't get off now. You gotta ride it till the end."

"The end being . . ." I gestured to my neck, eyes on his bandage.

"You got it."

"If they knew the truth, they wouldn't be out here."

"If they knew the truth, they wouldn't be here at all, and the 'swangs would've won the war."

"You sound like Dean."

The music faded away and the lights around us flickered once, twice, then went out. Someone screamed. From the tense silence that followed, a *tick tick tock* rose from the woods, quiet at first then building until my heart echoed each sound with a stuttering, hammered beat. The lights came back slowly, but they'd turned red, like a tidal wave of blood spilling across the ground and into the bay. Along the cliff, red spotlights illuminated hunched figures, their shadows slipping over the rock face. A drumming began, a war song.

I prayed this was the show and not an attack.

I don't know when I'd gripped Thad's arm, but he peeled my fingers back with a grimace. "No wonder you skipped college," I said under my breath, watching the red light play off the water and looking eerily similar to blood as the small rollers broke on the beach.

To the beat of the drums, the people atop the cliffs' edges began to writhe, dancing almost, as others on four legs joined them. In the night, against the red light, I only saw their silhouettes: the shape of a dog's head, a person falling to the ground, the dog jumping on them and tearing into them as their body flailed. Attacks happened all around the cliffs, the beats and ticking too loud for anything else.

Dramatics. Interpretive freaking dance. Seriously?

I blew a piece of hair out of my face and glanced around the party. Everyone was hushed, some with hands pressed against their mouths, others with their faces buried in their hands. Some trembled. I shook my head. These people were seriously out of their minds.

I turned to leave. "You're going to miss the grand finale," Thad said, looking very unexcited for said finale.

"What is it? A virgin sacrifice?"

Thad's mouth twitched in the corner, his light eyes dancing as he looked at me. In the night, violet flecks dotted his irises. I almost leaned closer to get a better look before I caught myself.

"Close. They pour blood over the first-years. A baptism

before Fields."

"You're joking."

"Yeah. But that would be pretty cool if they did. Could you imagine their faces?" He snorted into his cup as he took another long drink.

"That's sick. You need help."

He grabbed my arm as I tried to pass and leaned into my ear, his breath hot against my neck. "You're one to talk."

I didn't bother to dignify that with an answer. When I tried to leave this time, Thad let me. I went back up the trail beneath the canopy of lights, which had also turned red, casting a haunting shadow across the almost-dark trail. Drums thrummed behind me. My mind ticked in time with every tock. The skin beneath my eye began to twitch, and I regretted not pouring myself any of that punch before I left.

As I made my way up the path, an itch climbed up my spine, like I was being watched. Without being obvious, I searched deep into the woods' shadows, examining their dark folds for glowing eyes with upside-down reflections. My ears strained for the huffing and chuffing the 'swangs made. From my right, a twig snapped. I jerked to a stop.

Hello? I thought in my head, casting out the word like a fishing line. *Hex?*

No one answered, which somehow felt worse. I hadn't considered the fact that a 'swang other than Hex might be hunting me. One who might not want to save me, if "save" could be used to describe Hex's goals. I spun in a circle, heart hammering and ready to fight, when I hit something solid.

Instantly I thought 'swang.

My hands were up a split second later, my mind assessing possible weapons. Only then did I truly consider what I'd run into. *Dean.*

Honestly, I would have preferred a 'swang.

I dropped my hands, feeling stupid, but grateful the red twinkling lights didn't cast enough light for him to see my embarrassed flush. "Shouldn't you be at the party?"

Dean's smile glinted. "Just returning. Shall I walk you back?"

"Just leaving."

"Didn't find our little reenactment to your liking?" He cocked his head, mocking me, amusement dancing in his black eyes. I wanted to *disembowel* him. Somehow I'd liked this man weeks ago. I'd felt safe and comfortable with him, which was an idiotic error on my part.

"I think it's interesting how hard you work to hide the truth from the students only to terrorize them with tricks of light and creepy drums."

"Maybe I'm conditioning them with tricks of light and creepy drums."

I blinked in surprise. This was all some test? Anger thickened my throat. "This is the perfect time for a 'swang attack. Everyone is out after curfew. Not locked up in our little prison cells like good little hunters. It would be a blood bath, and they don't know to be afraid or cautious. You stole that right from them. They're blind to their own massacre."

Dean's smile slipped away, and something dangerously *interested* snapped in his eyes. He leaned down to stare into my face; I cringed back, disgusted. "Fascinating," he murmured.

"How does that brave mind of yours work?"

"Wouldn't you like to know?" I snapped.

"Oh, I would. Dearly. Maybe you will show me some time?"

"Screw off," I growled. I shoved around him, stomping up the path. The food from dinner curdled in my stomach.

"Be careful, Ollie," Dean called quietly after me. I didn't pause or turn around, but his words reached me nevertheless. "Remember our bargain. Remember how easy it would be to give Max a call." I hurried along faster. "That grave might still be waiting for you."

I whirled around. The words had been so faint, so barely there, that I didn't know if I'd heard him right. He couldn't know about the graves. "What did you say?"

"You're walking a dangerous tightrope," he said instead. "I would hate to see you fall off it."

With that, he slipped down the path, disappearing into the party. My fingertips began to tremble, then my hands, then my entire body. I told myself not to run back to the main building, but I sure as hell walked fast.

The same guards let me back through the gates, but this time I didn't stop to talk because I didn't trust my voice not to crack. I hurried to the main entrance, card ready and clutched in my hand. After practically breaking the scanner in half to get it to read my card, the door unlocked with a beep and I threw it open. My footsteps echoed across the silent entry, the air in the prison damp and cold. I shuddered. I wanted my bed. Maybe tonight, the pain would be gone when I tried with the razor.

As I passed the stairwell down to the ward, someone reached out and grabbed me, ripping me into the shadows. I shrieked into a hand clamped over my mouth, the sound muffled. Kicking and thrashing, I was dragged deeper into the shadows. Only when I took a deep breath, readying to fight like a banshee, did I smell Luke. My nose twitched around his particular spice: caramel and cottonwood.

When I stilled, he released me. "You better have a—"

"Listen to me," he snapped. From his pocket, he pulled out a key card and waved it in my face. "I can get us into the west wing lab."

I squinted at the card and finally recognized Mr. Abbot's face. "How did you get that?" I whispered.

"Mr. Abbot's coward ass is drunk in a rook's nest. He won't miss it if we hurry."

"I passed Dean going to the party."

"I know," Luke said, palming the card. "I followed him."

I hadn't seen or talked to Luke in days. I wanted to ask what he'd been doing, but I reminded myself that I didn't care. My stupid eyes wandered down to his lips, remembering how they'd felt and tasted, his breath like the caramel candies he constantly ate. My breath hitched.

"Don't look at me like that."

My eyes snapped back up to his, totally busted. "Like what?"

"As if you haven't ignored me all week like a spoiled brat."

"Excuse me?"

"Not now. I want to see what's in that lab, and I figured you did too. Are you in or do you want to go pout in your room some more?"

I waved down the dark stairwell, focusing really hard on not kicking him in the balls. "Lead the way."

I followed Luke down to the lab, past the night nurse on duty in the ward and into the sterile east lab. I needed to see the big bad they were doing in the west wing. The lab might hold some answers that would help Peg and me figure out my situation when I went to her over winter break. I was also hoping if I saw whatever Dean was doing behind locked doors, hopefully it would make leaving a little easier. Though I hated Dean and his lies, this place and the people had gotten under my skin and close to my heart. I didn't want to leave.

My skin itched at the thought of more running. I gritted my teeth against the feeling and crossed my arms over my chest, waiting as Luke opened the large steel door into the west wing.

He swiped the card. The silence as we waited for the door to unlock was unbearable.

"Are you sure—"

The unlocking beep interrupted me. Without a glance spared for me, Luke pushed down the handle and shouldered the heavy door open.

A wave of cold air hit us. Luke shivered and the skin tightened over my face. The air inside circulated from a fan overhead and smelled of chemicals and decay. I forced my feet to move away from the door and farther into the dark room. No lights flashed on above us.

From his pocket, Luke pulled out a flashlight and flicked it on. A wall of narrow and shallow doors over to our right. Glass cabinets full of tools and specimen jars to our left. And right in front of us, inches from my hand, a body laid out on a table.

Surprised, Luke jerked, sending the light upward to illuminate an entire row of metal tables, long and narrow, stretching out before us. All occupied.

I'd prepared myself to see anything, but my heart still thudded in my chest as I traced the hulking lines of the body closest to me, the massive claws, the glinting fangs. A 'swang switched to its night-form even in death. From the wounds to its head, I easily recognized it as the one who had attacked Peg. Luke cut me a scathing look like he recognized it too. I shrugged. He had his secrets, so I had mine.

"They're examining 'swangs. That's not too weird," I whispered. Gross. But it made sense, I guessed.

Luke walked around to the front of the body and shined his flashlight into its damaged skull. "No, they're examining their brains. Look."

I really could have gone without looking, but I joined him at the front of the table with my breath held and peered inside its cracked skull. The brain was gone. Not that there had been much left after Peg had gone Rambo on its ass.

"Also," I said, swallowing as I tried not to smell too much of the thick formaldehyde wafting off the body, "not that weird."

Luke headed deeper into the room, and since he was the one with a flashlight, I followed. A few more bodies were covered, which Luke revealed with a calculated flick of his wrist. All 'swangs. Likely ones he and the guards had taken down during the attack over fall break. Hex's pack. These were 'swangs who'd come for me, to rescue me. I averted my eyes as Luke studied their heads, noting each was without a brain.

Holy shit. Did I actually feel bad for these monsters? For dying because they'd come for me? I almost raked my hand through my hair until I remembered where I was and what I might have accidentally touched in here.

When Luke had examined at all the bodies on the tables, he crossed to the refrigeration unit on the other wall. "Of all the things I expected," he murmured, "a morgue was not one of them."

"Not that unexpected," I defended. Ugh. What was wrong with me? Seriously?

Luke met my eyes. "Then why are only the highest up in the university allowed in? Why not the other doctors and nurses?"

I didn't get to answer before he tugged the thick handle on the first door, which was a couple feet tall and wide. I knew what to expect as I opened the door farther for him, and he pulled out the retractable table. But some part in my brain registered the shape of this body was different, and when Luke pulled back the sheet, we stared down at the face of a human.

Black scars stood out on his gray face like thick, freshly inked lines. Down his neck, chest, and shoulders were more, zig-zagging across his skin like a horrible constellation. He wasn't old. Not even close. I glanced up at Luke in time to see his horror, his shock slash across his face before he ripped the sheet back over the body. "You knew him," I said.

"No brain like the others." Luke's voice was as icy as the body between us. He shoved the table back inside the shelf and grabbed the door from me before he shut it as silently as he could.

"You knew him," I repeated.

"I went to his damned funeral. I saw them lower the casket." He raised his eyes to mine, cold and glaring. "He had a hunter's burial—a sacred sendoff, an honorable one, but his body is *here*."

This wasn't okay, I knew. This wasn't expected. The 'swangs, sure. They were the monsters, though the guilt still nagged at me for thinking of them like that. Examining their brains was a reasonable jump. But the hunters? They deserved more than experiments and cold slabs. They were human.

"I'm sorry." I knew it wasn't enough.

Luke shook his head and turned to the next door. His shoulders were tense, his jaw dancing with every clench of his teeth. He was barely holding it together. "We don't get many things," he said under his breath. I walked to the next door, trying to see his face, but he kept it turned away from me. "Peace certainly isn't one of them. Death is meant to be our resting time."

I didn't know what to say. Maybe there wasn't anything to say. Never before had I felt like more of an outsider than I did now. There was no comfort I could offer Luke, because I didn't understand. I felt more guilt for Hex's pack laying on the tables in the open than I did for Luke's friend. So I screwed my mouth shut.

One by one, Luke opened each door and pulled back the sheet. Some of the bodies were old hunters, some young, but Luke knew each and every one. Deaths, he said, that went back a month or so. They were all here, thirty dead, a number that didn't count those who'd perished outside of Alaska. All with missing brains.

"This isn't a coincidence," he said after closing the last door. His last homage to a fallen hunter.

"The brains?"

"The rat studies. The 'swangs." His eyes went to the doors. "Us. He's looking for a connection. For a way to make us immune to pain. Like you. It's the only way to explain why he took the hunters' brains too."

I couldn't meet his eyes. He might see the truth there. I understood this morgue all too well; I easily saw what Dean was looking for. He wanted to re-create a disease like mine. But maybe, like me, he had already figured out my disease wasn't really a disease at all.

Hex's words ran back through my head. *These people will hurt you. They'll cut you apart to figure out what makes you different.*

Like he'd read my thoughts, Luke said, "Like *you*. That's why Dean is so fixated on you." His flashlight seared into my eyes. "Ollie, he doesn't want you for some kind of super solider. He wants to study you, watch you, see how you react to fear and pain. Then he wants to . . ." His eyes traveled back to the refrigerator doors, to the bodies within. Then, more quietly, he said, "You were right. He's going to kill you."

"It's a disease," I said, praying Luke wouldn't hear the lie. "He can't recreate that. I'm not special."

"He can sure as hell try."

I threw my hands up. "Then why hasn't he killed me already? Why not get it over with and spill out my brains so he can pick through them and get his stupid fucking answers?"

"Because he's not done experimenting with you. He doesn't know all your strengths and weaknesses yet. He wants to see how far you'll bend until you break." I cringed at his words, but Luke didn't notice or care. "*Then* he'll kill you."

"Great," I mumbled, "something to look forward to."

"We're getting the hell out of here."

I didn't object, worried if we stayed a moment longer in this morgue, Luke would connect more dots about how special I really was. He didn't know the full truth about being able to communicate with the 'swangs in their night-form or the latest development in my specialness: feeling pain after being bitten. But I didn't underestimate him enough to think he couldn't make the leap and realize what I already had. What Dean might have realized too: that if I were laid out in this morgue, cold and naked and brainless, I would be with the 'swangs, not the humans. Perhaps he'd even known from the beginning.

Peg was right when she'd said it was too dangerous for me to stay here, but I couldn't bear for anyone to learn I was their enemy, a half monster. Let them know I was a murderer. That I was messed up and mean and a bitch. Let them know that. But not this. Never this.

Especially not Luke or Sunny.

Our hurried footsteps echoed across the lab, the hiss of the door sealing behind us, locking with a beep. We didn't talk as we fled through the east lab, but Luke's eyes flicked over to where the rats were kept for the fear conditioning tests. Was he thinking I was the ultimate conditioned rat? I was. We took the steps two at a time, only slowing when we snuck past the ward entrance. Then up more steps and slipping into the main entry.

The students were coming back from reenactment. Moving the party from outside to inside. We blended in with them easily, our shocked, freaked-out faces perfectly matching theirs but for completely different reasons.

A hand reached for mine, surprising me because Luke was on my other side. I looked over, half expecting to see Thad, but instead, Sunny looked back at me, her eyes wide and terrified, cheeks slick with tears. She was trembling and unable to form words. I should have been out there with her during the reenactment or made her leave with me. Like a good friend. Instead, she'd watched it alone. She whimpered, needing me to hug her like a normal friend.

Had she pictured her dead brother? Imagined what it had been like for him to be ripped apart and eaten? From her apparent anguish, she had.

But if I looked too closely I saw her stretched out in the morgue, her pretty head cracked open and brainless.

I backed away, pulling my hand from hers. Through the crowd, I saw Hatter threading his way to us, his eyes fixed on

Sunny's wretched face. A sob broke free from her mouth as I shook my head. I couldn't. I just couldn't.

"Ollie," Luke said, shocked. He and Sunny watched me back away, bumping into people as I made my retreat.

Hatter reached Sunny and pulled her against him, tucking her head beneath his chin so that she was turned away from me. If looks could kill, Hatter would have slayed me right there. I deserved it.

I deserved a slot in the morgue amongst the 'swangs. Where I belonged. If my friends looked too closely at me, they would see the truth.

Luke's shocked expression burned into my back as I fled into the Death Dome. He didn't follow.

I crashed up the stairs, once again the only one in the dorms, and raced for my room. I didn't wait for lockdown. I slammed the door shut behind me, forcing it to lock early. Locking the monster inside. I nearly fell to my knees as I staggered toward my bed, tears completely blinding me. Pain like I'd never felt tore through me, ripping me to ribbons. My ribs were scalding pokers stabbing my insides. My heart a steak on the grill, charred and burnt over and over.

I hit my bed with a heavy thump. Immediately, I reached for the razor under my pillow, the cold metal a new kind of disgust. But I had to know. I dug it into the pad of my thumb, watching mutely as a huge tear of blood welled in the new wound.

I didn't feel a thing. On the outside.

SEVENTEEN

Monday came quickly. I hadn't moved from my bed other than to use my little bathroom or stare at my reflection in the mirror. I'd thrown away the razor sometime on Sunday, not trusting myself to stop testing my lack of pain.

The doors unlocked with a resounding snap across the Death Dome. Numbly, I stood and dressed, pulling on whatever I'd left on the floor from Saturday night. I grabbed my backpack, not certain what books were still inside, and slid open my door. The students were mostly gone, only the late stragglers rushing by me.

A moment slipped by before I realized why everyone was on time today of all days. Finals. A day of testing. Testing that I'd studied for with Sunny. My stomach twisted, but I walked down the metal gangway toward the stairs, putting one foot in front of the other.

My first test—Fear Theory—was to the left, second floor of the west wing, but I went straight. I knew I needed to take the test, but I needed some air to clear my head. With a swipe of my card, I was outside.

Instead of the sun in my eyes, there was Luke. Hulking and bearing down on me with a vicious, ripping growl. He'd been waiting on me. Before the door closed, he had me back inside. I didn't object as he towed me toward the west wing, a string of curses constant on his lips.

He threw open my Fear Theory class door and deposited me inside. Every student's head snapped up, their precious quiet disturbed. "She got lost," Luke snapped at Mr. Abbot, who was ready to object. "Because she's stupid. A complete idiot. Total asshole."

"Miss Andrews." Mr. Abbot turned back to his book, which he was reading at his desk. "Please take a seat. You'll get no extra time at the end."

"She won't need it."

I started to walk away when Luke grabbed my backpack and pulled me back to whisper in my ear, "You better actually take the test, or I swear I'll put you in that morgue myself."

"Great pep talk," I muttered, trying to pull away from him. Finally, he let my backpack go, and I stumbled forward.

The classroom's door slammed shut, but I didn't hear him stomp away, so I figured he was going to wait right outside, ready to haul me to my next exam.

The professor handed me the exam and a pencil. Some

students watched me take my spot in the very back, their expressions concerned and friendly, but most ignored me. I dropped my backpack onto the floor and sat down, staring at the paper in front of me. I could leave it blank, but I had to pass if I had any hope of leaving for winter break. It wasn't a guarantee of Dean's trust if I passed finals and Fields. But it was a good start.

So I lowered my head and took the test. When the bell rung, I'd been done for twenty minutes. I'd aced the test; Sunny had prepared me well, even if we hadn't studied in over a week.

As I walked to the front, one of the last ones to turn in my paper, Luke stalked in. Before I handed over my test, he ripped it from my hand and looked over it, making sure I'd answered every question. When he was certain I'd completed the test, he tossed it at Mr. Abbot and towed me to my next class.

"What the hell is wrong with you?"

Luke slammed the door to his bedroom as I set my backpack on the floor. I was exhausted, mentally drained. Six exams in one brutal, tiring day. The Combat and Weapons Theory exams had been the worst and longest. But I'd dug into them, relished them, needing at least someone—even if it was the professor grading them—to know that I hadn't given up. That I could have made it as a civvie here at Fear University. I wasn't leaving over winter break because I was too stupid to handle the school.

I needed someone to know that.

"What do you mean?" I sighed and sank to the edge of his bed, pulling harshly on my cramping fingers to straighten them back out.

He flung a stack of books off his desk and onto the floor with a bat of his hand. I looked up, brows raised at his outburst. All ten fingers thrashed against each other, his chest humming with a low growl. "You know exactly what I mean! Why were you leaving this morning? What happened with Sunny after the party?" He stalked over to me and got into my face. "Why are you being such a bitch?"

Fine. I lost it.

The violence singing in my blood was a siren call impossible to ignore. Didn't want to anyway. I punched him in the mouth, satisfied when his head snapped back and blood spattered from his busted lip onto my knuckles. "Don't call me a bitch, asshole."

Recovering with a ripping growl, he grabbed my chin faster than a blink. "Don't call me an asshole."

His pupils were so wide and engulfing that his eyes looked entirely black. He was totally losing control with me. The first lick of fear sliced through me, and I loved it. Wanted it. Deserved it.

He shoved away from me, but I didn't let him retreat or gather himself. I didn't know why I did it, why I needed to see him completely lose control with me now, of all times, when I knew I was leaving. Maybe it was because I might never have another chance. Maybe it was because I wanted to tell myself he wouldn't hate me when he knew the truth about me. Maybe I really was a monster. But I didn't back down.

When he went to open the bedroom door, to stalk out and likely leave me here, I stepped in front of him and slammed the door closed. We stood so close that our chests touched, his dark eyes glaring down at me, each breath exhaling through flaring nostrils.

"Move," he commanded. He wanted me to step away, to relent like everyone else did around him, but I didn't. I knew he was afraid of acting like his father, but I wasn't. I craved that kind of violence.

Maybe that was what I wanted. To be hurt. Punished. Like a 'swang should be.

I took a step closer.

"Ollie," he warned, his voice rasping over my name like a curse word. Heat pooled between my legs. When I looked up at him, I pushed my breasts ever so lightly against his chest. Instantly, my nipples hardened.

"Where were you going this morning?" he asked, his voice deep and crackling like lightning.

I knew he meant this morning, but I said, "I'm leaving over winter break. I won't be back."

Instead of going ballistic, Luke's breathing turned slow and lethal. I'd never seen him fight 'swangs, but for some reason, I knew this was his killing face.

"You shouldn't push me."

"Why not?" I put my hand on his chest and trailed my fingers down to his hip, where I pushed aside the material of his thermal and hooked my finger in his jeans. From beneath my lashes, I looked up at him, my heart breaking. "Are you scared?"

That did it. He grabbed my neck, and I gasped as he slammed me against the door, my breath choking in my throat. His eyes raked down to my heaving chest, and I could've sworn they darkened.

The tiny sliver of fear sparked and grew into a flame.

I fisted his shirt in my hand and shoved. He didn't move an inch. Instead, he crushed his mouth to mine, prying open my lips and forcing his tongue inside. He devoured me, consumed me. I held on, working my mouth against his as I gasped for breath whenever he let me up for air.

One hand stayed on my throat, while the other raked down my ribs and under my shirt, forcing the material up until he was at the swell of my breast, fingering the edge of lace. Through my bra, he rubbed his thumb over my nipple. Fire flooded down into my stomach, dripping lower until it sizzled between my legs. I ached to have him inside me, to feel his powerful body above mine. I knew it would be rough with him, but that was exactly how I wanted it.

He shoved up my bra and palmed my breast, squeezing and making me gasp into his mouth from the pressure. I grabbed a hold of his hair and pulled until he groaned too. The hard length of him bulged against his jeans and pressed into my belly. When I reached for it, he growled and grabbed my chin, forcing my head back against the door.

"Is this what you wanted?" His voice was hot in my ear.

I gave him a few quick nods as I tried to catch my breath.

He didn't bother unbuttoning my jeans before he jerked my hips free. The material scratched down my skin, but he didn't pull them all the way off, leaving them below my ass. I tried to wiggle them down, but he trapped me.

He shoved his hand between my legs. There wasn't much room, and I ached to spread myself open for him. I groaned in frustration, but he pressed me into the door. His fingers bit through my flesh and shoved inside me. I threw back my head and would've screamed loudly if Luke hadn't clamped his hand over my mouth in time to muffle the sound.

"You're wet." He withdrew his fingers like he was angry with me for wanting him.

He released his grip on my mouth. "I li—"

The fingers that had previously been inside me went deep into my mouth. I gagged, but Luke pushed harder. "You're too wet," he hissed.

I gasped for air when he finally removed his hand. He didn't seem concerned at my near strangulation. His eyes roamed down my body, lingering on my trapped legs.

"I want you," I said, my voice hoarse.

"Oh, it's too late now. You're going to get me."

He hefted me up and slung me over his shoulder. I yelped, getting an up-close and personal view of his ass. We crossed the room to his bed. A bright, blazing flare of heat spread across my ass cheek and I hissed in indignation, knowing he'd spanked me. Luke slapped me again, and I jerked in his hold, growling and kicking at his chest.

"Stop that, you asshole," I said, jabbing my elbows into his back. His muscles were so hard that I knew I was only injuring myself.

"Keep struggling, Ollie," Luke hissed. "That's what I like."

To illustrate his point, he plunged his finger deep into me, going deeper as I clenched and howled in rage.

"Dream on," I sputtered, wiggling against his finger. I struggled against him, but I liked the feeling of his finger pulsing inside me as I thrashed. I pushed myself farther onto his hand. I was moaning by the time he threw me off his shoulder.

I landed on the bed, my trussed-up legs in the air. I reached for my jeans, but he slapped my hands away. "Hands up," he said. With a hand on my ankles, he leaned over my body and wrenched my arms above my head. My breasts were open to him, my shirt and bra shoved beneath my throat. I stared up at him and felt my wetness drenching the insides of my thighs.

His nostrils flared as he leaned back, eyes falling to my ass. I tried to pull my ankles out of his grip but he held on. His hands went to his fly. I couldn't see the length of him, but I felt it when it sprung free against my legs. He positioned his knees on the edge of the bed and hooked my ankles over his left shoulder. "Don't touch me or I'll lose it. Got it, Ollie?"

The way he said it made me wonder if the 'swang saliva left any residual effects inside of him. Something that would make him afraid to let me touch him. Like he might unleash on me.

"Luke," I gasped out, wiggling against him.

Knowing he could be so wild, turned me on. Knowing I was the only girl in the world who could take him, turned me on even more.

He guided himself through my clamped legs, found my

entrance, and shoved inside.

I groaned, my complaints lost in my mouth, my hands fisting the sheets over my head. My back came completely off the bed. Luke tightened his grip on my legs and pounded into me with his head thrown back, his neck turning red and corded with his strain. "Holy fuck," he hissed, eyes heavenward as he beat himself inside me. He looked back down at me, his eyes hooded, his arms supporting my weight as he lifted me farther off the bed for a deeper angle. His jaw clenched and unclenched with each powerful stroke. I saw the side of his ass, muscles flexing, as he rammed into me.

I clenched my eyes shut at the sheer velocity of what I was feeling. Every inch of me stretched around him, opening for him to make me his until I was completely consumed. He was so big inside of me that he filled every inch of my body, though I knew it couldn't be possible. My lungs constricted, my heart in a vice. I couldn't breathe or move or whimper. He had me completely trapped.

That slice of fear shivered through me again, beginning between my legs and spreading out like a strobe light up my spine, pulsing through me until I was bucking against his hold, screaming as the orgasm ripped through me. Luke grunted as I came, shoving in and out of me faster.

I arced off the bed, my hands still above me and holding on for dear life.

He threw back his head and came violently, as I knew he would. Everything was electric inside me. I felt nothing but him, taking me completely.

Finally, he stilled deep inside me. He leaned over my legs

and rested his head on my shins. His expression was so vulnerable, so unguarded that I remembered his command from earlier and shivered. Luke felt my reaction and reared off of me, as if he thought he'd hurt me.

His absence made me flinch. I sat up on the bed as he paced away. He stopped by the door with his head bowed.

He trembled.

Suddenly, seeing him like this, I knew I'd pushed too far. This was my fault.

Luke said something. "What?" I managed to choke out.

He turned around and looked at me, his heartbreak echoing out through his wide eyes. "I'm sorry," he repeated, his voice rasping. "I'm sorry I hurt you."

"Luke." I might cry. "You didn't hurt me. But what—"

"I did!" he shouted. "I hurt you and you couldn't even tell."

I recoiled like he'd slapped me. "You didn't. I liked it, Luke."

Disgust washed over his face. Disgust toward me, like I'd been expecting. Just not for this. "What's wrong with you?" His question was quiet, damning. "How can you like being hurt? Are you that fucked up? Can you feel *anything*?"

I stilled. My heart might have stopped beating. "What happened to *you*?" I shot back.

Luke shook his head, shoving a hand through his hair. "This is fucked up," he said mostly to himself. Then to me, he said, "We can't do this. We're too screwed up for each other."

He was right. We were both screwed up. I'd seen that

tonight first hand. His father had screwed him up. 'Swang saliva had screwed him up. I looked away from Luke and told myself this made things easier. "Fine."

"I mean it, Ollie."

I stood from the bed and pulled up my jeans and righted my shirt. "I do too."

On my way to the door, he blocked me. "But you're not leaving."

"You said we're too screwed up to be together!" I flung my hands up in frustration.

His expression softened, the old, fight-for-control Luke returning. "I meant the school. You can't leave."

"Whatever you command, Luke." I shoved past him, and this time, he let me. It wasn't until I was outside in the cold air that I finally breathed.

I didn't know whether I was happy or sad that I'd finally broken him. Either way, I'd done it, and amongst his broken pieces I'd found a broken man, a man who wouldn't let himself be touched. Guilt lashed up from my stomach, making me sick with myself. He needed his control, and I'd taken it from him. He would likely hate himself for this. So why had I done it? To claim a piece of him before I left? To mark my spot?

Ollie was here, whipped across his back like twenty lashes.

I choked on a sob, but I stuffed it back down my throat and squared my shoulders. It was done now. I was destructive enough to know that I'd set out to make him hate me, and I'd done it. The worst damage possible. Mission accomplished.

Can you feel anything?

No. No I can't.

Now I needed to focus on passing Fields so I could meet Peg during break and never come back. By then, no one would even want me back.

EIGHTEEN

ields started at sundown on Tuesday and would last all
night.

We stood by the iron gates at the estate's entrance,
bare tree branches scratching above our heads in the frosty
night air. A guard far up in the closest rook's nest called out
names one by one, and the student shuffled through the gates
with two guards, like a death row prisoner on his final walk.
No one knew where they were going or what to expect.
Fields were the same every year, but they were also Fear
University's greatest secret. Another rite of passage that the
older students didn't share with the younger ones.

Yet another measure of fear. A way to control students.
To dole out the right kind of fear at the right time. To build

warriors with blindfolds on and trembling swords pointed in the right direction.

I hated it.

From the back of our group, someone puked. Another few cried softly in the back. No one spoke. It didn't help that there were no lights around us to splinter the dark shadows at our feet. Though we were still inside the gates, the scare tactics worked almost too well.

Not on me, of course. I couldn't give two shits about Fields. I needed to do well enough to pass so that I would have a measure of freedom during winter break to go to Peg's house. I knew I would pass. I had another worry.

My eyes cut over to Sunny. She huddled deep in her coat, her face almost obscured by her ear muffs, scarf, and hood pulled down tight over her face. I didn't need to see her face to tell she was freaking out. Her shoulders were brushing her ears, fingers fretting constantly inside the pockets of her jacket. I wanted to tell her it would be okay, but I knew she wouldn't appreciate it after Saturday night.

I wanted to apologize for leaving her but I couldn't. If I did, if she understood, I wouldn't be able to leave Fear University. Since I'd come here months ago, Sunny had become my family. My only family. Luke and Hatter too. No matter what, they couldn't see the truth of who I was. They would hate me. And that would kill me.

Gritting my teeth, I returned my glare back to the gates, daring the guards to pick me next.

They didn't. Two more students left, one at time, through the gates. Our group got smaller and smaller, the space between us growing wider with each departure. We were little islands separated by great oceans of fear. I imagined I smelled it oozing from their pores as they trembled deep in their coats. It made the November air thick and heavy, forcing the students to take deep gulping breaths.

This would traumatize them more than the Halloween reenactment had. I understood now why the older students kept so many secrets from the younger ones: they were too scared, too horrified from their own experiences to talk about them. Dean, the other professors, and a handful of hunters, including Luke, were slowly scarring the students around me and steering them from one horror to the next.

Conditioning them.

It was all so carefully orchestrated, so thought out, that it was almost pathological. Give the first-years the right fear. The good fear. Fear of the night. Fear of the 'swangs. But not the truth. Because to know the truth was to run. And they couldn't afford any more running. They needed bodies in the war.

Luke had been right about this place, this war, not being right for civilians. They would crumble here because they hadn't been raised to expect it like the other students had.

Up in the rook's nest closest to the gate, a walkie-talkie squawked. Time to walk the next student over. The guard leaned over the rook's nest and said, "Change of plans. Everyone else is testing in pairs from now on to speed things up a bit. Up next . . . Ollie Andrews and Sunny Lyons."

My stomach dipped. I shot a glance at Sunny, but she pointedly ignored me as she slipped through the crowd toward the gates. Reluctantly, I followed, the students around me refusing to look me in the eyes as I passed. These were the same people who sat at my lunch table, slapped me on the back in the halls, laughed at my jokes. Now, they shifted away from me as I weaved through them, too terrified to look fear in the face and see me. I didn't think of them as cowards, I felt sorry for them. This wasn't right, wasn't fair. And no one knew.

The gate opened a tiny fraction, enough for us to suck it in and shove ourselves through. "Sunny . . ."

She ignored me and joined the guards outside the fence. There were four to walk us over, which surprised me. I sighed loudly through my nose, earning a glare from Sunny.

We traipsed through the woods, walking a narrow path parallel to the bay. Our footsteps echoed off the packed dirt, mingling with sounds of the bay's small waves and the nocturnal creatures out scavenging before winter. The trees towered above us, blocking out the moon, so that we relied only on the guards' powerful flashlights sending mighty beams sweeping across the forest's shadows. More guards and hunters were positioned along the trail and in tall platforms in the trees, where they kept their eyes trained on the woods around them, huge rifles ready in their arms.

No one talked. No one looked at me. But while the silence and foreboding nature of the hike made Sunny shiver with fear, it made me want to roll my eyes. The walk represented another test to see how the students reacted to the darkness, to be outside the safety of the fences.

As we made our way to wherever Fields was held, I

thought about all the over-processed dramatics, like making us stand outside in the cold and walking through the woods at night. It was too much. Enough that any normal student would be useless from fear when they arrived at the testing. I furrowed my brow. Dean had to know this. He was pushing them too hard before the actual testing had even begun, which could mean one thing: Fields wasn't an actual test. It had to be something relatively easy. Maybe they were evaluating a student's fear to see how they reacted, how they managed all this buildup. It made sense.

At any time, I expected the guards to dump us in the middle of the woods. Then, in the shadows of the trees, a few hunters would make clock sounds, like we were about to be attacked. Maybe Dean would be sitting up in a platform with a pen and notepad to scribble down our reactions.

A stupid test, but one I was happy to go through. Easy to pass. Even for Sunny.

When my nose was dripping snot and my eyes watering from the cold night's air, we finally made it to the top of the hill the path led us up. On its crest stood a large pen with thick bars around its perimeter and a large, vaulted ceiling of mesh razor wire and bright spotlights shining down into the cage. From inside the bars came a scream and a thrashing sound. Sunny jumped and grabbed my arm, her eyes bulging.

"It's okay," I murmured. "You're fine."

Realizing what she'd done, she let me go and stepped away, not meeting my eyes.

Not the woods scenario then, I thought. Something a little different. More involved. I scrutinized the cage for any clues and strained my ears to hear anything that might be helpful. But nothing else came.

The guards rushed us around to the front of the cage and into a small holding room with no windows and two doors, one leading back outside and the other presumably leading into the cage. The door leading back outside locked behind the guards on their way out. We were alone.

In here, the sounds of whatever happened in the cage couldn't reach us. I decided to be thankful for Sunny's sake; she already looked pale enough, her hands shaking so hard that she shoved them under her arms.

The room was small with a low ceiling, where one long fluorescent light clicked and hummed above us. The walls and floor consisted of cold concrete. Along the doorless side walls sat low-slung benches; Sunny took a seat and hung her head between her knees like she might pass out. Unable to sit, I paced, pulling off my gloves and heavy jacket. In the cage, I doubted I would be worried about my warmth, and the holding room was making me sweat.

I would never, ever get used to being locked up.

I turned to Sunny and took a deep breath. "I know you don't like me right now, and I understand. But we might have to work together in there. I want you to know that I have your back. I won't let anything happen, okay?"

Sunny lifted her head but didn't meet my eyes, her trust in me shattered. "I have to pass the test too," she said under her breath.

"I'll make sure you pass it."

My words caught her attention, and she squinted at me

under the bright fluorescents. "What about you?"

"It doesn't matter."

"What the fudge does that mean?" Now she glared at me, unrelenting, and pushed up her glasses like she meant serious business.

"It means we need to focus in there and work together."

She didn't believe me. "So I'm supposed to forget the other night? That you've been ignoring me all week?" Her body relaxed slightly, and actual concern crept into her voice. "Ollie, what the hell happened? What aren't you telling me?"

"I—"

I didn't get to finish. The cage door unlocked and a red light above it began flashing. From an intercom, Dean's voice crackled. "Enter the testing area."

Sunny lurched up with a squeak. I nodded toward her jacket and thick layers. "Take off anything you don't need. I think we'll have to face a 'swang in there."

"What?" She kept swallowing like she might be about to throw up. "I can't—"

"You can. Ditch the jacket. Let's go."

The cage. The scream. All the lights. It had to be a 'swang. But there was no way in hell Dean was making students fight in their first year. We had to be separated from the 'swang by something. To test our fear. Our reactions. It would be easy. We would both pass.

I waited for Sunny at the door, and, when she'd jerked off her extra layers, I heaved it open. Together we entered the cage.

The spotlights blinded me, but they gave off enough

warmth I knew we wouldn't regret taking off our jackets. The enclosure spanned almost twenty feet long and the same wide. On the opposite end stood another door, this one much larger than the one we'd come through. The floor consisted of a stained concrete, rusty splotches scattered throughout, some fresher than others. Sunny whimpered behind me.

No divider separated us from the other end of the cage.

I glanced up, shielding my eyes against the lights. Behind us and far above our heads was a large, completely black glass window. A viewing room. I turned around fully and looked up at the glass, putting my hands on my hips.

The glass blinked, like a light came on behind it, and the blackness dissolved. Dean stood alone in a room similar to the holding room we'd been in. He smiled down at me; it was the dangerous smile, the smile he'd given me at the Halloween party. The one that had been a promise and a threat at once.

My stomach sank. This wasn't going to be a test. This was payback. A way to get me in line.

"I will be conducting your testing personally," he said, voice coming out over the intercom again. "It's you and me right now. Oh, and Sunny. Better be careful with her, Ollie. I know your previous history with saving young girls."

I didn't let myself react to his words. There was nothing he could say to me about that girl that I hadn't already told myself every night since my time in the Tabers' basement. As flatly as possible, I said, "I wouldn't expect anything less."

Dean narrowed his eyes, warning me not to speak again.

"Most testing normally involves a more sedate, drugged opponent. Along with guards lining the cage's walls, ready to put the animal down in case things get out of hand. But you're Ollie Andrews!" Dean swept his arms wide, glinting smile still in place. "You can do anything, right? So I sent the guards away and requested a *livelier* opponent." He leaned toward the glass, his smile slipping away, as his eyes drilled into mine. "And Ollie? I would be careful." His eyes flickered over to Sunny. "Bad things happen when you step out of line, and a death during testing wouldn't be unheard of. So next time, when you think about questioning my methods, you should consider what I can do to you."

My fists clenched at my sides. Sunny's terrified gaze turned toward me. "You should remember the last old man who locked me in a room and tried to hurt my friend," I hissed up at him. "Because that will be your fate soon."

He waved away my words like they were nothing. I'd really pissed him off if he was willing to hurt Sunny, a descendant from an Original family. It was a big risk, and I wondered if he was lying about the guards. Surely he'd positioned some outside the cage, just out of view, in case this went sideways.

"Pick a weapon." He pointed down to the wall in front of me, where a panel slid back and revealed a rack of weapons. "Ten seconds."

"What's going on?" Sunny's voice cracked. She stood close to me, our shoulders brushing, and grabbed my hand. "What does he mean?"

"Nine seconds."

I shook my head. "Not now. Get ready. This is going to

be worse than I thought." I mumbled the last part, talking mostly to myself. Why hadn't I considered Dean using Sunny against me? I'd played right into his hands.

This test would be anything but easy. It would be a life or death fight.

"Eight seconds."

I squeezed Sunny's hand. "We have to get some weapons."

With a jerking nod, Sunny scuttled over to the weapons and frantically pawed through them. I spotted the stingray whip quickly and picked it up, testing its weight in my hand. In Weapons Theory, I'd learned the mechanics of it and how to use it, but I'd never actually used it. Surprisingly, the whip's leather grip fit my hand perfectly, naturally.

"Seven seconds."

"What should I choose?" Sunny whispered, glancing over her shoulder to me.

"Have you practiced with the throwing knives?" She nodded. "Use them. You can keep your distance that way. Stay behind me as much as possible, but get off as many shots as you can."

Sunny picked up the pack of throwing knives, their blades slender and lethal. As I reached for another set of daggers, the weapons panel slammed shut. We would each get one choice. Sunny whimpered.

"Six seconds."

"It's okay," I murmured. "We can do this."

Sunny cinched the belt of knives around her waist with quaking hands. She pulled out a knife and hesitantly tested its weight a couple times in her hand. I turned and cracked the whip, checking its length. It was onyx-tipped point with razor-sharp barbs. I controlled it with ease, like I'd always held it. More importantly, it would help me keep my distance and defend Sunny until Dean called the test complete.

"Five." Dean's voice boomed over the intercom, making Sunny jump.

"Ollie, I'm sorry for being mean." There were tears in her eyes. She already looked defeated.

"Four."

"Not now, Sunny. Focus."

I stepped beside her and slightly in front of her, facing the opposite door, whip in hand. I was ready. I could do this. My heart beat solidly, evenly. My palms were dry, my grip solid on the whip. I breathed deeply.

"Three."

"Perausog. Perausog," Sunny said under her breath, like a prayer.

Dog. I smelled dog. From the door came a slight chuffing sound. Familiar. If I strained hard enough, I heard it.

Tick tock tick tock

"Two."

"Be careful, okay?" Sunny whispered beside me.

"Stay behind me. Don't let your fear get the best of you. He wouldn't risk you dying."

Tick tock

"What about you?" Sunny whispered.

A light above the door on the other side of the cage flashed green. A muffled howl came from the other side.

"I don't matter," I said between my teeth, red murder haze settling around me.

"One."

The door unlocked.

"Tick fucking tock," I growled.

With a snap, the door sprang open, flipping upward. From the darkness, two bright eyes glowed. A snarl. Sunny whimpered behind me. I stepped in front of her to shield her from the 'swang should he attack right away.

I crouched, ready for the creature to come bounding from the narrow shoot. Instead, he stalked forward, slowly stepping out into the bright lights. The 'swang was almost as large as Hex, his shoulders, rippling with thick muscles beneath his heavy fur, level with my eyesight. His lips pulled back in a snarl, exposing his sharp fangs, saliva dripping in a thick stream from his mouth. One of his tall, curved ears had been nearly chewed off, and a large scar stretched over his left eye and down across his snout. Long, splintered claws clicked across the concrete as he paced back and forth in front of us.

"Your test," Dean said from above us, "will be to subdue or kill the creature."

Not surviving. Not lasting a certain amount of time.

The 'swang roared up at the glass, his claws curling and chipping off parts of the concrete beneath him. From behind me, Sunny pulled out a knife, the metal knocking against her rings. I didn't look away from the 'swang as I whispered back to Sunny, "Don't throw until I say."

The 'swang's head snapped toward me at the sound of my

voice. I took a deep breath and focused on his eyes. *I don't want to hurt you.*

If the 'swang was surprised when he heard me in its head, he didn't show it. *Ah, so you're Hex's little prize. The one everyone has been talking about.*

Are you in his pack? If I convinced the 'swang not to hurt us, to just make a show for Dean, we might survive.

The 'swang lifted his lips wider, like he was trying to smile, but the effort made his scarred face look more grotesque. *No, pretty girl. I don't belong to Hex, and I have no qualms about killing you.*

So much for talking my way out of this. *Fine. Then I will hurt you, asshole.*

I cracked my whip, its tip lashing across the cage and coming within inches of the 'swang's face. He didn't flinch.

The stingray whip for the prodigy. The 'swang let out a low growl. *Only the best can carry the whip.*

Shut up.

Your friend's fear smells divine.

"Throw!" I sidestepped and lunged. A knife whizzed by my ear as I flicked the whip again. The 'swang howled and leapt toward us. Sunny's knife lodged itself into his neck, solid and deep. She might scoff at being in the accelerated classes, but they paid off now. My whip's tip dug through his chest. He didn't slow down. I snapped back my whip to hit him again, but it was too late. He sat back on his haunches and rose up onto his back legs as he swiped a paw toward us.

I had enough time to shove Sunny at of the way, but by doing so, I'd put myself squarely in the path of the 'swang's claws.

My head snapped back at the impact. The fleshy meat of my cheek, jaw, and neck shredded like fragile, expensive silk beneath a chainsaw.

The 'swang hit the ground, his claws dripping blood. By some grace, I stayed on my feet.

Not so pretty anymore.

I didn't have time to respond to the 'swang's thought before he leapt onto me, sending me staggering back, holding both our weight. He'd knocked the breath from my lungs, but I kept my eyes trained on the 'swang's mouth. If he bit me, it would all be over. The pain would consume me, revealing my secret to Dean. I couldn't let that happen.

The sharp breeze from another knife whooshed by my cheek and sunk into the 'swang's snout. He let out a cry and released me, slinking back and swiping at the knife with his paw. I didn't hesitate. I attacked, rage replacing my blood, becoming my life force, the violence achingly familiar to me.

More knives whisked by me, one after the other. I slashed my whip back and forth, the continuous cracking mingling with the 'swang's ripping growls. I cut through his hide again and again until streams of his blood slickened the floor beneath his massive paws.

I slung back my arm and sent the whip zinging forward again, aiming for the 'swang's face, hoping to take out an eye with the onyx tip. The 'swang twisted away and caught my whip in his mouth. He jerked and I fell forward, scraping across the concrete like I weighed no more than a doll, but I wasn't letting go of my whip.

"Ollie!" Sunny screamed.

I'd slid within the 'swang's striking distance, too close to that gaping, smiling mouth of his. He sprung toward me, ready to pin me to the floor. When he was a breath away, I rolled to the side, tucking head over heels in a tight ball. He landed between me and Sunny, and I sprang to my feet on the other side of the cage.

"Hey!" I shouted at the 'swang, sending my whip's tip ripping across his back. "Look at me!"

He didn't. He prowled toward Sunny, who reached to her belt, finding all her knives gone. She hadn't kept count. Over the 'swang's shoulder, she met my eyes, but she didn't retreat, though her fear made her chin quiver.

Without touching her, the 'swang sent her staggering, one knee crumbling beneath her and hitting the concrete. Sagging onto the ground, she looked like she was being drained, like a straw had been stuck into her brain to suck out her life. Her face went pale and waxy, her mouth locked open in a horrified, silent scream. Black tendrils, like slender ribbons beneath her skin, snaked out from her temples and looped around her eyes, down her nose, and into her mouth.

The 'swang fed off her fear. And Dean wasn't stopping the test.

With a howl of rage, I sprinted toward the 'swang's back. With a sideways flick of my wrist, I sent the whip's length cracking toward the 'swang. I'd never used the weapon before, but somehow I knew exactly how to gauge the distance, the force I would need from my wrist, like I was born with a whip in my hand. Perfectly, the leather end wrapped around the 'swang's neck, tightening with each circuit.

I leapt onto his back, straddling his massive shoulders and pulling the whip tight.

The 'swang reared up onto his hind legs. He was so big that I was only a couple feet away from hitting the ceiling. Beneath me, he hit the ground again and began thrashing.

Sunny slumped onto the ground and didn't move.

In that tiny split second, seeing her on the ground and worrying she might be dead, I understood true, heart ripping, gut sinking fear. I'd caught a glimmer of it that night in the Tabers' basement. But now, I knew that real fear came from being afraid for someone else. From trying my best to save her, and knowing it might not be enough. That was fear, but I couldn't dwell on it.

The 'swang backed up and I fell forward onto its neck. I struggled to hold on to the whip's end and keep the coil tight enough. Before I righted myself, he flung himself into the cage's bars, crushing me beneath his weight.

I screamed.

My vision went white from the impact, my breath stolen.

He reared again, claws scratching over the concrete, and fell backward. My back connected with the bars, and I scraped down every inch of the metal. The 'swang's weight crumpled into me, folding my body beneath him like an accordion.

My ribs broke so loudly I heard the cracks. My body folded over, nearly in half, unnatural and horribly wrong. Inside me, my lungs jammed together, slammed against my spine. Somewhere deep in my pelvis there was a scraping, a shifting. A second later my right leg went numb. I might not be able to walk, so I needed to hang on.

Hang on and pray.

The 'swang hit the concrete and rolled. For a second, my world went black, the concrete an unmovable pressure against my side sending my crushed ribs swishing around in my chest like melting ice in a glass. Above me, the 'swang used his weight to grind me into the ground.

For me, there was only that one moment, crushed beneath the 'swang and the ground.

There was nothing else.

I became nothing but a scream of rage and white-knuckled grip on the whip's handle.

The 'swang completed his roll, and I once again saw the lights blazing above us. I tried to clear my addled thoughts with a shake of my head, my breathing ragged and wheezing. I coughed, my throat wet and thick. Splatters of blood landed on my hands gripping the whip.

I made the mistake of looking down. Half of my collarbone stuck out from a ragged, bloodied hole in my skin. My shirt clung to me in tatters, scraped off by the grit of the concrete.

I coughed again and nearly fell off as the 'swang staggered to his feet.

From the side, a flash of color darted in, sliding in front of the 'swang. It was Sunny, dark hair streaming behind her, a yell on her blue lips. She swiped upward with both arms, knives clenched tight in her grip. The 'swang's throat tore open, like a rip of thick paper in a quiet room, the blood spilling onto the ground. He staggered but managed to hit Sunny's back with his paw. She tumbled wildly over the floor, connecting with the cage's wall in a sickening crunch.

Seeing her crumpled against the wall energized me enough to ignore the sickening squelch of my breathing, the way my ribs had shifted into my back. I shoved my weight backward and hauled on the whip's end. Over the 'swang's heaving head, I looked at the blackened glass.

And smiled at Dean, blood dripping from my mouth and face.

The 'swang hit the floor, his front legs giving way beneath him. A horrible gasping filled the air and it wasn't just me. I stood and limped away, dragging my right leg, jerking the whip tighter with each halting step. The 'swang went still but I didn't stop pulling. His back legs twitched. A blue tongue lolled out of his mouth and he wheezed, body shaking with spasms.

"Sunny?" I choked out, not taking my eyes off the bulging 'swang's eyes. My back hit the bars, but I walked my hands higher up the whip and kept pulling.

Across the cage, Sunny groaned and unfolded her body. "I'm okay," she said groggily.

"Ollie!"

Only one voice could reach me through my murder haze. I glanced toward the side, keeping one eye on the 'swang. Luke pressed against the bars, horror spreading across his face as he took in the cage's brutal scene. Hatter crouched beside him, hands reaching through the bars, and pulled Sunny to him. A handful of other hunters gathered around the cage, their faces shocked and confused. Someone yelled at Dean to unlock the door.

"Keep the whip tight!" Luke shouted. "We'll get to you. It's okay."

Was he talking to me? I spat blood onto the ground. I knew it was going to be okay, because I'd made it so. I jerked the whip one more time. With the slack, I tied it around the bars, looping the leather around and around until I tied it off in a knot that didn't give the 'swang any slack. From behind me, he whimpered, the sound so sad and awful that a shard of guilt tore through me.

I'm sorry, I said to him, finishing off the knot that would keep him in place. *I didn't want it to end like this.*

"Someone get a medic!"

"Ollie, you're okay! Don't touch it. Don't go near it!"

I ignored Luke. The 'swang thrashed against the concrete. Suffering. I spun around, searching for a knife. One lay on the other side of the cage. I limped over, right leg dragging, and grabbed it. The 'swang didn't move as I crossed to him. His eyes rolled up to me and registered the knife in my hand.

"Ollie, no!"

Just end it, he said. His voice was broken.

I'm sorry.

Me too.

I stabbed the knife into his eye.

Only when he was still beneath me did I look up at the glass. The glass didn't clear and Dean didn't speak again. But the cage doors unlocked with sharp beeps and Luke, Hatter, and too many guards to count rushed in.

I fell to my knees, a sob lodged in my throat as I blacked out.

NINETEEN

I woke in the ward the next morning. Sunny lay in the cot next to me. Beside her, still gripping her hand, Hatter sat on a stool, slumped over and snoring.

Slowly, with as little growling as possible so I didn't wake them, I eased off the cot. My ribs were wrapped so tightly I barely managed to breathe, much less pull myself into a sitting position. With a deep breath, I used my free arm to jerk myself up as I swung my legs over the edge. The floor of the ward tilted and spun, but I'd managed it.

I knew I was too injured to be moving, but I did it anyway to prove to myself that I still could. Sitting at the edge of the cot, my body flushed with searing heat and then freezing cold. I shook with chills even as sweat rolled down my forehead. If I kept my eyes up and away from the tight sling around my shoulder to brace my shattered collar bone, the wide swath of bandages beneath my sports bra to support my broken ribs, the way my right leg scraped across the floor, and the stitched-up seeping claw marks across my neck and jaw, I could convince myself I was fine. That I was still invincible.

I felt fine. Felt invincible. If I just didn't look down.

"He's meeting with Dean," Hatter said quietly, surprising me. I glanced back at him. He hadn't moved from Sunny's side, but he must have heard me trying to get up. It didn't surprise me that he hadn't offered to help. Apparently, I was still on his shit list.

He turned away from me, ending the conversation. The only sound as I left came from my foot dragging as I hobbled across the ward.

The stairs proved harder than I thought, and by the time I'd made it up them, my vision slanted sharply off-kilter and my body hummed with a pulsing pressure that made my ears pop. The two more flights of stairs to Dean's office were too much to consider. A few students clustered in the main entry as I limped through, their conversations hushing as I appeared, their eyes hovering on the thick bandage on my face. Keeping my head down, I shoved out of the main door and trudged toward the barracks.

Eventually I made it. Though I was practically dragging myself as I collapsed face-first onto Luke's bed. It sent a rattling in my ribs that set my teeth on edge and twisted my stomach. I groaned.

Bright side: at least the 'swang hadn't bitten me. That

would have made today really suck.

I laid there for a while until my breath came a little easier. It wouldn't take Luke long to find me here, but I shifted around on the bed, trying to find a position that didn't cause my body to feel like a balloon about burst. As I rolled over, I spotted a paper on Luke's bedside table. I almost ignored it, but the only thing written on it was a single name.

Frowning, I reached for it, not bothering to acknowledge how my broken ribs scraped against my lungs. I pulled the page out from where it was half buried. Once I had it in my hands, I read the name scribbled across it over and over.

Olesya Volkova.

Volkova. I'd seen that name before. I stared at the page until the quickly scrawled ink blurred. Why had Luke written this name down? The books on the table revealed nothing that would have prompted a note like this, and I'd never told him my full first name unless he'd read my file in Dean's office, which I doubted.

My head snapped up. The binder of the Originals. The Volkova family had been listed with the other original families.

Olesya Volkova.

I'm your father, Olesya.

From the front of the barracks, a door slammed. Heavy boots stomped down the hall. I set the paper aside, back where I found it, and looked innocently at the door as Luke barreled in.

"What the hell, Ollie?" he shouted. "Are you insane? You have a broken pelvis and collarbone! You need to be in the ward!"

No finger tapping. No controlled unwrapping of his caramel candies. Nothing. Straight to wild Luke, uncontrolled and uncontrollable.

"How was your meeting?" I asked, ignoring him.

Something happened in my chest, beneath the bandages and broken ribs. Something that had to do with my heart. Luke had a page in his room with my first name and an Original family last name. Hex was my father. I was part aswang.

So what did this page mean? Anything or everything?

I surfaced from my thoughts. Luke was still yelling at me. When he saw I hadn't been paying attention, he stopped, shoulders heaving. He raked his hands roughly through his hair, tugging at the ends. A tic traveled up and down his jaw. A long moment passed, filled with his ragged breathing. I'd never seen him work so hard to get himself under control.

Looking at him hurt that part of my heart, so I stared at my hands with my head cocked, wondering what the hell was happening to me. I wanted to cry. I wanted to laugh. I wanted to scream.

Olesya Volkova.

All this time, I thought I was a murderer, a runaway. No home. No family. Just me and running and trying to stay alive. That's all I ever was. Now, I had no clue.

What am I?

Luke was talking again. "What?" I asked, interrupting him.

"Christ." He crossed the room and sat down on the bed beside me. "Are you okay, Ollie?" He went to touch me, but his hand froze in the air inches away from my wounded cheek as if he remembered the line in the sand between us. Too screwed up to be together. And now, I thought ruefully, remembering how the 'swang had ruined my face, too ugly. I turned away from him.

"I'm sorry I didn't get to you faster," he said, voice rasping. "I had no idea what Dean had planned."

"That's not it."

"What's wrong?" he asked. "What else has happened."

Slowly, my eyes met his. He hadn't shaved in a couple days. The scruff made his chiseled face look harsher and sharper, more angled and haunted. Black circles darkened the skin beneath his eyes. He looked like hell.

"Everything is wrong," I whispered.

Olesya Volkova.

The name meant nothing to me. Olesya was a common Russian name. But that page did mean one important thing: Luke was keeping secrets again.

I didn't trust him, but unlike him lying about how dangerous the day-form 'swangs were, I couldn't be mad at him for this secret. I had my own lies to hide.

He scooted closer and put his arm around me. "I'll protect you," he said, but he spoke the words into the wall without looking at me. "I know I wasn't there at the cage, but I'll do better. I'll be better. I promise."

"You wouldn't say that if you knew the truth."

He stiffened beside me. Maybe we'd never been good enough friends to tell each other all our secrets, but we'd been close. At one point, I'd hoped he would be the one I never lied to. Now the lies were building up so high that I hardly saw him over them. Finally, he spoke. "What is the truth, Ollie?"

I shrugged. I couldn't trust him, and he couldn't trust me. It broke my heart.

"I know you're not telling me the truth about some things," Luke said, his voice low and controlled, his grip tightening on me. "It's fine if you want to lie to me, but remember Dean will never let you rest, never ease up on you. He'll keep at you until he gets you killed, and when you're dead, all your secrets will be revealed when he examines your brain."

I gritted my teeth to keep from shuddering. "Are you lying to me?"

His eyes flicked to the table where the page with my first name on it rested. "No," he lied.

I turned my head away, hoping he wouldn't see the moisture building up in my eyes. "Then I'm not lying either," I said. *And I love you. I love you even with your secrets and lies. I love you in spite of this place. I love you, but I'm a monster, and you'll hate me when you know the truth.*

I clamped my mouth shut to keep those words from spilling out, because he could never know I was the monster he'd trained his entire life to kill. He couldn't know I was the monster his father had abused him for. He could never love me enough to ignore the monster inside me.

"You're going north."

The words surprised me. "Now?"

"For winter break. Dean wants you to go north to Barrow

with me and a group of hunters. He says it'll be good experience for you."

"Good experience," I said numbly. All my plans of leaving, of going to Peg, were gone. If there were answers to have about me, I would have to find them myself. "I take it I'm not getting my pardon after all. Once a murderer, always a murderer."

"If you cooperate up north, he said he would still honor your deal about the pardon."

I snorted. Yeah right. "Did I at least pass Fields?"

"You did. He said he made it harder because of your abilities. Everyone is talking about it," he said, disgust heavy in his voice. "They're saying you're some great talent, but they have no clue he tried to kill you. Ollie, this is what I was afraid of, but if you come north, I can keep you safe." His grip tightened and he finally looked at me. "Winter break would give us time to figure out what Dean wants with you."

He wants to make monsters from a monster. He wants my head cracked open, brains exposed for his knife. He wants me dead but not before I provide him with an army. I said none of it out loud.

"Your father is in Barrow," I said instead.

Luke's fist clenched in his lap. "Don't worry about him."

"Dean will have him testing me or . . ." Or experimenting on me. Maybe north was an excuse for me to die.

Luke shook his head. "Dean has to be careful after Fields. Some of the professors and hunters are watching him closely. They say he's going too far with the testing, that you were too young. The other students faced off with some old 'swang that's so beat down he doesn't even try to do anything. It's what all the first-years do for Fields. They just had to stay in the cage for five minutes to test their fear. By the time we figured out he'd sent everyone away, it was too late. You were already killing it."

"He was really going to let us die if I couldn't kill it?"

"The 'swang was old and slightly sedated, and Dean had a gun up there with him. I don't think he would've let it get that far."

I looked away as Luke kept talking about how everyone was saying my test was the best they'd ever seen. Instead, I thought about Dean and the bodies in the morgue. He never would have used that gun to save us. I was easier to handle dead than alive. If I'd died with a decent excuse, Dean could have studied my brain. And would have realized what I was.

That was why he was sending me north.

Dead with a pretty bow on top. Monster free-for-all. Instructions included.

And Dean would never be punished for trying to get me killed, because everyone here, including Luke, didn't think the President of Fear University was capable of killing a student. But he was. He really, really was.

"Sunny and Hatter are coming north too. Hatter won't leave her here alone with him."

I sighed. "He won't leave her or Dean won't? He used her as leverage last night. I doubt he would be bothered to do it again."

"Dean said if you didn't come back with me, Sunny wouldn't either." His voice sounded reluctant, like he'd hoped I wouldn't figure that part out.

"Is that the full truth?"

Luke nodded, but he was lying again. That wasn't the full truth. I thought about the page beside me. All the 'swangs would be up north. Including Hex. If I wanted the truth, and I did, I would need to talk to him, which meant going where Dean wanted me to. Playing into his hands. If I managed to stay alive, I would be able to find my answers. Maybe, just maybe, I could figure out a way to stay and make Dean pay. To keep my family, my home, and Luke.

If I was going to stay instead of run, then I needed answers.

I'd never been the type to stay. I was a runner. A low-life. A murderer. Like my mom, I wasn't the type to keep promises or stay when I was needed.

"We need time," Luke was saying. "We can figure out what Dean is planning."

"He wants monsters," I said quietly.

"Ollie . . ." Luke leaned into me, resting his head against mine. "You're not a monster. You're just too good at killing monsters. That's all. Nothing is wrong with you."

Everything was wrong with me.

I met Luke's eyes and waited for another lie. "Do you really believe that?"

But I was really asking if my broken lover, beaten down and beaten up by his insane father, infected with saliva, turned into a vengeful, angry man by the university he believed in, still believed in *me*, even though we were too screwed up to be together, even though I was a monster and he was a monster hunter.

Unwavering, Luke met my eyes and nodded. "I do."

Truth. He still believed. That alone was enough for me to stay and fight. For as a long as possible, I wanted him to believe that nothing was wrong with me. I loved him.

"North it is then."

North to kill 'swangs.

North to search for truth amongst the blood and bones.

North for pretty answers to ugly questions.

North for Olesya Volkova.

ACKNOWLEDGMENTS

First of all, thank you, Nate. How you can tolerate me and still manage to love me, I will never understand. Thank you, Mom and Dad, for teaching me to dream and that hard work kicks luck's ass every time. Sorry I said 'ass.' And sorry for all the f-bombs in this book and for the awkward sexy stuff too. Thank you, Wylla, Mandy, and Drax the Destroyer. Y'all hang out with me all day while I'm writing and never, not even once, look at me funny for talking to myself. Big thank you to Jessica West and Red Road Editing for understanding my vision of Ollie and making her grammatically correct. Jessica, your friendship and enthusiasm makes my life complete. Another big round of gratitude goes out to Najla Qamber Designs. Thank you for yet another beautiful cover, and thank you to you and your wonderful family for all the personal accounts and stories about the aswang. Thank you, Katie, my favorite aunt, for helping me with all the medical questions I had (and thank you for always asking if it was "real life" or not. I appreciate the concern, even though we both know I don't go outside enough to actually get hurt). Thank you to my "Not a Street Team" members. Y'all are the best not a street team ever. And a huge, massive thank you to my Reviewers Club. Last but not least, I would like to thank The Hype PR, all the bloggers who spread the word about *Fear University*, and all the early readers, who called dibs on Luke.

Licks for all your faces.

ABOUT THE AUTHOR

Meg Collett lives deep in the hills of Tennessee where the cell phone service is a blessing and the *Internet* is a myth of epic proportions. She is the mother of one giant horse named Elle and three dogs named Wylla, Mandy, and Drax the Destroyer. Her husband is a saint for putting up with her ragtag life. For more information and to sign up for her newsletter, go to www.megcollett.com.

Enjoyed *Fear University*?
Please consider leaving a review!

CPSIA information can be obtained at www.ICGtesting.com
Printed in the USA
BVOW08s0225280916

463527BV00001B/31/P

9 781517 002145